Darklands 2

'An unusually intelligent, humane and curiously English volume . . . haunting prose . . . the stuff of sweat-inducing dreams.' *Christopher Fowler, Time Out*

'I find it hard to pick a favourite...Most of these are by newcomers to the genre, and if the quality is anything to go by, horror fiction is in good hands for the foreseeable future.' *Starburst*

'Maintains a high standard...Many are dystopian nightmares, others are flashbacks narrated, in true 90s style, by perpetrators rather than victims. If you want to know the answer to the question, "Where is the New Gothic?", look no further.' *City Limits*

'Ambitious, all-original...distinguished by memorable contributions from John Burke, Elizabeth Young and Kim Newman.' *Charles Shaar Murray, Daily Telegraph*

Also edited by Nicholas Royle

Darklands

About the author

Nicholas Royle was born in Sale, Cheshire in 1963. He graduated in modern languages from the University of London, then combined writing with a series of full-time jobs for six years before going freelance in 1992. He has had more than seventy short stories published in anthologies and magazines both in the UK and abroad.

Both *Darklands 2* (in 1993) and its predecessor *Darklands* (in 1992) won the British Fantasy Society's Best Anthology award. In addition his story, 'Night Shift Sister', won the Best Short Story award in 1993.

His novels, *Counterparts*, and *Saxophone Dreams* are forthcoming from Penguin.

With thanks to the BFS, Di and Mike Wathen, Chloë, Giuliana, Mike, David Almond, Chris Reed, Steve Jones, DUSFS, Anne Billson, Mum, Dad, Jools, Job, Uninvi, Julie, Jenny, Dill, Del, Alison, Kate, Nel, Mark, Flora, Phyllis van Thal, the contributors, and MSA for the mouse.

Happy Birthday JL.

Contents

Introduction	ix
Introduction to the new edition	xiii
Under the Pylon – Graham Joyce	1
Waiting For a Train – Joel Lane	17
Eyes Like a Ghost's – Simon Clark	27
Always – Michael Marshall Smith	45
One Day You'll Learn – John Burke	57
MacCreadle's Bike – Conrad Williams	79
The Light on the Cliff – Ian Cunningham	89
Recovery – Julie Akhurst	99
Two Strands of Wire – Roger Stone	119
Coffee – Jean-Daniel Brèque	131
Organ Donors – Kim Newman	139
Lethality – Elizabeth Young	185
The Elevator – Garry Kilworth	203
The Alternative – Ramsey Campbell	213

Introduction

An hour before sitting down to write this introduction I was in the dentist's chair having a couple of fillings and a scrape and a polish. I'd had part two of my root canal treatment the week before so by now I was on first name terms with the receptionist. But still, the waiting room, with its *Reader's Digests*, swollen tropical fish and excellent acoustics (you can hear each drill in each different treatment room), remained a place of fear. I went in and lay down for the hygienist, a woman I'd never seen before, and she took an enormous spade to my mouth and began scraping tea and coffee stains off the *back* of my teeth. How was I to know she hadn't just walked in off the street wearing a mask, a white coat and an air of confidence? She clearly favoured the robust approach and after the dentist had come in halfway through to administer *three* injections she set to with renewed vigour. After all, her eyes seemed to be saying, I couldn't feel it now. I felt it. The anaesthetic took a while to kick in. But then she knew that.

She finished and as I peeled myself off the chair I asked her if patients generally complained of pain during her treatment. Just a little discomfort, she said. I sat in the waiting room until the anaesthetic was just beginning to wear off, then they called me in for the real thing. I went in. I lay down. 'Just move up a couple of inches, would you?' The light went on and they loomed over me. Two minutes with the high-speed drill, which for some reason always makes me think of road accidents, sirens and Steve McQueen in *Le Mans,* then my dentist brought out the slow drill, prefacing its use with the remark, 'A little vibration.' I had to stop myself laughing, but it was dangerous hysterical laughter. My tooth became the road outside my window and his instrument the pneumatic drill that wakes me up every morning. The pain was . . . unusual.

Paying for it doesn't bother me. It's saying thank you. No matter what they do to me I always say thank you. As I left the surgery a man was walking past. 'Never go in there,' I wanted to tell him. 'Just don't go in there.' But I didn't because I hadn't yet regained control of my mouth.

There was a point to all this.

In real life we dislike pain and fear, we try to avoid them. But there's something attractive about experiencing fear vicariously, as long as we know we're safe. Safe and yet vulnerable. If a story frightens you it's because the writer has got inside you and touched a nerve. It's got to be a good story for that. A good writer can even scare you by writing about what frightens him or her, *even if* it's not something that would normally frighten you. I don't really know *why* we enjoy experiencing fear at one remove – I don't think I subscribe to the school of thought which says it's good for you because it enables you to face up to things; if I was going to be fastened to a torture rack for most of tomorrow I'm not sure that having read Kafka's *In the Penal Colony* would really make that much difference – but clearly many of us do.

There are twenty-three original stories in this book – good, intelligent horror stories about real people, their emotions and problems, relationships, their dreams and fears, what it's like to be human. It's not all fear and loathing: some of these stories are about other worlds, wondrous places, which exist just beyond our own (childhood, distant past, parallel universe); some give you the feeling of a dream and one or two plunge into nightmare;

some are frightening because of the terrible truth they reveal; two or three actually *physically* make me shiver each time I read them; one reduced me to tears and one shocked me when I thought I was unshockable.

The first *Darklands* sold out quickly and the feedback was good. Stephen Gallagher's *The Visitors' Book* has been reprinted in *The Year's Best Fantasy and Horror* edited by Ellen Datlow and Terri Windling, and in Heinemann's *Best Short Stories 1992* edited by Giles Gordon and John Hughes. Joel Lane's *Common Land* went into Karl Wagner's *The Year's Best Horror Stories XX* and Michael Marshall Smith chalked up his second consecutive appearance in Robinson's *Best New Horror* series (edited by Stephen Jones and Ramsey Campbell), with *The Dark Land*. The first book was a success and the only gimmick was top-quality stories. I am grateful to everyone who gave their support as I am to all those who have been involved in helping this book come about. Thanks to all the writers, including those whose stories were not suitable. I had to reject more than twice as many stories as are in the final line-up.

Anyone who liked the first book will love this second, final volume. If it's your first time, welcome.

Nicholas Royle
London, 14 August 1992

Introduction to the new edition

Although it says in the previous introduction that there are twenty-three stories in this book, there clearly aren't. There are fourteen. There were twenty-three in the Egerton Press edition. Thirteen of them are reprinted here along with one extra, original story by Ramsey Campbell, originally written for the first volume of the series. Don't ask. It's all too complicated. The remaining ten stories will form the backbone of a third volume if and when that gets the go-ahead, which I hope it will have done by the time you read this.

The success of the *Darklands* series has been very gratifying. The first two volumes won the British Fantasy Award for Best Anthology in consecutive years and received considerable critical acclaim. Stories from both books have been reprinted in several best-of-the-year anthologies and writers who were previously unpublished have gone on to sell stories elsewhere.

Since the original edition appeared well over a year ago, there is a need to update the authors' biographical information. Graham Joyce won the British Fantasy Award for Best Novel with *Dark Sister*, which he followed with *House of Lost Dreams*. His story, *Under the Pylon*, was reprinted in *Best New Horror 4*. Joel Lane won one of the prestigious 1993 Eric Gregory Awards for his poetry and a selection of his work appeared in *Private Cities*, a three-poet anthology from Stride Publications. He has sold several more stories, to Chris Kenworthy's three

Barrington Books anthologies *The Sun Rises Red*, *Sugar Sleep* and *The Science of Sadness*, as well as to two anthologies edited by Ellen Datlow, *Little Deaths* and an as yet untitled collection of feline horror stories. Simon Clark's story was chosen by Karl Edward Wagner as one of *The Year's Best Horror Stories XXI* and he has since sold two novels, *Nailed By the Heart* and *Blood Crazy* to Hodder Headline. Michael Marshall Smith's first novel *Only Forward* was a lead title from HarperCollins earlier this year and is being translated into about 104 languages. He has continued to sell short stories to anthologies on both sides of the Atlantic.

John Burke completed a new historical novel and has started work on a horror novel, *Nightmare Music*, set in Edinburgh. Conrad Williams was a popular winner of the British Fantasy Award for Best Newcomer, also receiving a nomination for Best Short Story; his short fiction has been appearing widely, from *Peeping Tom* to *Panurge*, *Northern Stories 4* to *Narrow Houses 3*. Ian Cunningham has been concentrating on tracking down a new ribbon for his printer, though he claims to have been developing his journalistic career. Likewise Julie Akhurst, who is currently in Australia launching a new women's magazine; a new story appeared in the small press magazine *Dementia 13* before she left the UK. Roger Stone has not been idle, selling stories to *Exuberance*, *Dementia 13*, *Premonitions* and Paul Lewis and Steve Lockley's laudable *Cold Cuts* anthology. On the outskirts of Paris Jean-Daniel Brèque keeps up an astounding rate translating huge science fiction and horror novels for the French market; his stories have sold to *Dark Voices 5* and *The Anthology of Fantasy and the Supernatural*.

Kim Newman followed *Jago* with *Anno Dracula* and so far this year he's published a new novel, *The Quorum*, and the first volume of his collected short stories, *The Original Dr Shade and Other Stories*, to be followed by a second volume, *Famous Monsters*, in November. Elizabeth Young has continued to work as a literary journalist and was co-author of *Shopping in Space: Essays on Contemporary American Literature* (Serpent's Tail). HarperCollins published another collection of Garry Kilworth's short fiction, *In the Country of Tattooed Men*, while his horror novels *Angel* and *Archangel* have appeared from Gollancz. Ramsey Campbell's introduction is up to date.

I believe there's an expanding market for *Darklands* stories and if all goes well this will be the second of many volumes. So now over to you.

Nicholas Royle
London, 23 April 1994

Under the pylon

Graham Joyce

Recently maligned in the introduction to his story in the otherwise excellent In Dreams *anthology edited by Paul McAuley and Kim Newman, Graham Joyce is in fact an agreeable man, a decent snooker player and a very talented writer. His story* Last Rising Sun *was one of the highlights of* In Dreams *and his first novel,* Dreamside, *one of the best horror/fantasy novels published in 1991.*

Born October 1954 in Keresley near Coventry, Graham Joyce went to teacher training college in Derby, decided not to teach and did an MA at Leicester University. 'I was a poet in those days,' he writes, 'and I won the George Fraser poetry prize. I felt sure this qualified me for a further period on the dole.' He has a good list of the sort of jobs writers are supposed to do before they get to write full time: 'Fitter's mate, slab-loader, kitchen porter, holiday camp greencoat, bingo-caller, supply teacher, legal supernumerary . . . somehow I became a development officer for the National Association of Youth Clubs. I did this for eight years and when in 1988 it began to feel like eighty years I quit and went to live on the Greek island of Lesbos to concentrate on writing. My girlfriend quit her job as a solicitor and we got married before driving down to Greece in a 2CV stuffed with luggage.' He sold Dreamside *to Pan just as they were preparing to come home skint. His other stories have appeared in* Interzone, Midnight Rose *and* New Worlds.

Under the pylon

After school or during the long summer holidays we used to meet down by the electricity pylon. Though we never went there when the weather was wet because obviously there was no cover. Apart from that the wet power lines would vibrate and hum and throb and it would be . . . well, I'm not saying I was scared but it would give you a bad feeling.

Wet or dry, we'd all been told not to play under the pylon. Our folks had lectured us time and again to keep away; and an Electricity Board disc fixed about nine feet up on the thing spelled out DANGER in red and white lettering. Two lightning shocks either side of the word set it in zigzag speech marks.

'Danger!'

I imagined the voice of the pylon would sound like a robot's speech-box from a science-fiction film, because that's what the pylon looked like, a colossal robot. Four skeletal steel legs straddled the ground, tapering up to a pointed head nudging the clouds. The struts bearing the massive power cables reached over like arms, adding a note of severity and anthropomorphism to the thing. Like someone standing with their hands on their hips. The power cables themselves drooped slightly until picked up by the next giant robot in the field beyond, and then to the next. Marching into the infinite distance, an army of obstinate robots.

But the pylon was situated on a large patch of waste ground between the houses, and when it came down to it, there was nowhere else for us kids to go. It was a green and overgrown little escape-hatch from suburbia. It smelled of wild grass and giant stalks of cow parsley, and of nettles and foxgloves and dumped housebricks. You could bash down a section to make a lair hidden from everything but the butterflies. Anyway, it wasn't the danger of electricity giving rise to any nervousness under the pylon. It was something else. Old Mrs Nantwich called it a shadow.

Joy Astley was eleven, and already wearing lipstick and make-up you could have peeled off like a mask. Her parents had big mouths and were always bawling. 'The Nantwiches,' she said airily, 'could only afford to buy this house because it's under the pylon. No one wants a house under the pylon.'

'Why not?' said Clive Mann. It was all he ever said. Clive had a metal brace across his teeth, and even though he was odd and stared at things a lot, people mostly bothered to answer him. 'Why?'

'Because you don't,' said Joy, 'that's why.'

Tania Brown was in my class at school (she used to pronounce her name Tarnia because of the sunshine jokes) and agreed with Joy. Kev Duffy burped and said, 'Crap!' It was Kev's word for the month. He would use it repeatedly up until the end of August. Joy just looked at Kev and wiggled her head from side to side, as if that somehow answered his remark.

The Nantwiches Joy was being so snobbish about were retired barge people. Why anyone would want to rub two pennies together I've never understood, but they were always described as looking as though they couldn't accomplish this dubious feat; and then in the same breath people would always add 'yet they're the people who have got it'. I doubted it somehow. They'd lived a hard life transporting coal on the barges, and it showed. Their faces had more channels and ruts and canals than the waterways of the Grand Union.

'They're illiterate,' Joy always pointed out whenever they were mentioned. And then she'd add, 'Can't read or write.'

The Nantwiches' house did indeed stand under the shadow of the giant pylon. Mr Nantwich was one of those old guys with a red face and white hair, forever forking over the earth in his backyard. Their garden backed up to the pylon. A creosoted wooden fence closed off one side of the square defined by the structure's four legs. One day when I was there alone old Mrs Nantwich had scared me by popping her head over the fence and saying, 'You don't wanna play there.'

Her face looked as old as a church gate. Fine white bristles sprouted from her chin. Her hair was always drawn back under a headscarf, and she wore spectacles with plastic frames and lenses like magnifying glasses. They made her eyes huge.

'Why?' I'd croaked.

She threw her head back slowly and pointed her chin towards the top of the pylon. Then she looked at me and did it again. 'There's a *shadow* orf of it.'

I felt embarrassed as she stared, waiting for me to say something. 'What do you mean?'

Before she answered, another head popped alongside her own. It was her daughter Olive. Olive looked as old as her mother. She had wild, iron-grey hair. Her teeth were terribly blackened and crooked. The thing about Olive was she never uttered a word. She hadn't spoken, according to my mother, since a man had 'jumped out at her from behind a bush'. I didn't see how that could make someone dumb for the rest of their life, but then I didn't understand what my mother meant by that deceptively careful phrase either.

'Wasn't me,' said Mrs Nantwich a little fiercely, 'as decided

5

to come 'ere.' And then her head disappeared back behind the fence, leaving Olive to stare beadily at me as if I'd done something wrong. Then her head too popped out of sight.

I looked up at the wires and they seemed to hum with spiteful merriment.

Another day I came across Clive Mann, crouched under the pylon, and listening. At that time, the three sides of the pylon had been closed off. We'd found some rusty corrugated sheeting to lean against one end, and a few lengths of torn curtain to screen off another. The third side, running up to the Nantwiches' creosoted fence, was shielded by an impenetrable jungle of five-foot-high stinging nettles.

It had been raining, and the curtains sagged badly. I ducked through the gap between them to find Clive crouched and staring directly up into the tower of the pylon. He said nothing.

'What are you doing?'

'You can hear,' he said. 'You can hear what they're saying.'

I looked up and listened. The lines always made an eerie hissing after rain, but there was no other sound.

'Hear what?'

'No! The people. On the telephones. Mrs Astley is talking to the landlord of the Dog and Trumpet. He's knocking her off.'

I looked up again and listened. I knew he wasn't joking because Clive had no sense of humour. He just stared at things. I was about to protest that the cables were power lines, not telephone wires, when the curtains parted and Joy Astley came in.

'What are you two doing?'

We didn't answer.

'My Dad says these curtains and things have got to come down,' said Joy.

'Why?'

'He says he doesn't like the idea.'

'What's it got to do with him?'

'He thinks,' Joy said, closing her eyes, 'things go on here.'

'You mean he's worried about what his angelic daughter gets up to,' I said.

Joy turned around, flicked up her skirt and wiggled her bottom at us. It was a gesture too familiar to be of any interest. At least that day she was wearing panties.

I had to pass by the Dog and Trumpet as I walked home later that afternoon. I noticed Mrs Astley going in by the back door, which was odd because the pub was closed in the afternoon. But I thought little of it at the time.

Just as we were accustomed to Joy flashing her bottom at us, so were we well inured to the vague parental unease about us playing under the pylon. None of our parents ever defined the exact nature of their anxieties. They would mention things about *electricity* and *generators*, but these didn't add up to much more than old Mrs Nantwich's dark mutterings about a *shadow*. I got my physics and my science all mixed up as usual, and managed to infect the rest of the group with my store of misapprehensions.

'Radiation,' I announced. 'The reason they're scared is because if there was an accidental power surge feedback . . .' (I was improvising like mad) ' . . . then we'd all get *radiated*.'

Radiated. It was a great word. Radiated. It got everyone going.

'There was a woman in the newspaper,' said Joy. 'Her microwave oven went wrong and she was *radiated*. Her bones all turned to jelly.'

Tania could cap that. 'There was one on television. A woman. She gave birth to a cow with two heads. After being *radiated*.' The girls were always better at horror stories.

Kev Duffy said, 'Crap!' Then he looked up into the

pyramid of the tower and said, 'What's the chances of it happening?'

'Eighteen hundred to one,' I said. With that talent for tossing out utterly bogus statistics I should have gone on to become a politician.

Then they were all looking up, and in the silence you could hear the abacus beads whizzing and clacking in their brains.

Joy's parents needn't have worried. Not much went on behind the pylon screens of which they could disapprove. Well, that's not entirely true, since one or two efforts were made seriously to misbehave, but they never amounted to much. Communal cigarettes were sucked down to their filters, bottles of cider were shared round. Clive and I once tried sniffing Airfix but it made us sick as dogs and we were never attracted to the idea again. We once persuaded Joy to take off her clothes for a dare, which she did; but then she immediately put them back on again, so it all seemed a bit pointless and no more erotic than the episode of solvent abuse.

It was the last summer holiday before we were due to be dispatched to what we all called the Big Schools. It all depended on which side of the waste ground you lived. Joy and Kev were to go to President Kennedy, where you didn't have to wear a school uniform; Clive and I were off to Cardinal Wiseman, where you did. It all seemed so unfair. Tania was being sent to some snooty private school where they wore straw hats in the summer. She hated the idea, but her father was what my old man called one of the nobs.

Once, Tania and I were on our own under the pylon. Tania had long blond hair, and was pretty in a willowy sort of way. Her green eyes always seemed wide open with amazement at the things we'd talk about or at what we'd get up to. She spoke quietly in her rather posh accent, and for some reason she always seemed desperately grateful that we didn't exclude her from our activities.

Out of the blue she asked me if I'd ever kissed a girl.

'Loads,' I lied. 'Why?'

'I've never kissed anyone. And now I'm going to a girls' school I'll probably never get the chance.'

We sat on an old door elevated from the grass by a few housebricks. I looked away. The seconds thrummed by. I imagined I heard the wires overhead going *chock chock chock*.

'Would you like to?' she said softly.

'Like to what?'

'To kiss me?'

I shrugged. 'If you want.' My muscles went as stiff as the board on which we perched.

She moved closer, put her head at an angle and closed her eyes. I looked at her thin lips, leaned over and rested my mouth against hers. We stayed like that for some time, stock-still. The power lines overhead vibrated with noisy impatience. Eventually she opened her eyes and pulled back, blinking at me and licking her lips. I realised my hands were clenched to the side of the board as if it had been a magic carpet hurtling across the sky.

So Tania and I were 'going out'. Our kissing improved slightly, and we got a lot of ribbing from the others, but beyond that, nothing had changed. Because I was going out with Tania, Kev Duffy was considered to be 'going out' with Joy, at least nominally; though to be fair to him, he was elected to this position only because Clive was beyond the pale. Kev resented this status as something of an imposition, though he did go along with the occasional bout of simulated kissing. But when Joy appeared one day sporting livid, gash-crimson lipstick and calling him 'darling' at every turn, he got mad and smudged the stuff all round her face with the ball of his hand. The others pretended not to notice, but I could see she was hurt by it.

Another time I'd been reading something about hypnotism, and Joy decided she wanted to be hypnotised. I'd decided I had a talent for this, so I sat her on the grass inside the pylon while the other three watched. I did all that 'you're feeling very relaxed' stuff and she went under easily; too easily. Then I didn't know what to ask her to do. There was no point asking her to take her clothes off, since she hardly needed prompting to do that.

'Get 'er to run around like a 'eadless chicken,' was Kev's inspirational idea.

'Tell 'er to describe life on Jupiter,' Clive said obscurely.

'Ask her to go back to a past life,' said Tania.

That seemed the most intelligent suggestion, so I offered a few cliched phrases and took her back, back into the mists of time. I was about to ask her what she could see when I felt a thrum of energy. It distracted me for a moment, and I looked up into the apex of the pylon. There was nothing to see, but I remembered I'd felt it before. Once, when I'd first kissed Tania.

When I looked back, there were tears streaming down Joy's face. She was trembling and sobbing in silence.

'Bring her out of it,' said Tania.

'Why?' Clive protested.

'Yer,' said Kev. 'Better stop it now.'

I couldn't. I did all that finger clicking rubbish and barked various commands. But she just sat there shaking and sobbing. I was terrified. Tania took hold of her hands and, thankfully, after a while Joy just seemed to come out of it on her own. She was none the worse for the experience, and laughed it off; but she wouldn't tell us what she saw.

They all had a go. Kev wouldn't take it seriously, however, and insisted on staggering around like a stage drunk. Clive claimed to have gone under but we all agreed we couldn't tell the difference.

Finally it was Tania's turn. She was afraid, but Joy dared her. Tania made me promise not to make her experience a past life. I'd read enough about hypnotism to know you can't make people do anything they don't already want to do, but convincing folk of that is another thing. Tania had been frightened by what happened to Joy, so I had to swear on my grandmother's soul and hope to be struck by lightning and so on before she'd let me do it.

Tania went under with equal ease, a feat I've never been able to accomplish since.

'What are you going to get her to do?' Joy wanted to know.

'Pretend to ride a bike?' I suggested lamely.

'Crap,' said Kev. 'Tell her she's the sexiest woman in the world and she wants to make mad passionate love to you.'

Naturally Joy thought this was a good idea, so I put it to Tania. She opened her eyes in a way that made me think she'd just been stringing us along. She smiled at me serenely and shook her head. Then there was a thrum of electrical activity from the wires overhead. I looked up and before I knew what was happening, Tania had jumped on me and locked her legs behind my back. I staggered and fell backwards on to the grass. Tania had her tongue halfway down my throat. I'd heard of French kissing, but it had never appealed. Joy and Kev were laughing and cheering her on.

Tania came up for air, and she was making a weird growling from the back of her throat. Then she power-kissed me again.

'This is great!' whooped Kev.

'Hey!' went Clive. 'Hey!'

'Tiger tiger!' shouted Joy.

I was still pinned under Tania's knees when she sat up and stripped off her white T-shirt in one deft move.

'Bloody hell!' Kev couldn't believe it any more than I could. 'This is brilliant!'

'Gerrem off!' screamed Joy.

Tania stood up quickly and hooked her thumbs inside the waist of her denims and her panties, slipping them off. Before I'd had time to blink she was naked. She was breathing hard. Then she was fumbling at my jeans.

'Bloody fucking hell!' Joy shouted. 'Bloody fucking hell!'

The lines overhead thrummed again. Tania had twice my strength. I had this crazy idea she was drawing it from the pylon. She had my pants halfway down my legs.

Then everything was interrupted by a high-pitched screaming.

At first I thought it was Tania, but it was coming from behind her. The screaming brought Tania to her senses. It was Olive, the Nantwiches' deranged daughter. Her head had appeared over the fence and she was screaming and pointing at something. What she pointed at was my semi-erect penis; half-erect from Tania's brutal stimulation; half-flaccid from terror at her ferocious strength.

Olive continued to point and shriek. Then she was joined at the fence by Mrs Nantwich. 'Filthy buggers,' said the old woman. 'Get on with yer! Filthy buggers!'

A third head appeared. Red-faced Mr Nantwich. He was just laughing. 'Look at that!' he shouted. 'Look at that!'

Tania wasn't laughing. She looked at me with disgust. 'Bastard,' she spat, climbing quickly back into her clothes. 'Bastard!'

I ran after her. 'You can't make anyone do what they don't want to,' I tried. She shrugged me off tearfully. I let her go.

'Filthy buggers!' Mrs Nantwich muttered.

'You can't make anyone!' I screamed at her.

'Look at that!' laughed Joe Nantwich.

Olive was still shrieking. The power lines were still throbbing. Clive was trying to tell me something, but I wasn't listening. 'It wasn't you,' he was saying. He was pointing up at the pylon. 'It were *that*.'

I never spoke another word to Tania, and she never came near the pylon again. I was terrified the story would get back to my folks. I didn't see why exactly, but I had the feeling I'd reap all the blame. But a few days later something happened which overshadowed the entire incident.

And it happened to Clive.

One afternoon he and I had been sharing a bottle of Woodpecker. He'd been *listening* again.

'Old man Astley's found out.'

'Eh? How do you know?'

He looked up at the overhead wires. 'She's been on the phone to the Dog and Trumpet.'

He was always reporting what he'd 'heard' on the wires. We all knew he was completely cracked, but it was best to ignore him. I changed the subject. I started regaling him with some nonsense I'd heard about a burglar's fingers bitten clean off by an Alsatian, when Clive took it into his head to start climbing the pylon. I didn't think it was a sensible thing to do but it was pointless saying anything.

'Not a good idea, that.'

'Why?'

Climbing the pylon wasn't easy. The inspection ladder didn't start until a height of nine feet – obviously with schoolboys in mind – but that didn't stop Clive. He lifted the door we used as a bench and leaned it against the struts of one of the pylon's legs. Climbing on the struts, he pulled himself to the top of the door, and standing on its top edge he was able to haul himself up to the inspection ladder. He ascended a few rungs and seemed happy to hang there for a while. I got bored watching him.

It was late afternoon and the sky had gone a dark, cobalt shade of blue. I finished off the cider, unzipped my trousers and stuck my dick outside the curtains to empty my bladder. A kind of spasm shot through me before I'd finished, stronger even than those I'd felt before. I ignored it. 'So the burglar,' I was telling Clive, 'knew the key was on a string inside the letter box. So when the owners came home they got into the hallway and found,' I finished pissing, zipped up and turned to complete the story. But my words tailed off, 'two fingers still holding the string . . .'

I looked up the inspection ladder to the top of the pylon. I looked at the grey metal struts. I looked everywhere. Clive had vanished.

'Clive?'

I checked all around. Then I went outside. I thought he might have jumped down, or fallen. He wasn't there. I went back inside. Then I went outside again.

Spots of rain started to appear. I looked up at the wires and they seemed to hum contentedly. I waited for a while until the rain came more heavily, and went home.

That night while I was lying in bed, I heard the telephone ring. I knew what time it was because I could hear the television signature blaring from the lounge. It was the end of the late night news. Then my mother came upstairs. Had I seen Clive? His mother had phoned. She was worried.

The next day I was interviewed by a policewoman. I explained we were playing under the pylon, I turned my back and he'd disappeared. She made a note and left.

A few days later the police were out like blackberries in September. Half the neighbourhood joined in the fine-toothcomb search of the waste ground and the nearby fields.

They found nothing. Not a hair from his head.

While the searches went on, I started to have a recurring nightmare. I'd be back under the pylon, pissing and happily talking away to Clive. Only it wasn't urine coming out, it was painful fat blue and white sparks of electricity. I'd turn to Clive in surprise, who would be descending the inspection ladder wearing fluorescent blue overalls, his face out of view. And his entire body would be rippling with eels of electricity, gold sparks arcing wildly. Then slowly his head would begin to rotate towards me and I'd start screaming; but before I ever got to see his awful face I'd wake up.

We stopped playing under the pylon after that. No one had to say anything, we just stopped going there. I did go back once, to satisfy my own curiosity. The screens had been ripped away in the failed search, but the nettles bashed down by the police were already springing up again.

I looked up into the tower of the pylon, and although there was nothing to see, I felt a terrible sense of dread. Then a face appeared over the Nantwiches' fence. It was Olive. She'd seen me looking.

'Gone,' she said. It was the only word I ever heard her say. 'Gone.'

Summer came to an end and we went off to our respective schools. I saw Tania once or twice in her straw boater, but she passed me with her nose in the air. Eventually she married a Tory MP. I often wonder if she's happy.

Inevitably Kev and I stopped hanging around together, but not before there was a murder in the district. The landlord of the Dog and Trumpet was stabbed to death. They never found who did it. Joy moved out of the area when her parents split up. She went to live with her mother.

Joy went on to become a rock and roll singer. A star. Well,

not a star exactly, but I did once see her on *Top of the Pops*. She had a kind of trade mark, turning her back on the cameras to wiggle her bottom. I felt pleased for her that she'd managed to put the habit to good use.

Just occasionally I bump into Kev in this pub or that but we never really know what to say to each other. After a while Kev always says, 'Do you remember the time you hypnotised Tania Brown and . . .' and I always say 'Yes' before he gets to the end of the story. Then we look at the floor for a while until one of us says, 'Anyway, good to see you, all the best.' It's that *anyway* that gets me.

Clive Mann is never mentioned.

Occasionally I make myself walk past the old place. A new group of kids has started playing there, including Kev Duffy's oldest girl. Yesterday as I passed by that way there were no children around because an Electricity Board operative was servicing the pylon. He was halfway up the inspection ladder, and he wore blue overalls exactly like Clive in my dream. It stopped me with a jolt. I had to stare, even though I could sense the man's irritation at being watched.

Then came that singular, familiar thrum of energy. The maintenance man let his arm drop and turned to face me, challenging me to go away. But I was transfixed. Because it was Clive's face I saw in that man's body. He smiled at me, but tiny white sparks of electricity were leaking from his eyes like tears. Then he made to speak, but all I heard or saw was a fizz of electricity arcing across the metal brace on his teeth. Then he was the maintenance man again, meeting my desolate gaze with an expression of contempt.

I left hurriedly, and I resolved, after all, not to pass by the pylon again.

Waiting for a train

Joel Lane

I remember clearly the excitement I felt when I first came across Joel Lane's fiction in Karl Wagner's The Year's Best Horror Stories XV. *His story,* The Foggy, Foggy Dew, *had something of Ramsey Campbell about it, and something of Dennis Etchison, but the author already had his own voice and it was a compelling one. I was pleased when his story* Common Land *was picked from the first* Darklands *to be reprinted in volume XX of Wagner's* Year's Best, *particularly since that story had marked his return to writing horror fiction after a year spent despairing of the lack of suitable markets.*

Joel Lane was born in October 1963 in Exeter. He lives in Birmingham, where he works in educational publishing and sets many of his stories. These have appeared in Ambit, Critical Quarterly, Panurge, Exuberance *(issue four was a Joel Lane special featuring two stories, an interview and bibliography),* Skeleton Crew, Fantasy Tales, Dark Dreams, Winter Chills *and* Best New Horror 3. A *selection of his poems is due to appear in an anthology from Stride Publications in 1993.*

'Waiting for a Train,' he says, 'is about loneliness and need. When I was much younger I used to see isolation as being somehow inevitable. Now I see it as something that can be prevented and overcome; but so many people just miss the opportunity.' Waiting for a Train *also happens to be the grimmest, most disturbing story he has written so far.*

Waiting for a train

Everything was still and clear, as though the day were holding its breath. Frost took the colour out of the trees. Jason cupped his hands and blew into them as the sound of the approaching train echoed from beyond the red bridge. The platform was crowded, but nobody moved towards the line as the dark head of the Inter-City train emerged from the tunnel. No doubt they were waiting for the second-class carriages. Jason was so relieved at not having to queue to get onto the train when it eventually stopped that he didn't immediately realise he was the only one.

The carriage was half full of dazed-looking commuters, their sleep still ingrained in their faces like stubble. Most of them wore scarves and gloves. On the platform a crowd of people were still waiting, huddled in postures that suggested a lack of expectation. Some of them were reading books or newspapers; others stared through the train with eyes it was impossible to meet. Behind them, two porters were trying to wheel a huge box down a stone ramp that was badly in need of repair.

The carriage window framed a series of landscapes. A gravel yard was filled with the rusting shells of cars, piled ten or twenty deep. The Dunlop tyre factory occupied a valley, surrounded by a pale forest of electricity pylons. Further out, the bare fields were a crumpled quilt with its stitches broken; three cooling towers breathed shadow into the white sky. The only things moving were flocks of birds in the distance, their arrowhead formations tilting on an invisible mirror. Jason tried to lose himself in the view, pretending the frames moved in time rather than in space. There was a tightness in his chest which he identified as hunger. He couldn't remember when he'd last eaten.

Wasn't the buffet carriage nearer the front of the train? He stood up and walked through a series of long half-empty carriages, where the passengers sat immobile (in silence or with headphones), their eyes shut. The buffet compartment had no seats of its own; all the food was tightly sealed in plastic, to be taken away. Jason bought some coffee and a sandwich, then sat down in the nearest seat. He had no luggage to worry about. All the people in this carriage appeared to be eating; none of them were sat together or talking. His sandwich turned out to be rancid, part dry and part soggy, with a pale spot at one corner. The coffee was barely drinkable; there was a greyish sediment at the bottom of the cup that made him wish he'd left it alone. This had to be worth a complaint. Between Jason's seat and the buffet carriage, a man with shiny-gelled hair was quietly eating a large beefburger which smelt of rot and tomato ketchup. Jason could see white things moving through the meat, like loose teeth that had gone soft. He got up quickly and walked in the opposite direction.

Between carriages, he pushed down the window and let the frozen airstream scour his face. His eyes watered, blurring the view. There were no factories out here; only fields of white and gold stubble and bare trees like stained-glass windows without the glass. Beyond the ragged line of hedges, Jason thought he could glimpse the edge of a lake. Slowly, his nausea faded until he felt calm and sure of himself. The landscape was too real for him to pass through it. He twisted the door handle; it flew out of his hand as the door slammed against the carriage wall. The wind surrounded him like a bandage which slowly came unravelled as he stepped out towards the field. Before his feet could touch the grass, the railway tracks rushed up to brand him.

It was night, somewhere close to Wolverhampton and heading north. The train was almost empty. Jason had been playing cards with himself for hours, and wishing he had some music to listen to. A red gleam in the distance made him look up. There was a fire somewhere, outlining the rooftops in between; it seemed close because it was so bright. Around it, white streetlamps climbed into the sky. The train passed a factory with strange metallic pipes draped around its walls; an automatic light patrolled the vacant shop floor. Pieces of glass twinkled from a row of giant scrapheaps. Then he was looking down at the back yards of terraced houses, reaching almost to the railway. He could see the concrete paving, the washing lines, the curtained windows that framed inaccessible lives. Then more scrapheaps, towers, structures of aluminium and glass. And then the tunnel, vast and familiar as an empty bed.

The dark made him feel exposed. Was nobody else awake? Towards the back of the carriage, some people were slumped in their seats; an elderly couple were sleeping with their heads together, like a double exposure. All the faces were like curtained windows. Stepping quietly, Jason passed through the automatic doors to the next carriage. Three women were sitting at a table in semi-darkness. Their hands were moving; when he got closer, Jason saw that they were passing a single photograph around between themselves, always the same way. It was too dark to see what image they were sharing. He looked around: there was nobody else in sight.

Between that carriage and the next, someone was standing by the window and looking out. Jason could see the side of her face, and a shadowy reflection superimposed on the outlines of hedges and trees. She was young, about Jason's age, and had short black hair and a pale face. As he stepped past her, the girl turned. 'Hello.' Jason stared at her. Nobody had spoken to him on this train. She looked tired and edgy; perhaps she too was having trouble sleeping. 'Who are you?' she said.

'I'm Jason.' It was draughty in the space between carriages. The floor jerked sideways, making him feel unstable. 'Who are you?' She reminded him of Adele, his girlfriend at technical college. Behind her head, a few station lights were moving very slowly. The sound of the train dried out to a waiting vibration.

'Carol,' she said. 'Look. I want you to see something.' She turned back to the window and pointed with her eyes. Jason could see people standing on the station platform, and others sitting at the back. Nobody moved towards the train. In the thin light from behind them, their clothes and faces had no colour. They were very still, as though they had been waiting a long time. Carol turned round. 'Why don't they do something?' she said. 'Every station. I half want to get out and join them.' She looked at him. 'Stay here a bit.' The lights began to slide away to the right; the train was breathing again. Above the blackened rooftops, grey clouds stood out against the night. Jason stood next to Carol, trying to share what she saw. Occasional lights revealed a flat wasteland where clumps of grass were mixed with various debris: rubber tyres, scrap metal, burnt plastic, coils of wire. Carol gripped his hand. Her fingers were cold, but no worse than his.

Her mouth was warm, though. When they started kissing, Jason felt something shift inside him, like a hand of loneliness reaching up through his lungs. Carol's need matched his so exactly that she could have been his double. 'Stay with me,' she repeated, 'don't go away.' He could hear the uneven beating of her heart. They lay down together. The difficulty of making love in a confined space, the slight discomfort and confusion, gave him an unexpected sense of reality. The train's jolts and vibrations passed through them both, as though they were part of it and not just its passengers. The journey was theirs.

After the climax, they slipped apart. Jason felt numb and helpless, as though a current had been switched off. Carol recovered herself more quickly. She straightened her clothes and glanced at the window. 'They're still there,' she said. 'It's cold.' She wrapped her arms around herself and gave him a kind of frightened smile. 'Stay with me. I want you to see something.' She took his hand and led him through the door to the toilet: a tiny room with a wash-basin, a hand-towel and a condom machine.

'What is it? What's up?' There was nothing to see in here. There wasn't even a window. Carol looked even paler than before. She fumbled in the pockets of her denim jacket and brought out a little plastic box. It was full of new razor blades. Before Jason could say anything, she cut herself across the inside of her left wrist. A gash opened and, seconds later, began to bleed. She knelt down and held her wrist over the toilet bowl. Blood ran through the fingers. Jason knelt beside her and stroked her hair; he didn't know what else to do.

After a minute or so, Carol flushed the toilet. 'It goes over the tracks,' she said. 'The whole fucking line. It's my signature. Backwards and forwards.' She was crying quietly. The tears ran from her face into the rusty water. Jason tried to pull her away, but her muscles were rigid. Someone else would have to find her. As he closed the door behind him, he heard Carol flushing the toilet again. What did it mean, he wondered, when the acts you lived by were only gestures? But he didn't have time to think about it. The train had stopped; in the window, a city's distant lights were sprawled like a constellation. There must be some problem with the line ahead. Jason twisted the door-handle and carefully pushed the door half open. One sideways step, and he was able to climb onto the metal struts between carriages. From there, it was easy to pull himself up onto the carriage roof. He crouched there, with his hands and feet lodged in a metal grid. The cold made his fingers ache. Soon the train started up again; Jason tensed himself against the wind. Not far ahead, he could see the mouth of a tunnel where the railway passed under a road. He saw half the train disappear, its roar muffled by the sleeve of darkness; and when he was near enough to see a lorry on the road above the train, he put his hands over his face and stood up.

There was a brick-red glow on the skyline, the effect of either distant rainfall or fire. Jason could see pieces of the sky in the windows of derelict buildings. Quite a few people got on the train at Coventry; but most of them stayed on the platform. This time, he saw them clearly. He saw how many of them were crowded onto each seat, behind each face. Waiting for the train. Whatever it was that came to take them to another place or to reunite them with their families, it wasn't the train. It was just a vehicle, a machine on rails; not the train. Around him, people were storing luggage and looking for empty seats. Three of the newcomers sat around a table just across the aisle from Jason. They were his parents and his younger sister. He turned to face them; they didn't react.

Half an hour later, they were still ignoring him. Only his sister, Catherine, had thrown him a few secretive glances. Twice his father muttered something to his mother, and she nodded. They both looked tired and uneasy. How much longer could they keep this up? Suddenly, all three of them stood up and headed for the far end of the carriage. Jason had a clear view of the window where they had been: a sign read STAFFORD. He'd have to follow them out. But other people were blocking his way; by the time he'd got out onto the chilly platform, they had disappeared.

Wherever he looked, unreal faces stared him out. The wind from the departing train shuffled them like cards. It was a game of patience he couldn't win. For a moment he leaned against the wall, trying to gather his thoughts. The sky had clouded over, and the light was draining back into the sun. He tried to read the timetable to find out when the next train was due. Then he realised where his parents and sister must have gone. Trying to keep his mind clear, he walked through the ticket barrier and past the taxi rank just as the streetlamps were coming on, their light grainy with mist. The traffic sounded like a perpetual and vacant laughter.

Up the hill, past the school and the car park. Shops and offices gave way to houses with security lights that flashed on as Jason passed. Then the hospital, a series of grey buildings with grass verges surrounded by razor-wire. His parents' house was on the far side of the park. He'd been this way many times before. Just inside the gates, some children were playing on a climbing-frame made of scaffolding. A line of poplar trees flanked the pathway that divided the park into two areas – one neat and formal, the other uneven and wild. The dead leaves on the path must have fallen months ago.

Beyond the trees was a place he didn't recognise. Hints of light touched the gaps in the sky. The buildings ahead were formless and carried no signs. Tarpaulins hung from scaffolding like a huge window display. Jason walked faster, trying to recover his sense of direction. Telegraph wires made his scalp prickle as he turned around a corner, and found himself at the edge of a patch of wasteground which sloped down towards the town centre. He could see a blurred finger-painting of distant red and white lights against the night. The ground was littered with rusty cans and green glass. Some loose bricks suggested a past or future building site. Jason stared up into the clouds whose dirty grey stuck to the night like lichen. Suddenly he knew where to go.

It had been in his mind all the time, the only fixed point he had to rely on during that terrible Christmas at home. He was away from them now; their faces were blurred. Their voices couldn't reach him here, though the static in his head was almost as hard to endure. Not much further now. At the lower end of the wasteground, a gap in the wall let him through onto the railway line. The tunnel mouth was only a few yards ahead. Jason walked along the track until he couldn't see anything; then he lay down and put his head on the rail. The train took a long time coming. It always did.

Eyes like a ghost's

Simon Clark

Born 1958 in Wakefield, Simon Clark has appeared in Dark Dreams, Fear, BBR, Skeleton Crew, Peeping Tom, Aklo *and* The Year's Best Horror Stories. *His most disturbing story – before this one – was* Out From Under *in* Blood & Grit *(BBR Books). He draws a realistic picture of the world, then introduces something so shocking you almost gasp. Then it gets weird.*

In his early teens he experimented with reanimation; insects mainly, but he also attempted to revive a dead blackbird. The jump leads from his father's Lada slipped and hit the bumper, resulting in an arc which blasted the chrome work. 'The damage took some explaining.'

On why writers write, he suggests, '. . . to communicate something that is hugely important to them at an unconscious level: they don't even realise what it is, yet strive to communicate it.' Whereas some writers vanish behind their work, his presence is always felt, as is the sense of what he's communicating. However weird it gets, he remains a very human writer.

Eyes like a ghost's

I found the cassette in the boxful of books I'd bought at the cancer shop. I never even realised it was in there until I'd brought the box home, balanced on the PVC hood of my daughter's pushchair. Elizabeth would have played merry hell about that. The hood was already splitting in three places. Well, at the time, Elizabeth would be hammering at the till keys in the supermarket, so what the eye doesn't see . . .

'Dad! A computer game!'

My seven-year-old son, who had been rooting in the box, rattled the cassette box excitedly above his head.

'I shouldn't think so, Lee,' I said, pulling my gloves off. 'Someone'll have left it there by mistake.'

'Oh . . . music.' He pushed 'music' out from his lips with disgust.

'Probably.'

'Music, crap music.' He threw the tape back in the box and returned to the television. Bart Simpson was spraying 'EAT MY SHORTS' on the school wall.

'Someone phoned up,' called Lee, swinging his legs over the arm of the chair. 'They said, "Can I speak to Martin Price?"'

'Well, that's my name,' I said. 'What did you tell them?'

'I put the phone down.'

'Didn't you ask if you could take a message?'

Lee didn't answer. The television had greater pulling power than me.

I toyed with the idea of delivering a lecture on manners but apart from the likelihood of it falling on deaf ears, the tape Lee had pulled from the box caught my attention. For some reason I felt pleased. The tape hidden amongst the books seemed a minor bonus. I intended a closer look but an annoyed yell from the kitchen signalled my daughter wanted release from her pushchair. And a biscuit . . . And a drink . . . And toys . . . And . . .

The tape would have to wait.

* * *

YOU CAN'T SEE ME, BUT I SEE YOU

I am Joseph Lawton. This happens:

I ride with you on bicycles I have painted golden, to where the trees paint the watery face of the river that shines beneath the sun. There we drink wine, eat sandwiches and you describe your paintings: tight, tight canvases all covered with ice-cream smiles, cats and gnomes and fishes and laughter.

Later, I play my guitar as you lay across the blanket and look up at the sky.

The sky is as blue as my guitar and full of music.

* * *

'The man on the telly said it was going to snow.' Lee gleefully bounced up and down on the sofa while looking out of the window. 'Snow, snow faster. Ally-ally aster.'

'Lee, stop bouncing. How many times have I got to tell you?'

He ignored me. 'Can we get the sledge out?'

'If it snows. Have you seen my slippers?'

'Saw Jug chewing them.'

'Oh, bugger. Did you stop her?'

'No.'

'Thanks a lot, Lee.' Barefooted I crossed the room to where I'd left the box on the sideboard. *The wood's scratched to high heaven as it is* . . . Elizabeth would scold. Not that she really minded. I knew she loved me and the kids more than anything. A long time ago she'd stopped worrying about pristine furniture and spotless carpets. I don't believe there's such a thing as a houseproud parent.

On top of the box lay the cassette. It might as well have been calling my name. I picked it up. Someone had turned the inlay card inside out as if ready to make a contents list but for some reason had never got round to it. Pencilled very firmly in the corner of the card were the letters JL.

I glanced across at the stereo. A few minutes remained before Elizabeth returned home. I tapped the cassette thoughtfully against my chin.

I'd taken three steps toward the stereo when I stopped suddenly. My bare toes sank into wet pile.

'Lee.' I sighed. 'Did you spill your pop this morning?'

'No,' he replied innocently, then continued his snow watch.

Kids make you philosophical. I dropped the cassette back in the box and went to hunt for a cloth under the kitchen sink.

* * *

MILES OF SMILES

I am Joseph Lawton. This happens:

'This is for you,' I say. I give her the ring with a diamond. She puts it on the third finger of her left hand. On the middle finger of her other hand is another ring set with an emerald as big as a man's eye. She looks down at her new ring for a while; her hair the colour of Turner sunsets falls across her face. Then she sits on the end of the bed and cries. I put my arm around her shoulder. These moments, I think, are precious.

Later she stands and tells me she will make a stir-fry.

I lean back across the bed, play the guitar and sing. It sounds like the golden bells that hang in the smiling trees of paradise.

I know I love her, because they told me so.

* * *

'See you tonight, Martin. Chops all right?'

'Perfect, love.' I kissed Elizabeth, then Lee, then Grace, sitting so warmly wrapped up in her pushchair that only her eyes peeped over the blanket.

They waved me good-bye in a line as I drove away from the house. I watched the figures grow small in my mirror, still waving like a family from the Waltons.

My hand groped across the back seat amongst the toys and my plastic sandwich box, then closed over the small, sharp cornered box of the cassette. I snapped the tape into the car's stereo.

For a second nothing much happened, just the hiss of the old tape. Then emerging from the hiss, almost growing from it rather than a recording came a voice.

'Yeah.' A male voice; in his twenties perhaps. No accent. You could imagine the man nodding as he spoke, as if acknowledging he was ready.

More tape hiss then in a flat voice, 'This is it.'

I was ready to eject the tape in favour of the radio. My surprise find was turning out to be a non-event. Then the music started.

A guitar, slightly out of tune, as if the strings lacked the proper tension. I'd played electric guitar in the youth club band as a teenager, but I wasn't even sure if I was listening to an electric or an acoustic.

The strumming chords were fumbling, hesitant. A pause. Then the guitar started again. This time vigorous, with a newfound sense of assurance.

When the man began to sing I nearly switched off. The

voice sounded flat and very nearly tuneless.

A wannabe pop star, I decided, with all the talent of a no-hoper in a tailspin, had simply been filling a Sunday afternoon. But my hand paused on the switch. The dirge had almost been laughable, yet as I listened to the lyric a quirky kind of charisma began to shine through.

The first song sounded faintly psychedelic with repeated reference to 'the black bear that sleeps by my head', and 'I may be tall but I feel so small'.

I became so engrossed in the songs, their stark beauty so unearthly, that I drove on a kind of autopilot, not noticing the queues of traffic over the bridge into town.

The strange lyrics and hypnotic guitar filled the car. I upped the volume. There was a trembling tenderness and sincerity in the voice; the words wound their way around my brain like spiders' webs. They stuck. The songs made me think of a child who had seen or experienced something profound; something they did not understand, yet which they desperately, desperately tried to describe using the only imagery they had available to them. The effect was of an attempt at communicating a transforming experience but failing. Yet even in failure some essence of the message filtered through – and its power winded me.

* * *

SMILE? THIS MIGHT HAPPEN TO YOU

My name is Joseph Lawton. This happens:

'There's one! And there's another!' cries Sophie excitedly.

'How many's that?' I ask. 'Have you kept count?'

'Have you, silly?' she laughs. We are both giggling. The cat watches us; it jumps from the sofa to the drawers then back again. She knows.

'What do you think they are?' She holds my bare arm under the table lamp. 'Can you feel them? Do they itch?'

At first I'm not sure. 'No . . . Not itch. No, but I felt a tingling.'

'Hold still, silly.' She looks at my arm so closely her hair washes over my skin like cool silk. 'They are on both arms. Look. There must be . . . four, five . . . Six. That's just on this forearm . . . Here. Oh! I think they really are, you know.'

'What?'

'Ancient writing. Yes! Sumerian cuneiform.' She looks up at me, her eyes shining. She is beautiful.

Then I gaze at my arms. They are covered with white marks under the skin, like tattoos without colour. It started yesterday as I lay on the bed playing my guitar. This morning my arms are covered with ancient cuneiform symbols – stars, squares, spiky pennants, snowflakes, crooked crosses, tactile swastikas: ghosts' tattoos. Something marvellous is happening to me.

'I recognise this one,' says Sophie. 'This is Ishtar. A Sumerian goddess.'

'Ishtar,' I whisper. She looks quickly up at me with her eyes shining like diamonds. 'She is sending you a message. We have to copy these down and take them to someone who can read them.'

On the little table in the corner of the room the television shows a film in black and white. A ghost with sparking eyes and graveyard teeth plays a violin as the gates to a thundering hole in the earth open. There is movement behind the gate. The ghost plays faster. I recognise the music. Because it is mine.

* * *

'I'm going out on site,' I told Brian. 'I'll be about an hour.'

Brian, his mouth crammed with a sausage sandwich, could only manage a nod.

I didn't switch on the stereo until I parked my car at a rural paddock surrounded by trees without leaves. In eighteen months it would be buried beneath executive homes. Now it looked bleak.

I listened to the tape from end to end. It had its hooks deep inside of me.

More songs, some spangled with bizarre surrealist imagery. Some very plain. These plain ones were perhaps the most effective. They were sparse descriptions of what the singer might have been seeing from his window at that very moment. But all the songs carried this potent charge that was electrifying. And always the plod, plod, plod of the guitar. Often the songs did not end in the conventional way. They simply fell apart as if some joker had stolen the last sheet of music; then the singer faltered to a halt. Sometimes you thought the songs would continue as a change of key seemed to herald a new verse. Then the song would abruptly end. As I listened, gazing at the bare winter fields I thought of God at the egg-crack of creation, rehearsing making Man and Woman only to break off in failure to toss away a part-formed torso, a fragment of head.

The collection of songs ended in a scrabble of fretwork sounds followed by the ringing thump of the microphone falling on the floor. The singer spoke for the last time; the voice weary, defeated: 'That's it. There is no more.'

I listened to the tape one more time before driving back to work.

When I walked through the door I thought I'd walked into the wrong office. I saw my name plate, MARTIN PRICE, on my desk, I knew the names of the dozen people sat at their desks, but just for an instant they looked like strangers.

Brian, peeling the wrapper from a Mars Bar, looked out of the window.

'It's starting to snow,' he said.

* * *

CONCRETE HANDS CLAP THE FUNERAL CLOWNS

My name is Joseph Lawton. This happens:

I know there are people who are suffering and who are unhappy now, while I, happy, warm and at peace, sit and play my guitar. Sophie stands at the kitchen table, buttering bread, slicing red cheese. She looks up and smiles at me. Sad people thoughts push roughly into my brain.

I try to forget. I cannot.

All over this world people are suffering pain. Someone must be to blame. My thoughts spill into the song. Maybe with the stars on my arms I can help.

'A sad song,' says Sophie, licking butter from her ring with the green stone as big as a man's eye. 'Oh, look. Don't cry. Don't be sad.' She walks to me, her bare legs look pale beneath her tasselled skirt. Her hands that touch my face are cool and buttery.

The sorrowing voices of all the people that suffer fill my head. I imagine them crying out to me. Only I can save them. Only I can save them. They cry and they cry.

And that's when I know Sophie must die.

* * *

I think you'll find this interesting. I found the tape in a box of books in a charity shop. God knows who the singer is, but there's a weird kind of charisma there, almost hypnotic. When you hear it you'll know. I thought you might consider it for one of your special limited edition albums. Anyway, have a listen, Bob, and let me know what you think. In the meantime I'm going to try and find the guy. I've got a couple of leads. Christ! Now I know what it feels like to be a detective!

I posted the copy of the tape to Bob Finch, an old school mate.

He now owned three record shops and did some record producing. Very small time but his records were highly regarded.

Then I drove to the area of town which can adequately be described as 'bedsit land'. Tree-lined Victorian avenues; redbrick houses sub-divided into flats and bedsits. From some windows red bulbs glowed.

I parked the car and pulled an envelope from my jacket pocket. One of those brown municipal ones that litter drawers in every household. This one had fallen from a children's illustrated book of fables I found in the box of books from the cancer shop. Pencilled on one side: *Ishtar – Sumerian goddess – arrives at the gates of the underworld – threatens to break down the gates and set the dead upon the living.* On the reverse, a computer-printed label gave an address in this street. Flat 7b, Park View. The name, Joseph Lawton. I felt a rush of triumph. Coincidence be buggered! That matched the initials JL on the cassette inlay card. I had found him!

* * *

I OWN DEAD COW HANDS. I OWN A VEGETABLE SOUL

My name is Joseph Lawton. This happens:

I wake Sophie who sleeps by my side. I tell her about my dreams. I tell her I must save thousands of sad lives.

'How?'

I tell her she has to die.

She looks at me as the sunshine pushes its way into our bedroom. Then she sits up, holds my armful of stigmata to her little bare breasts, and looks hard into my eyes and says, 'All right.'

I feel happy, I feel sad, I feel GHOST. No. I don't know why I said that.

I feel transforming.

I make breakfast – a bowl each with one Weetabix and a handful of bran. Milk. There's milk in the bowl for the cat. I have cat-shaped thoughts in my head. Black cat thoughts.

We go shopping.

In Poundstretcher I pick up a knife. It flashes like a solid sliver of light. Pure, pure light. Hygienic-looking.

'Is that the one?' she asks.

'Yes.' I put the knife in the basket. The time is 9.30.

She admires a picture of a black cat in a yellow frame. I take it from her and put it in the basket. 'I'll put it on the wall for you,' I say, then I pick up the knife and study the way it flashes Morse under the fluorescent lights. What messages, I wonder. The blade is long and clean. I know I will need it soon.

We go to the tills where she puts three packets of cherry sweets into the basket. Smiling, Sophie talks to the girl at the till. We pay £3.40. The time is 9.50.

* * *

Before I left the car I sat listening to the tape, looking up at the huge brick facade of the house; a moulded brick plaque bore the legend PARK VIEW 1875. Which one of those lighted windows held Joseph Lawton? What did he look like? I imagined a young man with Christ-like hair; aesthennic build; a pair of burning eyes. Reclusive. Like one of those Victorian poets who starved in garrets. I pictured him walking, shoulders hunched, down this tree-lined avenue, so completely absorbed by his blistering visions that on one level he saw nothing; yet on a deeper level he saw everything.

This seemed so important to me now. Last week I found my old guitar in the loft, restrung it and was busy learning the songs from the tape by ear. They were an inspiration to me.

* * *

ORANGES, ORANGES, ORANGES IN YOUR HAIR

I am Joseph Lawton. This happens:

I sing to Sophie who sits on the wooden chair at the kitchen table. She looks at the picture on the wall. The cat within its yellow frame.

Her hair looks orange in the afternoon light. She smiles and fiddles with her ring with the green stone as big as the eye of a ghost.

I go drench the knife in boiling water and leave it on the drainer to dry. I know I will need the knife soon.

It is 3.30pm.

I begin my preparations. I take the blank cassette tape from the box under the bed. I blow the dust from the tape deck. The guitar has fresh strings. Microphones are checked and plugged into the deck.

The sheets of paper on which my songs are written are spread carefully on the table. There is a special order to this. Like a ceremony.

Sophie glances at my arms covered with the ghost white tattoos; Sumerian symbols of life, death, hope, love, death, re-birth, bitterness, black cats, tactile feelings, love-dove-shove . . . 4.15. Everything is ready.

* * *

Evening. Dark. Cold. Snow on the ground.

I stood in the avenue with its huge Victorian town houses and trees long since stripped of their leaves.

Loud voices argued nearby. That's the kind of area it was.

'He is!'

'He's not.'

'He's going to do it, I tell you. He is actually going to do it.'

'He's not.'

'Look at him. He's decided. He's crossing the street.'

Ignoring the voices I approached Park View. Most of the window frames looked rotten. The front door had been roughly painted purple. But there were enough scratches on it to show every colour it had been painted since 1875. A dozen door bells set in an illuminated plastic panel caught my eye. A few had cards bearing handwritten names. Joseph Lawton was not amongst them.

* * *

I FEEL UNREAL. I FEEL ALONE

I am Joseph Lawton. This happens:

On the rug, the black cat sits licking her paw. It is 5.30.

'Sophie, are you frightened?'

'No,' she replies with a little shake of her head and watches me with her clear eyes.

'There is no hatred in this,' I explain. 'I have read the messages. I must save lives. When I kill you I will be doing it for love.'

She agrees.

'I hear them shouting from the street. Sophie, they have voices like ghosts – all in pain and crunching out. I have to save them.'

She sits on the settee, wearing a purple skirt and a white T-shirt. It bears the picture of a black cat playing with a ball of wool.

I smile, hoping it will stop her worrying. Lightly, I run the knife, like a single-toothed comb, through her hair. No, don't be frightened sweet Sophie, smile and smile and smile.

Once those voices that crunch and crack from the pavement are gone I will be happy again. We can ride the golden cycles to the river once more.

It all goes quickly. The knifing.

She took it very well. That pleases me. She doesn't cry out or wriggle.

She just sits there as I press the knife into her neck. Three times there. Four times through the cat picture on her T-shirt.

I pull the knife out of her, wash it, and put it in the drawer.

When I return she still sits on the sofa, the hair about her white face looks very red.

'Will it take long?' she asks. 'My neck is sore.'

'Not long, sweet Sophie.' I hold her hand and stroke her hair. 'After you've left this place, will you still love me?'

She makes a little smile; then her eyes go cloudy.

At 6.15pm. she is dead. I prop her up with cushions so she can still see me. Then I switch on the tape deck. The voices in the street stop screaming at me; my arms are clean; and yet I feel as if all the magic that I once knew has gone. My world is cold and lonely now.

Now the guitar is in my hands. I sit on the chair by the table.

'Yeah.' I nod to Sophie. 'This is it.' Softly, I begin to play my guitar.

* * *

I pushed open the door of Park View and stepped inside. I stopped suddenly. It was as if I'd been there before. Incongruously the place smelt pleasantly of cooking smells, especially garlic.

With no trace of hesitation I half-ran up the stairs to the second floor. No carpets made the sound of my feet echo up and down the stairwell.

When I reached a door with 7b written large in black felt tip I stopped. For some reason I was holding my breath. Then it came. I don't know why but for some reason the place I was in suddenly scared me. The squares of carpets outside doors looked too thick, the doors too big for their doorways; nail heads swelled from the skirting boards in a way that was somehow disgusting, grey metallic stumps forcing outwards.

I closed my eyes to stop the images lodging like parasites inside my head.

The sickening feeling went as quickly as it came. I felt calm. Somewhere in the distance came the sound of a girl singing. A ballad, slow, haunting. Outside, trees gently waved in the breeze. The sense of peace was beautiful.

I knocked on the door. 'Mr Lawton. I happened to come across a tape of your songs in a . . .'

Maybe that was better. Mentally rehearsing the greeting I knocked again.

'Hello?'

The door remained closed. I realised the voice came from behind me. I turned to see a girl. In her twenties, ginger hair; she wore a vaguely hippy-style dress and plain white blouse. There was a black cat in her hands which she stroked nervously.

'Hello,' I smiled. 'I'm looking for the tenant.'

She wrinkled her freckled nose. 'Sorry?'

I looked back at the door. 'Does a man live there? A musician?'

'No . . . no. That one's empty. It's been empty for months.'

Gone. I was on the verge of swearing furiously, but the fury did not come. I felt a lightness oozing through my body; a pleasant sensation. And life looked different now. I looked, no, I felt different. Enlightened. I would become a different person. Something was happening to me. Something special.

'Is there anything else you want?'

Her voice pulled me back. I must have been staring.

'Yes there is,' I said firmly. 'I need a place to stay. The empty flat will be fine.'

She stroked the cat in a shy but quietly pleased way. She liked me. 'The landlord comes to collect the rent about now. You could ask him about the flat.' She looked up with the tiniest of shy smiles. 'If you want . . . if you're not in a hurry . . . you could wait for him in my flat. I've got some tea.' She rubbed the cat's head. The green stone in her ring caught the light with an emerald flash.

As I followed her through the door she paused and looked back up at me. 'What's your name, mister?'

I smiled, feeling a liquid heat run through my body. 'My name?' I reached out and ran my fingers through the cat's coal-black fur. 'My name's Joseph Lawton.'

I followed her inside and shut the door.

* * *

Martin!
Thanks for the letter. From what you say the songs sound fascinating. But check your stereo for gremlins. The tape you sent me was blank!
Good luck, Bob Finch.

Always

Michael Marshall Smith

At the 1991 British Fantasy Convention Michael Marshall Smith picked up two awards – the Icarus award for Best Newcomer and the Best Short Story award for The Man Who Drew Cats *which appeared in* Dark Voices 2 *and was reprinted in* Best New Horror 2. *I've been speaking to his friends and they think it was a flash in the pan. Why else would it be called the Icarus Award? They meet in rooms across North London, these so-called friends, and discuss the timetable for his downfall. Should they wait until after the January 1994 publication by HarperCollins of his brilliant novel* Only Forward? *Or nip it in the bud now, just as he sets to work on his second novel and may be about to land a feature commission? But these things have their own momentum: his agent, muttering darkly about a complete life change, is leaving the country; his lease in Kentish Town prohibits the keeping of a cat; and the corner video shop tore up his card when he failed to return* Look Who's Talking Too.

He was born in Knutsford, Cheshire, in May 1965 and grew up in the US, South Africa and Australia before returning with his family to England in 1975. He went to Cambridge, fell in with the wrong crowd (Footlights) and ended up in a Radio 4 comedy show, And Now in Colour . . . *His favourite authors include Ray Bradbury, Stephen King, Kingsley and Martin Amis, Jack Finney, Ramsey Campbell and Thomas Wolfe – 'the proper one, not the 70s loser'.*

His Darklands *story,* The Dark Land, *is reprinted in* Best New Horror 3. *This story is very different, the effect is different – but devastating.*

Always

for Sarah

Jennifer stood, watching the steadily falling drizzle, underneath the awning in front of the station entrance. She waited for the cab to arrive with something that was not quite impatience: there was no real hurry, though she wanted to be with her father. It was just that the minutes were filled to bursting with an awful weight of unavoidable fact, and if she had to spend them anywhere, she would rather it were not under an awning, waiting for a cab.

The train journey down from Manchester had been worse, far worse. Then she had felt a desperate unhappiness, a wild hatred of the journey and its slowness. She'd wanted to jig herself back and forwards on her seat like a child, to push the train faster down the tracks. The black outside the window had seemed very black, and she'd seen every streak of rain across the glass. She'd stared out of it for most of the journey, her face sometimes slack with misery, sometimes rigid with the effort of not crying, of keeping her hands and body from trembling and twitching with horror. The harder she stared at the dark hedges in shadow fields, the further she tried to see, the closer the things she saw.

She saw her mother, standing at the door of the house,

wrapped in a cardigan and smiling, happy to see her home. She saw the food parcels she'd prepared for Jennifer whenever she visited, bags of staple foods mixed with nuggets of gold, little things that only she'd known that Jennifer liked. She saw her decorating the Christmas tree by herself in happy absorption, saw her in her chair by the fire, regal and round, talking nonsense to the utterly contented cat spreadeagled across her lap. She tried to see, tried to understand, the fact that her mother was dead.

After her father had phoned she'd moved quickly through the flat, throwing things in a bag, locking up, driving with heavy care to the station. Then there had been things to do. Now there was nothing. Now was the beginning of a time when there was nothing to do, nowhere to hide, no way to escape, no means of undoing. In an instant the world had changed, had switched from a home to a cold hard country where there was nothing but rain and minutes that stretched like railway tracks into the darkness. Nothing was the same any more, nothing would ever be the same: and her mind screamed as it tried to bend itself to fit a world in which her mother was no longer there.

At Crewe a man got on and sat opposite. He had tried to talk to her: to comfort her or to take advantage of her distress, it didn't matter which. She stared at him for a moment, lit another cigarette and looked back out of the window. She judged all men by her father. If she could imagine them getting on with him, they were all right. If not, they didn't exist.

She tried to picture her father, alone in the house. How big that house must feel, how hollow, how much like a foreign place, as the last of her mother's breaths dissipated into the air. Would he know which molecules had been inside her, cooling as they mixed? Knowing him, he might. When he'd called, the first thing, the only thing she could think was that she had to be near him, and as she waited out the minutes she tried to reach out with her mind, tried to picture him alone in a house where the woman he'd loved for thirty years had sat down to read a book by the fire and died of a brain haemorrhage while he made her a cup of tea.

As long as she could remember there had been few family friends, been no need for them. Her parents were two sides of the same coin, and had no need for anyone else. So different, and yet the same person, moving forever in a slow comfortable symmetry. Her mother had been home, her father the magic that lit up the windows; her mother had been love, her father the spell that kept out the cold. She knew now why as the years went on her love for her parents had begun to stab her with something that was like cold terror: because some day she would be alone. Some day she would be taken in the night from the world she knew and abandoned in a place where there was no one to call out to, nowhere to turn.

And now, as she stood waiting for a cab in the town where she'd grown up, she numbly watched the drizzle as it fell on the distant shore of a far country on a planet the other side of the universe. The trees by the station road called out to her, pressing their twisted familiarity upon her, but her mind balked, refused to acknowledge them. This wasn't any world she knew.

In three weeks it would be Christmas, and her mother was dead.

The cab arrived, and the driver tried to talk to her. She answered his questions brightly.

At the top of the drive she stopped for a long moment, throat clenching. Everything was different. All the trees, all the pots of plants her mother had tended, all the stones on the drive had moved a millimetre. The tiles had shifted infinitesimally on the roof, the paint had faded a millionth of a shade. She had come home, but home wasn't there any more.

Then the front door opened spreading a patch of warmth on to the drive, and she fled into the arms of her father.

For a long time she stood there, cradled in his warmth, only then realising how badly she'd needed to see him. He was comfort, he was an end to suffering. It had been him who had talked her through her first boyfriend's abrupt departure, him who had held her hand after childish nightmares, him who had come to her when as a newborn ball of needs she had cried out in the night. Her mother had been everything for her in this world, but her father the one who stood between Jennifer and worlds outside, in the way of any hurt.

After a while she looked up, and saw the living room door. It was shut, and it was then that she finally broke down.

Sitting in the kitchen in worn-out misery she held close to her the cup of tea her father had made, too numb to flinch from the pain that stabbed from every corner of her mother's kitchen. On the side was a jar of mincemeat, and a bag of flour. They would not be used. She tried to deflect her gaze, to find something to focus on, but every single thing spoke of her mother: everything was something she wouldn't use again, something she'd liked, something that looked strange and forlorn without her mother holding it. All the objects looked random and meaningless without her mother to provide the context they made sense in, and she knew that if she could look at herself she would look the same. Her mother could never hold her again, would never see her married or have children. And she would have been such a fantastic grandmother, the kind you only find in children's books.

On the kitchen table were some sheets of wrapping paper, and for a moment that made her smile wanly. It had always been her father who bought the wrapping paper, and in years of looking Jennifer had never been able to find paper that was anywhere near as beautiful. Marbled swirls of browns and golds, of greens and reds, muted bursts of life that had lain curled beneath the Christmas tree like a bed of flowers. The paper on the table was as wonderful as ever, some a warm pink, the rest a pale sea of shifting blue.

Every year on Christmas morning, as she sat at her customary end of the sofa to begin unwrapping her presents, Jennifer had felt a warm thrill of wonder. She could remember as a young girl looking at the perfect oblongs of her presents and knowing that she was seeing magic at work. For her father would wrap the presents, and there were never any joins. She would hold the presents up, look at them every way she could, and still not find any Sellotape, or edges of paper. However difficult the shape, it was as if the paper had formed itself round it like a second skin.

One evening every Christmas her father would disappear to do his wrapping: she had never seen him do it, and neither, she knew, had Mum. In more recent years Jennifer had found the joins, cleverly tucked and positioned so as almost to disappear, but that hadn't undone the magic. Indeed, in her heart of hearts she believed that her father had done it deliberately, let her see the joins because she was too old for a world where there could be none.

She could remember once, when she'd been a very little girl, asking her mother how Daddy did it. Her mother had told her that Dad's wrapping was his art, that when the King of the Fairies needed his presents wrapped he sent for her father to do it. He went far off to a magic land to wrap the King's presents, and while he was away he did theirs too. Her mother had said it with a smile in her eyes, to show she was joking, but also with a small frown on her forehead, as if she wasn't sure if she was.

As Jennifer sat staring at the paper her father came back in.

He seemed composed but a little shocked, as if he'd seen the neighbours dancing naked in their garden. He took her hand and they sat for a while, two of them where three should be.

And for a long time they talked, and remembered her. Already time seemed short, and Jennifer tried to remember everything she could, to mention every little thing, to write them in her mind so that they would still be there in the morning. Her father helped her, mixing in his own memories, as she scrabbled and clutched, desperate to gather all she could before the wind blew them away.

Looking up at the clock as she made another cup of tea she saw that it was four o'clock, that it would soon be tomorrow, the day after her mother had died, and suddenly she slumped over, crying with the kettle in her hand. Because the day after that would be the day after that day, the week after the week after, next year the anniversary. It would never end. From now on all time was after time: there was no going back, no undoing, no last moment to snatch. There would be so many days, and so many hours, and no matter how many times the phone rang, it would never be her mother.

Seeing her, her father stood up and came to her. As she laid her head on his shoulder he finished making the tea, and then he tilted her head up to look at him. He looked at her for a long time, and she knew that he, and nobody else, could see inside her and know what she felt.

'Come on,' he said.

She watched as he walked to the table and picked up some of the wrapping paper.

'I'm going to show you a secret.'

'Will it help?' Jennifer felt like a little child, watching the big man, her father.

'It might.'

* * *

They stood for a moment outside the living room door. He didn't hurry her, but let her ready herself. She knew that she had to see her mother, couldn't just let her fade away behind a closed door. Finally she looked up at him, and he opened the door.

The room she walked into seemed huge, cavernous. Once cosy, the heart of the house, now it stretched like a black plain far out into the rain, the corners cold and dark. The dying fire flickered against the shadows, and as she stepped towards it Jennifer felt the room grow around her, bare and empty as the last inaudible echoes of her mother's life died away.

'Oh Mum,' she said, 'oh Mum.'

Sitting in her chair by the fire she could almost have been asleep. She looked old, and tired, but comfortably warm, and it seemed that the chair where she sat was the centre of the world. Jennifer reached out and touched her hand. Kissed by the end of the fire, it was still warm, could still have reached out and touched her. Her father shut the door, closing the three of them in together, and Jennifer sat down by the fire, looking up at her mother's face. What had been between the lines was gone, but the lines were still there, and she looked at every one.

She looked up to see that her father had spread three sheets of the pink wrapping paper on the big table. He came and crouched down beside her and they held Mum's hand together, and Jennifer's heart ached to imagine what his life would be like without her, without his Queen. Together they kissed her hand, and said goodbye as best they could, but you can't say goodbye when you're never going to see someone again. It isn't possible. That's not what goodbye means.

Her father stood, and with infinite tenderness picked his wife up in his arms. For a moment he cradled her, a groom on his wedding day holding the slender wand of his love at the beginning of their life together. Then slowly he bent, and to Jennifer's astonishment he laid her mother out on the wrapping paper.

'Dad...'

'Shh,' he said.

He picked up another couple of sheets of paper and laid them on top of her. His hands made a small folding movement where they joined, and suddenly there was only one long piece of wrapping paper. Jennifer's mouth dropped open like a child's.

'Dad, how...'

'Shh.'

He took the end of the sheet lying under her mother, and folded it over the top. Slowly he worked his way around the table, folding upwards with little movements of his hands. Like two gentle birds they slowly wove round each other, folding and smoothing. Jennifer watched silently, cradling her tea, seeing at last her father do his wrapping, and as he moved round the table the two sheets of paper were knitted together as if it were the way they'd always been.

After about fifteen minutes he paused, and she stepped closer to look. Only her mother's face was visible, peeking out of the top. The rest of her body was enveloped in a pink paper shroud that seamlessly held her close. Her father bent and kissed his wife briefly on the lips, and she bent too, and kissed her mother's forehead. Then he made another folding movement, brought the last edge of paper over and smoothed, and suddenly there was no gap, no join, just a large irregular paper parcel perfectly wrapped. Jennifer cried a little, knowing she would never see her mother's face again.

Then her father moved and stood halfway down the table. He slid his arm under his wife's back, and gently brought it upwards. The paper creaked softly as he raised her body into a sitting position, and then further, until it was bent double. He made a few more smoothing motions and all Jennifer could do was stare, eyes wide. On the table was still a perfect parcel, but half as long. He slid his hand under again, and folded it in half again, then moved round, and folded it the other way, gentle and unhurried. For ten minutes he folded and smoothed, tucked and folded, and the parcel grew smaller and smaller, until it was two feet square, two feet by one, six inches by nine. Then his concentration deepened still further, and as he folded he seemed to take especial care with the way the paper moved, and out of the irregular shape emerged corners and edges. And still the parcel grew smaller and smaller.

When he finally straightened there was on the table a tiny oblong, not much bigger than a matchbox, a perfect pink parcel. Jennifer moved closer to watch as he pulled a length of russet ribbon from his pocket, and painted a line first one way round, then the other to meet at the top. As he tied the bow she looked closely at the parcel and knew she'd been right all along, that she'd seen the truth as a child. There were no joins, none at all.

When he had finished her father held the little shape in his hands and looked at her. He reached out and touched her face, his fingers as warm as they'd always been, and in their touch was a blessing, a persistence of love. All the time she'd been on this planet they had always been there, her father and mother, someone to do the good things for, and to help the bad things go away.

'I can only give you one present this year, Jen, and it's something you've already got. This is only a reminder.'

He held up the parcel to her, and she took it. It felt warm and comforting, all her childhood, all her love in a small oblong box. She felt she knew what she should do, and brought the present in close to her, and pressed it against her heart. As she shed her final tears her father held her close and wished her Happy Christmas, and when she took her hand away, the present was gone from her hand, and beat in her heart.

The journey back to Manchester passed in a slow blur of recollection, and when she was back in her flat she walked slowly around it, touching objects in the slanting haze of early morning light. She wished she could be with her father, but knew he was right to tell her to go back. As she sat in the hallway she listened to the beating of her heart, and as she looked at reminders of Mum she let herself feel glad. It would take time, but it was something she already had: she had her mother deep inside her, what she'd been, the love she'd given and felt. She was her mother's pride and joy, and while she still lived her mother lived too: her finest and favourite work, the living sum of her love and happiness. There would be no goodbyes, because she could never really lose her. She could never speak to her again in words, but she would always hear her voice. She would always be inside her, helping her face the world, helping her to be herself.

And Jennifer thought about her father, and knew her heart would soon be fuller still. She knew it would not be many days before another parcel was delivered to her door, and that it too would be perfectly wrapped, its paper a pale sea of shifting blue.

One day you'll learn

John Burke

John Burke was born in Rye, Sussex, in March 1922 and brought up in Liverpool. Since 1965 he has been a full-time author.

His first novel, Swift Summer *(1949), won an Atlantic Award in Literature. In 40 years he has written more than 120 books, including 45 film and TV novelisations, among them such titles as* Dr Terror's House of Horrors, Moon Zero Two, UFO *(as Robert Miall). He edited three volumes of* Tales of Unease *for Pan. His non-fiction includes* An Illustrated History of England *and* A Traveller's History of Scotland *(John Murray). Currently he is working on a novel about Anglo-Scottish clashes in the 16th century.*

Although they now live in Scotland, for many years John Burke and his wife Jean lived in Southwold, Suffolk. During their first year there they became aware independently of each other that their house was haunted. A man would come downstairs from the top floor and sway in the open doorway of their bedroom. He was very gloomy and appeared puzzled. Asking around, they got clear descriptions that made it obvious that some resonance had been left on the air by their predecessor-but-one, a widower who had kept a housekeeper at the top of the house and gone up for dismal drinking bouts with her before tottering back down to his own bedroom.

No one has ever published a collection of John Burke's horror stories. Someone ought to. His finest stories – like Don't You Dare *in Alex Hamilton's* Splinters, And Cannot Come Again *in his own* New Tales of Unease, *and* Lucille Would Have Known *in Ramsey Campbell's* New Terrors Two *– are about hauntings, whether by ghosts or dreams. We gather from the first line of* One Day You'll Learn *that we're on familiar territory, but that's no reason to feel reassured.*

One day you'll learn

Not until after her death did his mother actually come to live with them full-time.

She had always been grudgingly independent, contriving to make them feel guilty that they were not doing enough for her and didn't really want her in their home, while at the same time saying of course she preferred her own little place and wouldn't dream of being a burden on anyone. Once when she had suffered a mild attack of some ill-defined gastric trouble she stayed a week in their spare bedroom, gallantly not criticising her son's erratic working hours, the way the kitchen was kept or not kept, or the way poor dear little Emily was being brought up.

'I don't want you to worry about me. You really don't have to tiptoe upstairs when you come in so late, Henry. It's your house, not mine.'

'Mother, I was out at a committee meeting.'

'Good heavens, it's not up to me to ask for explanations. None of my business how you spend your evenings, I'm sure. I just hope you don't leave poor Prunella on her own too often, that's all.'

'One evening, *that* was all.'

'She never complains, of course. That I *will* say about her.'

And the next day, to her daughter-in-law: 'Prunella, you

mustn't fuss over me. Poor little Emily hardly sees the two of you. She's the one you ought to be thinking about, not an old nuisance like me.'

When at the end of the week she considered herself, if not recovered – for she would never fully recover from the aches and agonies which had plagued her all her life – at any rate fit enough to return to her loneliness, she thanked them wistfully, and added: 'I don't suppose I'll have to bother you again. I know I haven't long to go.'

Leaving, she smiled her forgiving, tight-lipped smile.

At nigh on seventy she was in fact spry and with hardly a day's real illness behind her; but for the last thirty years had been skilled in the understatement of massive inner torments. Nobody understood. It was useless consulting her doctor. 'No good at all, any of them. No idea of what I go through.' Called in nevertheless during her spell in the spare room, the doctor had confided to Henry: 'She's what we call a church-window patient – hundreds of small pains.'

Mrs Calder would not have been amused. Amusement was something she created on her own terms, within herself, unable ever to accept it from without.

She had called herself Mrs Calder since just before Henry's birth, though she had never married. Around that same time she had moved from Wiltshire to Derbyshire and found a part-time job – referred to thereafter as 'a position' – with an estate agent. It had all been Henry's fault. Before that she had been a teacher in a well-paid position, getting on in years and with a headship in sight when seduced by a science teacher in the same school.

'If he'd been any good at all,' said Mrs Calder, 'he'd have been a scientist instead of just teaching, wouldn't he?'

Henry's early shy questions about why he had no father at home, as most other boys had, were met at first by solemn hints about a tragic accident. When he was older and his questions grew more searching, her version of the truth was so brusquely uncommunicative that for some while he did not grasp its true significance. Then a school friend's casual prurience conveyed enough for him to piece the relevant fragments together. Yet even the truth remained implausible. It was impossible to believe in his mother having ever had relations with a man, ever slackened the hostility of those lips, ever put her arms in abandonment around anyone. She could not bear to be touched, let alone touch. If he tried to kiss her at Christmas or on her birthday, she flinched away.

One year he saved up his skimpy pocket money to buy her an Easter cake from the local confectioner. When he set it before her she stared with bleached blue eyes at the cake and then at him.

'You mean you've thrown your money away on that rubbish?'

'Mum, it's a present; a treat.'

'I know what they charge at that shop. It's a disgrace. You're to take it back and make them give you your money back.'

'Mum, I couldn't do that.'

'You'll do as I say.'

'Please. I wanted to—'

'Wanted to show off. Just like *him*. Throwing money around that he hadn't got, and then . . .' She pushed her hands out as if to thrust the cake over the far edge of the table. 'Then,' she said, 'you'll be off when it suits you, just like him.'

It was a cold childhood. He was well fed and warmly dressed. Like their rented cottage above the canal he had to be always neat, always brushed and washed, with everything fitting to the inch. But the very security was cold. If he made any impulsive gesture, trying to snuggle close to his mother or coming home from school full of a brief excitement about a fair or about a film at the local cinema, his enthusiasm was soon put into perspective.

'It's obvious who you take after.' Or: 'I don't know what's to become of you. Lord knows I've done my best, but I just don't know. It's cruel.'

By the time he was in his twenties and had found, with his flair for electronics, a job – 'a position' – in a nearby components factory, he had also read enough books to know the jargon about complexes and frustrations and traumas, and enough newspaper and magazine features to know about the deep-seated psychological problems of unmarried mothers. But her condemnatory blue gaze never yielded a flicker of grateful awareness.

'Hm. You've certainly got his smarmy way with you. For all the good it'll do you.'

At one stage he suggested raising a mortgage through the firm's housing scheme so that they could buy a house and she would feel secure.

'What's wrong with the one we've got? After all I've done, now it's not good enough for you?'

'Paying rent on a place we'll never own is just throwing money away.'

'You're the one who throws it around. Save it. You'll need it one day, when I'm gone. One day you'll learn.'

He needed it sooner than they could have foreseen.

He met Prunella.

It took only a few light, laughing, affectionate weeks to melt a way through the ice which had inevitably formed around him. He could not believe it, could hardly believe in Prunella's existence. But her smile, the fullness of her lips, the generous and uncomplicated brown eyes always glowing questions or loving answers at him, the touch of her hand as if she could not bear to be near him without brushing against him and seizing his hand, setting the warmth of her cheek against his, all brought a frightening but exhilarating thaw.

'You mean you've *got* to marry her?' his mother demanded with frosty conviction.

'No, Mum, I don't mean any such thing.'

'I've never heard of anything so awful.'

'You'll like Prunella,' he said. 'You'll love her. You've just got to.'

'Oh, I've got to, have I?'

Prunella was invited to tea. When Henry walked her home afterwards, she said: 'Poor dear.'

'What, me?'

'No, silly. Your mother. She must have suffered a lot.'

'And I've had to share it.' He tried to make it a joke.

'Now we'll both share it.'

Prunella was too warm and alive to conceive of any such thing as an insoluble problem, an incurable sickness.

The next morning after breakfast Mrs Calder said: 'I didn't sleep a wink all night, worrying about you. That girl. It doesn't bear thinking of.'

'Then try thinking some pleasant thoughts for a change.'

He so rarely dared to get angry with her. She looked almost pleased. He had given her proof of all her worst thoughts about him. 'You don't know what it is to suffer. You never have.' Her eyes gleamed with the appetite for condemnation. 'One day you'll learn.'

In the week before the wedding, the night-time distortions began.

The first hazy dream, drifting between sleeping and waking, began happily enough. He was walking away from the altar with Prunella; they were outside the church and everyone was cheering; and they stopped for photographs to be taken. Suddenly he was doubled up by pain. His stomach was wrenched in on itself, dragging him down. As he wrapped his arms across it, trying to contain the agony, a violent muscular spasm knocked his legs from under him. He fought to straighten up. Prunella and the wedding guests were just a shifting blur, hurting his eyes. Ashamed of what he must look like, he forced his arms up into the air, as if to pull himself upright.

Hands and arms freed themselves. The bedclothes fell away. Gasping for breath, he looked up at the faint light from outside across his bedroom ceiling. Somehow he was sure that in the next room his mother was awake, too: and content to be so, relaxing after her moments of concentration.

But that was crazy. All part of the meaningless nightmare that would wane in daylight.

At breakfast he looked across the table and saw that she was smiling at her plate, unusually content with whatever visions she might be conjuring up.

That night he tried not to go to sleep, afraid of what she might have in store for him. Then he turned over, furious. It was ridiculous. He was too keyed up. Too many things on his mind: preparations for the wedding, the extra work he had been tackling in the factory to make up for the fortnight he would be away on honeymoon. He would stop being absurd, and sleep.

He slept.

There came pain in his chest. He was suffocating. A lid closed over him; there was something soft across his face; and when he tried to sit up, the padding of the lid held him down.

He had been buried.

You always were afraid of the dark, weren't you? Afraid of being shut in. That time you were trapped in the cupboard under the stairs ...

He tried to choke words out. They clogged in his throat. Then he heard her laughing. He had rarely heard her laugh, and certainly never like that before. He grabbed his dressing-gown without even realising he had managed to stumble across the room from the bed, and hurried into his mother's room, ready to challenge her and put a stop to all this.

She was lying on her back, sound asleep, her lips gently puckered.

As she was putting the kettle on in the morning he said, blunt and matter-of-fact: 'You realise it's only a couple of weeks to the wedding? A fortnight on Saturday. You haven't asked about the arrangements.'

'I don't need to. They're all in hand.'

'I know they are. That's what I want to sort out with you. After we leave the church—'

'I won't be at the church, of course.'

He stared. 'Naturally you'll be at the church.'

She was buttering toast with firm, attacking strokes. 'There won't be time. Not with all the things I have to do here for the reception.'

'Mother, we're not coming here for the reception.'

'And where else would you go?'

'Prunella's parents have fixed all that. I just want us to run over the details.'

'So your home isn't good enough for these folk?'

'It's got nothing to do with that. The bride's parents always take charge of—'

'I'm not accepting anyone's charity.'

He tried patiently: 'Come on, Mum, I'm sure you know the proper way of doing things. It's all fixed. After the ceremony we all go to—'

65

'I won't be at the ceremony. I've told you that. I'll be here, and I shall expect you all to come here.'

She was daring him to answer back. He looked at the thin lines etched across her forehead and the parallel line of her almost invisible lips, and something snapped. 'You drove my father away, didn't you? It wasn't that he deserted you. You frightened him off. *Frightened* him.'

Her eyes shone as if he had never before offered her such an acceptable compliment.

She came neither to the wedding nor to the reception afterwards. He explained to his new in-laws that she had become overwrought and was not well enough to leave the cottage for a few days; and warily fended off various offers to call on her with wedding cake or keep an eye on her while the newly-weds were away.

On their wedding night Henry felt a sharp twinge of dread. How could she reach out and plant her perversities from so many miles away?

Prunella's warmth and love and ecstatically demanding body banished any such spectre.

He raised the mortgage on a trim little house a mile along the canal from the cottage in which he had been brought up, and while he and Prunella were still both working they managed comfortably. Mrs Calder made no apologies for her behaviour at the time of her wedding; but a week after they had moved in she came round without warning, equipped with a bag full of cloths and plastic bottles of polish and detergent. 'Yes, I guessed it'd be in this sort of state.' Ignoring Prunella's protests, she went down on her hands and knees and set about cleaning and polishing.

They fell into a routine of inviting her for Sunday lunch. The moment the meal was finished, Mrs Calder was on her feet, carrying dishes out and insisting that the washing-up should be done immediately and that she would be the one to do it. She couldn't bear to sit for a moment with dirty plates on the table or by the sink.

When she heard that a baby was on the way, her reaction was so close to what Henry had predicted that he nearly burst out laughing. Perhaps that was the best thing: to laugh at her, laugh her petty stupidities out of existence; but not, of course, ever to invite her to share such laughter.

'Oh, how dreadful. I did hope you'd have more sense. How you'll make ends meet, with only one of you working—'

'We'll manage,' Prunella said happily.

Her mother-in-law looked round the room, condemning it as it was now and visualising the possibilities of it growing so much worse.

When the baby was born and named Emily, she said: 'Emily? That was a servant's name in my day.'

Then, unexpectedly, she seemed to mellow. It was too conventional: she showed signs of becoming a doting grandmother.

'Do be careful of the little mite. I'm sure she's not eating enough.' And: 'I do think I got those mitts just right, don't you?' And: 'But of course I can push my little angel down to the post office on my own.' And: 'She needs her Gran, then, doesn't she?'

It was all so out of character that it gave Henry the shivers. When he tried to explain his revulsion, Prunella studied him quizzically and said he really had to get over these childhood hang-ups of his. The poor old thing hadn't had much joy out of life. Now she was finding something which meant something to her, and they ought to be thankful. It was a bit late for the poor old thing to learn what loving was about – Prunella's arm slid round Henry's neck and he could smell the sweetness of her throat – but how could they possibly begrudge her the pleasure now?

Loving . . . or acquisitiveness?

Mrs Calder had not merely volunteered as baby-sitter when they wanted to go out together, but as the months went on pestered them to go out more often. On two or three occasions they returned to find Emily seeming to murmur to herself in her sleep, as if precociously trying out words and ideas she had just been taught. And there would be a placid, faraway look in Mrs Calder's eyes.

Once she must have sensed Henry's unease and the likelihood that he was framing some criticism, and she was swift to forestall him with a new, winning sentimentality. 'Such a treasure, isn't she? I don't know what you've done to deserve her. You can see she takes after me, bless her. Such a pity she has to grow up.'

'Mother!' Even Prunella experienced momentary alarm.

'All the pain,' sighed Mrs Calder. 'And the filth. Being mauled by filthy men. Such a terrible shame.'

That night when Henry, nagged by indefinable doubts, was restless in bed, Prunella drew him closer. To her it had been funny. 'Come on, filthy man – come on and maul me.'

The next time they went out, Henry insisted on paying a girl to baby-sit, without telling his mother. They spent an agreeably relaxed evening; but returned to find the girl gone and Mrs Calder in her place on the settee.

'I came round and found you'd gone out. Whatever possessed you, not asking me?'

'Mother, we don't want to bother you every time.'

'It bothers me a lot more, thinking of someone like that girl here. I sent her packing, I can tell you. Wasting your money on useless little sluts like that. Do you want poor little Emily to pick up *her* habits?'

For a few weeks they did not spend an evening away from the house. Prunella fidgeted. Wasn't Henry being just a bit neurotic? His mother was a conscientious baby-sitter, she adored Emily, nothing could possibly go wrong.

'She doesn't want Emily to grow up.' It came to Henry out of the blue; or out of some terrible, impenetrable darkness.

'That's just one of those things she says. You know what she means.'

'I'm not sure I do. And I'm damned sure *you* don't.'

Prunella looked unhappy. Henry felt equally unhappy. For different reasons. They were utterly different unhappinesses.

Then, with no indication that any one of her current ailments was worse than any of its predecessors, Mrs Calder collapsed and was rushed into hospital.

'You see,' she whispered when Henry came to her bedside. 'I was right. I knew all along. You never did understand what I had to go through.'

'Mother, you mustn't try to—'

'Not that I'm finished yet.' She was very quiet and very steady. 'You'll not get rid of me that easily. I'm not going far away.' She gazed complacently into a distance which only she could measure. 'Not far away. I still have to look after Emily.'

'Mother, Emily's doing fine. When you're out of hospital we'll—'

'She's going to be looked after. That I promise you.'

Mrs Calder smiled. And died. But, as she had promised, she did not go far away.

There were only five mourners at the funeral: Henry, Prunella, two elderly ladies from the church who had sat in the pew behind Mrs Calder every Sunday morning, and an old age pensioner living near her cottage who said over the cold meats, with a disapproving sniff in a certain direction, that he had often cleared her path of weeds because nobody else ever came to see her.

When it was all over and they were tidying up in a methodical style of which the departed woman would surely have approved, Prunella cried for a few minutes, because the poor old thing hadn't had much pleasure out of life, had she?

'And certainly never gave any,' Henry said sombrely.

'Darling, you mustn't say a thing like that, not so soon after.'

He tried to feel guilty; but could not.

'Gran.' The piping voice came from the bedroom over the stairs. 'Yes, Gran. Please.'

'She's dreaming,' said Prunella fondly.

When Henry slid into bed he was content to lie awake for a while in drowsy security. A great weight had been lifted. He felt warm and snug. Prunella was warm beside him, there would never again be that insidious voice persecuting and sneering and denigrating.

Emily's voice had been remarkably clear and precise. Suddenly more articulate and understandable, surprising for a child of her age.

Prunella's arms crept around him. He turned to her. Languidly they began to explore each other.

And Mrs Calder said: 'Disgusting.'

Henry jerked to one side. Looking at the end of the bed he saw nothing but knew who was there.

Prunella mumbled a reproach. 'Darling, what is it?'

'Disgusting.' It resonated once again. 'Couldn't you wait? Couldn't you wait to get rid of me?'

Henry pushed himself up on one elbow. Prunella moaned again, and her hand coaxed him back. Couldn't she see – or, no, not see, but be overpoweringly aware of who was there, watching and hating?

He tried to surrender to Prunella rather than that chimera. Loving excitement rather than freezing scorn.

After a few minutes Prunella went limp, and sighed.

It was impossible that she should be incapable of hearing the mocking laughter, almost out of earshot.

In the sober clarity of daylight Henry knew that the presence had not been banished. His mother was still in the house and intended to remain. He waited for Prunella to become aware of this of her own accord. Together they could fight it.

Next night and the night after were humiliating repetitions. On the fourth, Prunella feigned sleep as soon as her head touched the pillow. Henry lay awake, not daring to risk a descent into dream where gleeful derision might be waiting for him. Yet really, he began to sense, there was now to be little difference between sleeping and waking. His mother was here in the dark and in the light, even stronger-willed than when she had been alive.

It was nonsense. How could a woman dead and in her coffin continue projecting fright and fantasy into his living mind? She no longer had the resources for it. The brain died at death; thought faded; personal loves and hates faded; everything dissolved into oblivion.

'Gran, please.'

Though Emily's voice through the open bedroom door usually woke Prunella at once, this time she did not stir.

'Gran, when? Please.'

Henry slid out of bed and tiptoed into her room. Moonlight from the edge of the curtain filtered across her pillow and across closed eyelids. Emily was smiling yet puzzled.

'A picnic? Yes, Gran, but where?'

Again she was speaking with that eerie precision which had surprised him before and now was pricking him with unease.

'Gran, wait for me.'

Prunella swayed in through the doorway, yawning uncontrollably. 'Whatever are you two up to?'

Emily's eyes were suddenly open. She stared at her father, stared past him at her mother, and began to cry.

'Gran, the picnic . . . Don't go away.'

'Darling, you've been dreaming. Here, let's tuck you up.'

Prunella sat on the edge of the bed, straightened out the edge of the sheet, and stroked Emily's hair. Henry went back to their own room but sat propped upright against the headboard until Prunella returned.

She shook her head affectionately. 'Poor little scrap, I suppose it's a bit baffling. She's bound to miss her grandmother for a few weeks.'

Henry said: 'She's after her.'

'Sweetie, what are you talking about?'

'Mother,' he said. 'Mother's trying to get her hands on Emily.'

Prunella collapsed yawning into bed. 'Oh, dear. I do think you must be suffering some sort of – what do they call it? – delayed reaction. Emily doesn't understand what being dead really means. But you do, for goodness' sake.'

Do I?

On his way down the road in the morning he swore that his mother should not claim Emily. Somehow he would protect her, somehow stand between them.

During working hours it seemed silly and irrelevant. Only when he got home, opening and closing the front door, did the full force of her determination come surging to meet him. The truth was loud and clear and gaining substance. Prunella kissed him, whispered, 'I've had a little talk to Emily, and I think she understands,' and did not appear to notice that Mrs Calder was sitting by the corner in the shadow of the bookcase.

'I told you she'd be no good to you.' Prunella did not hear. Nor did she wake, as Henry did, in the small hours of the morning to hear that lost, plaintive voice calling out: 'Gran . . . when?'

He lay very still in bed, struggling to resist the exultant tide which spilled into the room, seething like some terrible flood forcing its way through a gap in the wall to drown everything in its path.

'Get back where you came from.' Henry said it aloud; and still Prunella did not stir.

'Emily will be better off with me than with that useless creature there.'

'You're not going to have her. I'd rather die than—'

'Die? Oh, no, we don't want *you* over here. Not for a long time yet.'

He sat up, shouting at her. Prunella jolted awake. And at once the room was silent.

'Henry, you're not having the horrors again?'

'She's still here. And it's getting worse.'

'Darling, no wonder Emily's disturbed. She can't help hearing some of the crazy things you shout.'

Not until almost dawn did exhaustion claim him. Then in dream he was led from the house to the graveyard and drawn down into the mind which lay festering below the earth. 'Don't be in any hurry,' she was intoning. 'You never were very brave, were you? You don't want to face what it means, coming over here. The waiting period – you won't like that. The mind goes on a long, long time, you know. Long after you're buried and rotting.' He groped up to half-wakefulness, but slid wearily back again, blearily vowing that when his time came he would be cremated. And his mother was convulsed with delight. Somehow she was no longer talking: just implanting visions and mockery in his mind. He thought cremation was quick and painless? He had no idea of the eternity of fear, waiting for the flames to scorch through the box, and then the eternity of pain in the burning . . . and the wounds and blisters which would never heal through all eternity.

Prunella studied him so glumly at breakfast and again when he got back in the evening that he did not dare say a word about Emily, even in the most casual way, or about his mother still sitting in the corner as if to welcome him home. They watched a television programme with which they would not usually have bothered. When a character in it was shot at close range and the scene cut quickly to another location, the thought beginning to formulate in Henry's mind was snatched up by his mother. She made him feel the bullets screwing one by one with infinite slowness through flesh and bone, each tissue with its own hell of infinite agony. He clapped his hands to his head as the clamour within grew intolerable.

But this was nothing, she was telling him. *One day you'll learn.*

He began to sob. Then Prunella's hands were on his, pulling them away, gripping them as she looked into his eyes.

'Darling, you can't go on like this. Look, what we need is a holiday. We'll leave Emily with my Mum and Dad, and—'

'No!'

'There's no need to shout. They'd love to have her, and she'll have a lovely time. And so can we.'

From her corner Mrs Calder made it silently clear that she was the one with whom Emily would have the loveliest time. She would see to that.

Henry said: 'We daren't go away and leave her.'

As he set off in the morning, Prunella walked to the gate with him. 'Couldn't you make an appointment with the company doctor?' Far beyond her shoulder, the old rented cottage in which he had been brought up was sharply delineated in a brightness of sunshine and reflected light from the canal. 'I'm sure he could find something to help you sleep,' Prunella was saying. 'Maybe recommend that you do have a holiday.'

Her voice faded as he walked away. His mother's did not fade, even though she had not spoken a word. The resonant silence jangled in his head as he went to the office, went on jangling as he coped with familiar daily routine, and receded only slightly when he stood on the terrace of the executive restaurant and looked down the drop of fifteen storeys to the car park. Of course he had no intention of falling. His mother knew that. She was slyly, insistently nudging him. He would never have the nerve to throw himself into oblivion.

Not that it would be oblivion, with her there waiting for him.

We don't want you over here.

It was Emily she wanted. So he must stay here, close beside Emily, holding on to her.

Prunella met him at the door that evening. 'Did you go to the doctor?'

'No.' He kissed her and spoke as briskly as he could manage, in spite of that figure of undying malevolence which was there and yet not there, always in the corner of his eye, never quite coming into focus. 'I'm sorry I've been such a misery lately. Dog-tiredness, that's all it's been.'

Throughout the evening he contrived to be cheerful, playing with Emily and making her giggle, then off the top of his head planning a wildly extravagant summer tour for the three of them. Prunella opened a bottle of port which had been set aside for the funeral but not opened for so few mourners. At bedtime he took his wife in his arms, and they were both laughing enough to drown the faint whisper of disgust he heard somewhere in the distance. The world was joy. At last she sank contentedly away from him. And as she lilted away into sated slumber, a chill pervaded the room and burned into his bare shoulders. Desperately he reached for Prunella again, to wake her; desperately pressed his mouth to her damp, sweet neck.

'Soon, Gran?' The childish cry was like birdsong on the night air.

He edged away from Prunella, tense.

'Come along, my lovey,' his mother was coaxing.

There was a rustle of bedclothes and the faint somnambulistic patter of feet out on to the landing.

Henry pushed himself out of bed. In the faint light, making her almost wraithlike, Emily was walking steadily towards the top of the stairs, clutching her teddy bear. He reached out to stop her, but she was dizzyingly surrounded by a swirl of darkness, and his mother's voice went on coaxing, luring, tempting.

'No!' Henry shouted.

He knew Emily had to be there, within that cloud, at a predictable spot of the landing. He groped for her; and found her. She jerked convulsively. He began pushing her back towards the bedroom. She dropped her teddy bear, and must have jolted awake, for he heard her crying in her own, waking voice. Childish frustration beat against him from one side, while his mother's rage came writhing from the other.

Henry tried to turn, reaching out an arm to brace himself against the wall. He stepped on the teddy bear, and his foot slipped.

He went over the top of the staircase, fell to one side, half spun round and then went headfirst until one final wrench twisted his neck.

His mother was screaming. She seemed to come rushing towards him along an interminable corridor between pits of crimson darkness, thrusting out her arms as if to push him away, as she had once pushed that Easter cake of his away.

No. Not you. We don't want you over here.

He tried to turn back, to call to Prunella and take her hand and be pulled back to her and to Emily and to reality.

But his body lay still and would not move again.

This was reality now.

He made words without a voice. 'You've robbed me of Emily. But not the way you meant to.'

'I'll have her yet.'

'No. Not now.' He was aware of her face as a swirling distortion, and her thoughts as a foul breath. 'We're on equal terms now,' he said.

And in eternity there would be no sleep, no need for sleep. Only eternal vigilance. Watchfulness, until Emily had lived out her life to the full and could find another world sweeter than this purgatory.

Also, in eternity, no days, no nights, no time. But he found himself moving towards his mother and saying mockingly, challengingly:

'One day you'll learn. Then we can both rest.'

MacCreadle's bike

Conrad Williams

Warrington's a funny sort of place, stuck there halfway between Liverpool and Manchester, not really having much identity of its own, the high-street chains and refurbished pubs having eradicated most of its character. I'm not sure that teaming up with Runcorn helped much either, creating a 'new town' at the very centre of the country. Canary Wharf, for instance, was built slap bang in the middle of London's Docklands. Being at the heart of things clearly isn't everything. But the Cheshire town did produce Conrad Williams, in March 1969.

He studied humanities at Bristol Polytechnic and has been writing since the age of seven. So far he's published a string of tales in the small press magazines Maelstrom, Chills, Works, Dementia 13, Mystique *and* Peeping Tom, *and has work due to appear in* Exuberance *and* BBR. *He's written two novels and is at work on a third. He was first published in* Dark Dreams *when he was only 18 and although it was an assured debut his work has grown in the years since.* MacCreadle's Bike, *his first story in anthology form, is a powerful study of the fine line teenagers tread between excitement and anguish.*

'The idea for the story,' he writes, 'came from memories of childhood when I looked out of my bedroom window at Seven Arches whilst listening to the rasp of motorbikes as joyriders scrambled over the school fields in the dark.'

MacCreadle's bike

Delicate Freddy shifted in bed; last night's letter spiralled to the floor.

He wanted to go to Pris, tell her things he'd scribbled in lager havoc but prose was awkward on his tongue; speaking love, a stuttering habit.

The walk took him ten minutes. Every morning the same, the only route. Its habitude had driven him to daydreams. Here's The Rope – where last New Year he was groped by a middle-aged woman reeking of Pernod. He'd been sickeningly aroused and at the smell of aniseed he was wont to switch off and reminisce. Pepper, Rifle and Sawdust knelt like buddhists at his approach.

'Delicate, we beseech thee, give us a sign of your immortality.' Rifle's eyes exploded, his lenses making graceful arcs before raining on the window.

'Bad mood rising,' quipped Pepper, hitching his jeans up around his hips. 'Pris awaits apologies galore.'

I will not cry . . . Delicate even managed to smile when the top of Pepper's head sheafed to flame, crisping him black.

Dare *you*? he glared at Sawdust, but he was leading the others into Rifle's house, hungry for the kitchen.

Delicate aped their casual swagger, that looping of the shoulders, the slow puncture of cheeks as they sucked in

81

sensually. They were razor adverts: clean panther sleek. Their clothes hung massively – beneath waxed barbell bodies. Delicate moved like starched shirts – pin-filled and cardboard-collared. He gave up the pretence when they reached the fridge. They were chugging Holsten and though he hated lager, he chugged too, lanced by bubble tears.

Seven Arches awaited them this evening. They'd take a case of Holsten, get wasted while oily walls swarmed around them. Sometimes, after the pubs shut, the girls came down to talk and help with the lager. Feeling amorous, Rifle usually took Della on to the embankment, returning a while later hot and red, zipping himself up. Delicate thought Della extremely beautiful save for the ragged scar encircling her throat like strange jewellery. Delicate, Pepper, Rifle and Sawdust were banned from all the pubs.

Twilight encroaching, they set off across the field. Pepper was singing *Purple Haze*. Rifle and Sawdust walked shoulder to shoulder discussing breasts while Delicate traipsed in their Siamese shadow, watching the long grass pulverised beneath his feet. Maybe Pris would come down tonight and he'd hold her awkwardly while they watched the Liverpool-Manchester trains clatter by. She always ignored the others and talked to him. Once she'd even laughed at a joke he'd told her – about copper wire being invented by skinflints wrestling over a penny.

Through broken school goalposts the Arches came into view. A brook ran beneath one; sometimes they threw stones at moorhens and swans. Rifle had once puked on a mallard.

Sometimes, in the winter months, used syringes could be found by the piss-stained weeds. But this was summer and, oddly, the junkies' tools were out of season; now only lager cans marked out territory.

Sawdust struck a match to the grainy light, his face glittered and spun. 'Delicate, you look delish in the dark. Love to love you baby.' Laughter.

Delicate fished for a riposte, could only muster 'Suck my dick', which he spoke half-heartedly, hoping they wouldn't hear. But they were already necking their beers. Delicate necked too. Soon, throats loosened by lukewarm Pils turned to safe ground: football, women, blackouts. Rifle leaned against the wall, told of his exploits with a vindaloo – how his arse had resembled the Japanese flag the day after. When they stopped laughing, all eyes fell to Delicate who was collecting hot wax on the ball of his thumb.

'So tell us about Pris, Freddy. What's got you on your knees beggin' forgiveness?'

Delicate leapt forward and carpet-bombed Pepper's body with punches. Pepper dropped paralysed. 'Leave it out, Pep,' he moaned, as Pepper glanced round, grinning, running his fingers through the gold black perfection of hair.

'Leave it out, Pep!' he mocked, falsetto. 'You turd. Tell us. Couldn't get it up?'

'Couldn't get *what* up?' guffawed Rifle.

Sawdust snorted lager through his nose. 'Noodle-dick!'

Delicate's face flared in the sputtering light. The others slumped, clutching hearts, throats. Within seconds they were dead; minutes, they were rotting.

Rifle burped apocalyptically.

''kay,' said Delicate. 'I'll tell you . . . she doesn't want to see me again.'

'Well pass the fuckin' Kleenex.'

'No . . . well,' and here he thought his ruthlessness might gain currency. 'I told her to eat shit an' die.'

'You told Pris to . . . fuck that's cruel, Freddy. Better watch her old man doesn't find out. He'll beat shit out of you.' Rifle looked disgusted. He cracked open another can of Holsten by way of consolation.

'You *wanted* to know.' But he sounded pathetic, hurt.

'Yeah, well we got more important things to drink about. Y'better apologise. Pris is a lovely bitch.' Sawdust turned his back on him.

Delicate drank deeply, reached the weak, watery depths of his can before groping for another. Oblivion would be a good state in which to confront Pris if she turned up.

In the distance, a motorbike roared at speed.

'Listen to that, Rifle,' said Pepper, fingers hitched in his belt-loops, unconsciously adopting the coolest pose should the girls arrive. 'Some thunder on the road tonight. What y'reckon? BMW?'

Rifle hissed his contempt. *'Harley* . . . Jeez, what a sweet, sweet sound. Lust for some wheels like that. I'd have *two* legends between my legs. Sweet.'

Came the rustle of bushes and a drunken giggle. The girls arrived, looking for drinks and fumblings in the dark. Over the rim of his can, Delicate espied Pris moving with cautious grace by the flames, weaving slightly. She really killed those halves of Dry Blackthorn when she got going. She made a point of shunning Delicate; perched herself on Pepper's knee, laid her head against his neck. When she drank from his can, Delicate looked away, sought Della's grotesque beauty. She was French kissing Rifle already, pressed up against him like a layer of clothing. Her hand fluttered at his groin and Delicate felt a heat inside him; he wished he had Rifle's cocky finesse, his danger.

Della caught him watching, winked, licked her lips and whispered in Rifle's ear. They laughed and strolled away to the embankment. The other girls – Simone, and a girl Delicate didn't know – were writhing over Sawdust who trilled 'Rock an' Roll' at the walls.

A candle went out. A train rumbled overhead, brakes squealing as it slowed for Warrington Central.

''lo Freddy,' whispered Pris.

To hide his tears he buried his face in the smoky warmth of her jacket. 'Sorry Pris.' Scrawled pledges danced at his eyes. 'I didn't mean to speak to you like that. I . . . love you like there's no tomorrow.'

Pris held him. 'Hush m'baby. Give us a kiss.'

Rifle came galloping in, his belt buckle jangling like a metal heartbeat. He was breathless. 'MacCreadle's out!' he was shouting. Della came into the candle's shimmering light stuffing a breast into her bra. She was clearly angry that their games had been interrupted.

'Hey, Delicate! Stop maulin' Pris. D'you hear what I fuckin' said? I *said* MacCreadle's out!'

Delicate watched as the tunnel collapsed on Rifle's head . . . but he was tired of making them die. After all, they were the only friends he had. 'Makes you say that?' His skin was drenched in Pris perfume. He felt wonderful.

Rifle's eyes like golf balls. 'Can't you hear? Listen.'

It drifted to them like slow mist: the throaty growl of the Harley.

'Could be anyone, mate,' said Pepper, his fingers shuffling under Simone's sweater.

'That's MacCreadle's bike, man. *Swear*. He's done his time. He's out!' Rifle took off towards the headlight stitching darkness.

'Who's MacCreadle?' asked Pris, but Delicate was shivering. He'd been just ten when they put MacCreadle away for some diabolical crime. His mother used to scare him by saying MacCreadle would come to slice him while he slept.

The motorbike was getting impossibly loud. When the headlight exploded across the walls like a strobe, Delicate's heart lurched. The engine's scream was cut leaving its cooling tick and Rifle whooping in the distance as he ran to catch up.

'MacCreadle,' said Pepper.

'How goes it, Pep?' came a low, smooth voice. His face, heavily bearded, looked like ice in the candlelight. Pale, pale.

'When did you get out, Mac?' asked Sawdust, running a trembling hand over the motorbike's bulk. It seemed to glow.

'Mornin'. Seen much of Patti?'

'Patti went down to the Smoke last August, Mac,' gasped Rifle, jogging into the tunnel.

MacCreadle grunted, then gestured at Delicate. 'Fuck's that?'

'That's Delicate Freddy. He's okay. Bit of a geek, no harm.' Pepper sounded apologetic.

'Delicate? Jesus. Looks the type of goon *everybody* rips the piss out of. That right?'

Delicate rose, trying – God, *trying* – to be cool. 'Nah. The guys muck about with me. S'all fun.' He tried to swagger but stopped when MacCreadle got off his bike. He was huge – a mass of branch limbs wrapped in denim and leather. The girls eyed him.

'Like you, man. Y'got balls to stick around.' He sized him up for a while, nodding. His eyes were like hot tar, swooning in the flame.

'Ever ride a bike, Deli-cate?'

'Sure. I've ridden bikes.'

'No.' He placed spade hands on Delicate's shoulders, gently massaged. His breath was Juicy Fruit. 'I mean, have you ever ridden a *bike*?'

Delicate's eyes flashed to the Harley and MacCreadle smiled.

'N-no.'

Delicate was led to the edge of the tunnel where they looked out at the night. He felt big, cocooned by power; their eyes were on him, awed and envious.

'You know, ridin' a Harley D is better than ridin' any woman. *Any* woman. You 'member that.'

The keys felt like cold silver in his palm.

They watched Delicate mount up, disengage the stand and rest his foot on the kick start. Only MacCreadle and Pris were smiling. The others were a blur of open mouths. Then loudly, beautifully, Rifle yelled: 'Go for it, Freddy!'

Delicate kicked down on the pedal and was astride a beast itching to bolt.

'Goose it, man,' mouthed MacCreadle and Delicate obliged, filling the air with demons. In a slow arc, he rolled the Harley outside. King of the Road, Man of the Moment. I'll show them. He tore about the field, churning grass to pulp and hurtled to a skidding stop in front of them. But the bronco bucked and he found himself on his back looking at the stars. The laughter, like stilettoes, pierced him to the core.

'. . . fuckin' nancy . . .'

'. . . like a granma . . .'

'. . . pussy rider, haw! haw! . . .'

MacCreadle picked him up. 'Show 'er some respect, man. Don't treat her like a toy – she'll kill you.'

Delicate saw MacCreadle mashed beneath a car . . . but no. He *couldn't* see it. Not this one. Not MacCreadle.

He clambered back on the bike, halting the tears and laughter; opened the throttle, scrambled up the embankment to the train tracks.

'WATCH ME NOW!' he screeched, blasting between rails, juddering like a tangled puppet.

The tracks hissed and sang with arrivals. Delicate closed

his eyes to the night, felt only the lunatic rush of air in his face, the hellish thunder of MacCreadle's bike. Sirens and screams heralded respect. Watch me *now*.

The light on the cliff

Ian Cunningham

Born 1962 in Surrey, Ian Cunningham took a degree in English and an MA in American studies from London University before moving into journalism. For the past six years he's worked as a researcher on one of the most research-intensive magazines in the world. At the age of 13 he won a school prize (an Alfred Hitchcock anthology) for his brutal crime novel set in Epsom and Cornwall (the only two places he knew), but The Light on the Cliff *is his first published piece of fiction.*

He's an open, friendly fellow who clearly loves life but approaches it with caution and knife-edge creases in his trousers. Among his many enthusiasms are 'W.B. Yeats, Henry James, H.P. "Saucy" Lovecraft, Patrick Hamilton, Ross Macdonald, Colin Watson; the cinema (especially anything involving Saul Bass or Ernest Borgnine); badminton (preferably with an inferior player [note: he is the world's worst squash player]); the opening titles of Z Cars *c1964; classic cars (especially the Cortina Mk 1); Edward Hopper; the opening bars of "Wow" by Kate Bush, etc.'*

He writes at a speed that makes Flaubert seem slapdash (the French novelist used to think nothing of spending a whole morning on getting just the right word) but when he does finish a story the wait is worth it. Here he betrays an artist's eye for beautiful and frightening imagery.

The light on the cliff

When I was a boy I liked to sit, perched, on the very rim of Ireland. There I would sit, hour upon hour, bare feet dangling over the cliff, looking out to sea. Later, I heard about the statue of a woman, a mile high, outside New York harbour, and for a time I would look out even more keenly than before, telling myself that I could make out a tip of her crown above the line where America started.

Or I would climb the hills behind our village and look down at the world. Brown plain below at my back; these hills under my feet; then the little plain before me, the village flung against the coast; a still, giant sea.

We were separate, apart in that last small reach of sand and rock before the land gave up at last to water. One pale road curved and corkscrewed its way from the land horizon to our village. Few travellers came in or out. We saw no soldiers, not even after we heard that Dublin was burning. Later, our hills again shielded us gently from what we knew lay beyond – the mingling of Irish blood in fields and copses and stables. We heard of it; we did not see it, though once I watched as, far inland, a thin brown strand of smoke climbed the sky. A big house in flames.

Our village had its own big house. It stood perhaps two miles away – strangely far, since the house gave birth to the village. I mean: there was no fishing, and thin soil: people came to work at the house and settled near it, or as near as they could. The house stood at the edge of a wood, at the top of one of the big cliffs. The village grew up, uncomplainingly, further down, on the flat part of the coast.

I had never known the house to be lived in. It was empty before I was born, and long before the other big houses were burnt. Why it died early I don't know: I never asked. But there were people in the village, my father among them, who had seen it as it was, when guests would come in carriages to sit out the afternoon and evening on its smooth summer lawns. Then the young lady of the house would play her harp to her guests and the sound of her playing and their applause would drift gently down to the village. So my father recollected.

But now the lady and her house were dead and no one had any reason to go up there or think about the place. Perhaps we were scared by the place even then; I don't know. I'm thinking of the time when my father woke up in the night and said he could hear the harp music again. He woke me up and my mother; my other brothers and sisters stayed asleep. He had the front room window open and was listening, not really frightened, more puzzled. I could only hear the sea, but he said he could hear music. Still, people told us the next day that during the night a fog had come up and a yacht had run aground up the coast: a lot of people were up that night. But the two people on the yacht weren't found, so I can understand now why harps were played.

I think I was fourteen at that time, and this thing that happened to me came a short time later. All day the thunderclouds had been rolling in off the sea, driving into the land like hard fingers. By late afternoon they were still mounting overhead, and the daylight had taken on that strange bright glare that comes before a storm. The first rain didn't fall until dark, but when it did it hurled itself down in a fury, dinning on the roof and invading the chimney so that the sitting room smelt of wet smoky turf. The yellow lamplight made dim mirrors of the windows, but outside I could hear the sea beginning to seethe. The first crack of thunder came.

There was no question of going out that night. We sat around by the fire, waiting for it to be late enough to go to bed.

The storm still raging, there was a sudden, impatient banging on the door which continued even as my father pulled it open. My uncle – his brother – almost pushed him aside in his haste to get out of the rain. His white hair was plastered to his head, his clothes darkened by water. Standing by the fire, he began at once to steam.

'Feckin' little bastards. Six of them gone this time.' In his exhaustion, he spoke to no one in particular, of his sheep. We knew he was getting too old to keep them together on nights like this. 'Will one of you give me a hand.' It was more a statement than a request, and his eyes were already on me, the eldest except for my father. I thought, 'Shit,' but I said, 'Where did they go?'

My uncle visibly brightened. 'They've not gone far, son. Just into the wood. You know the wood behind the field. They've not gone far now but if we leave them they'll wander. Thanks, son.' I was already on my feet. My younger brother said, 'I'll go with you two.'

'You will not.' My father had on his firm look. 'I'll come and give you a hand.'

'No, no, you're all right.' I started to put on my coat. 'I'll chase them out of the wood, down to Mick. They won't be gone far.' I didn't want to be a child to two adults. I would do the work and be credited for it.

My uncle took down the lamp from next to the door and lit

it at the fire. 'Are you right?' I opened the door. Cold salty rain, blown sideways, hit me in the face. My mother murmured, 'Look after your Uncle Mick,' as she closed the door behind me.

We walked down the lane towards the patch of land where Mick kept his sheep. The rain still teemed down, punctured now and then by lightning and the sea roared away, invisible, beyond the narrow strand to our left. At the edge of Mick's field we passed the shelter where he had managed to contain what was left of his flock. At the other end of the field, a dim white shape stirred suddenly, then disappeared into the wood behind. Mick grabbed my arm. His old man's grip was tight like a baby's.

'There he goes. There he goes. Get after him now.'

By the time I got to the edge of the wood the sheep was nowhere to be seen. I called back to my uncle to wait there, then plunged in.

I had the lantern, but beyond its dim light there was only darkness and there was no path. Twigs clawed at my face. The rain drummed through the canopy of leaves and branches, gathering in streams in my hair and down my neck. Up ahead, there was a loud snap and a bleat. I followed the sound, moving gradually uphill until I found myself on a narrow path between the wood and the edge of a cliff. I held the lamp up – no sheep – and started along the path.

I wondered if any of the sheep had fallen over the edge. I didn't know this stretch of cliff, nor how steeply the ground fell away under its lip. I stood in the rain at the edge of the cliff and waited for the next flash of lightning so that I could see over the edge. I had to wait for a minute until it came. Then, in that space of light, I looked over the edge of the cliff. Jammed on the rocks, perhaps a hundred feet below me, was a vast, silent sailing ship.

She must have been one of the last of the big sailing ships. How long she had lain there I don't know: the storm must have brought her in sometime after nightfall. Just the sheer size of her, and the surprise, frightened me more than I had ever been frightened. I stood in the wet darkness, gripping the lantern, waiting once more for the lightning so I could see her again and be certain. The lightning flashed. She was still there. I saw now she had four masts, the third one almost directly below me. I felt I could almost reach down and touch the tip. Then it was dark again. I heard the sea suck three times in, out, in, out, in, out, before the thunder came.

That was when I saw the small yellow light ahead of me and on the land side. A house? I hadn't noticed the light before, but I made for it, and as I came nearer I saw it was coming from a point some way above me, away from the path.

I stood underneath the beam. From up close, it seemed to soar out; motes swam high above my head. The light blazed out over the cliff, out to sea.

I climbed the bank, making for the source of the light. I told myself, as I climbed the wet grass slope, that with the light there would be people, ordinary men like my father and my Uncle Mick, who would help. They would wake me from this dream-like night and save whatever men were left on the ship, with sensible, heavy tools and ropes and bright lanterns. So I reassured myself as I climbed, because I felt afraid. There was a clump of low trees and shrubs at the top of the slope, and I pushed myself through at what seemed the thinnest point. I had to bow my head to get through this second thicket, and all the time I was aware, at the corner of my vision, of the thick milky light that poured in from the other side.

Music began as I stood in the small wood. It was harp music. The first notes were irregular, exploratory, like cautious footsteps on uncertain ground, but then they began to sound out firmly and decisively, with metallic, ringing twangs that grew louder and louder and filled the whole space, it seemed the whole world, with sound. Somewhere, strong fingers were working furiously. The echo of each receding note hung in the moist night, so that the very air around me and the ground under my feet, the leaves and twigs that touched my face, seemed to hum and shiver as if nature were playing in unison with the harp that a man had made.

The music groaned sweetly through my ears, into my head and my mind. I rushed forward, gouging myself through what remained of the thicket, until I stood, scratched and bleeding on the far side. I was at the edge of a lawn that lay like wet black ink except where the beam exposed a swathe of fresh grass.

Beyond the lawn was a house. It could only be *the* house, the big house that my father had spoken of. The light poured from it.

The music stopped abruptly, leaving the last notes hovering in the open air. A thin, mizzling rain fell in my eyes.

I began to run towards the house. In the silence, my feet slithered on the grass. I saw now that the light was coming from enormous French windows that stood open, facing the sea. I stopped running when I reached a paved terrace that seemed to run around the whole of the building. I crossed the terrace, panting, and stood in the lee of the house, to one side of the great open windows. Then I peered around and looked in.

The light seemed bright enough to cut my eyes. It came from a chandelier that tumbled like a white-hot waterfall from the high ceiling. Two men's bodies were in the room. One lay in a corner, like a pile of wet dark rags. A seaman's cap and an oilskin were on the back of a chair near him. The chair stood at a rich, long walnut table under the chandelier. On the table was another man, naked, his face down, his head furthest away from me.

By the table was a white harp, and next to it a pale, dark young woman in a long green gown. She was looking at the man on the table and she did not see me. I looked at the oilskins on the chair, and thought of a wreck and of seamen who had seen a light and climbed a cliff in search of help.

The woman raised a hand to the level of her head, then brought it slicing down to the bottom of the man's spine. I heard his body break. I saw her reach into him and pull the white spine from him, as I would wrench a backbone clean and complete from a cooked fish. Then she pounded into his soft flesh, stroked it, moulded it, hummed to herself over it, wrenched out the bloody, gutty gristle and arranged it just so, sculpting swiftly and surely, until she had made a new harp, from him, which she played.

Recovery

Julie Akhurst

Julie Akhurst was born in 1963 in Orsett, Essex, the daughter of two teachers, both of whom taught her while she was at school in Norfolk. She won two scholarships to Oxford and went on to work for a Kent-based publisher. From there she progressed to magazine work, rising through the ranks of a bestselling national monthly magazine. She's now features editor on a national weekly women's magazine, living in north London.

Her first published story, Small Pieces of Alice, *which appeared in* Darklands, *made it on to Ellen Datlow's recommended list in* The Year's Best Fantasy and Horror. *Subsequently she has sold stories to* Dementia 13 *and* Exuberance *(in addition to the two she sold to* H *and* Skeleton Crew *which folded before publication). She writes wonderful prose, confident and beguiling, with a touch as subtle, effective and deadly as a scalpel. An atmosphere of mounting unease and tension is created, then there's often a killer line, which may in itself appear harmless, until you realise the full implications, and it sets to work on you. The effects can be physical. This is a frightening story and, beware, its resonances stick around.*

Recovery

It took two minutes' fumbling at the stiff lock before Anne realised the door was already open. Because she stepped into the narrow, musty hall on to a doormat, she stood and scraped her dusty heels back and forth, though last winter's dirt was already ground deep into the thin carpet. She was buying time, getting her bearings, recovering her breath in the still, hot air.

There was a narrow shelf by the front door, where she dropped her keys, then she leaned back against the peeling paint, under the stained glass halflight. It all looked different, she thought, now that she was on her own. She touched the raised patterns of improbable flowers on the faded papers, trailing her fingers slowly from room to room. She ended up upstairs, in the back bedroom, averting her eyes from the drifts of dead flies, three-deep on the sill, breathing in the smells of summer dust, cabbage-water and old, dead flowers.

And there was the garden – *her* garden, though she didn't begin to know how she would cope with it. A long, narrow strip, bisected with green chickenwire; a tiny shed at the far end and a rusting brazier; fallen bamboos in neat rows to mark the graves of peaplants; the faint outlines of two flower beds; the rotting mulch that was last autumn's leaf-fall.

Next door was quiet and tidy, the stiff, dry laundry waiting to be brought in. In the distance, around the bend in the reservoir, two lawnmowers buzzed in competition, like ghosts of the small black bodies not two inches from her thumb.

Resolutions were already pouring in: to be orderly, industrious, to win their respect next door with the height of her peas, the regularity and whiteness of her laundry – to make this a real home. She would remember the names of plants, understand *Gardeners' Question Time*, get to know the people in the village and form a small circle of close friends whom she could invite back for coffee. Her forehead, her untidy hair pressed against the hot glass, she focused through a distorting bubble, held the shed tight between her eyelashes and wished very hard that above all, she would be normal.

Oh, hope of Israel, its saviour in time of distress, why are you like a stranger in the land, like a traveller who stays only a night?

'Seems like it could have been meant for you personal – a message from Jesus,' said the beaming lady on the door. She was shaking Anne's hand with conviction, holding it tight between her own two, flour-white and violet-scented.

'Not that you're only staying a night, of course.'

Anne sank into the laughter and the plump flesh and let herself be steered past groups chattering in low voices, towards an ante-room where the ladies of the congregation were serving coffee, arranging digestives on unmatched china.

'Now we don't want to scare you off, but neither do we like to let you go without a welcome, and that's why I'm here, dear. I'm Mary Shand, by the way, and this is my husband, Don – our *treasurer*,' she added impressively, and stepped back, the better to show him off.

Anne looked up into Don's crinkled smile, the flat hair arranged carefully on either side of his round, red face, and felt she could manage here. Keep it even, she thought – the voice quiet and low, not too eager, not too frigid, and she'd be all right.

'Like I said, the text this morning could have been just for her, don't you think, Don? She's the new lady at Kiln Cottages. Anne . . . ?'

' . . . Graham. Anne Graham,' she supplied.

'And what might you be doing here in the middle of nowhere, Anne?' he asked, inclining his head slightly, so that she could see the broken vessels in the eyewhites, the scaly flesh in the wide parting. This was what she'd been waiting for and she was ready for it. She breathed evenly and concentrated on keeping the smile in her eyes.

'I'm a writer.'

'Well, we're honoured,' said Mr Shand, and there was no trace of irony in his voice, no suspicion or mistrust.

'It's been some time since we could boast anyone in that line of country round here, isn't it, Mary?'

His wife nodded supportively, still beaming, the feathers on her hat bobbing.

'Myself, I work down at the reservoir, mainly on security, general upkeep – that sort of thing. Not a lot to do in this kind of weather, in fact, except maybe chasing off the bathers and boys with their toy boats. Last summer we even had some of those wind-surfers down for the day from Oxford causing trouble. They were soon sorted.'

There was a pause – significant but friendly – while he slid a finger inside his collar; working it round; easing the flesh from its starch-stiffened burden; mopping up the thin yellow line of new sweat; waiting for her to speak.

At last, 'Can I ask what it is you're writing?'

She was ready for that too.

'They're – well, memoirs, really,' and realised as she said it just how inadequate it sounded. To her surprise, though,

Mr Shand straightened up, satisfied.

'You'll have a more interesting life than any of us then,' he laughed, including his wife in the joke. 'We need young people round here with something going for 'em. You seemed to be getting a good deal out of the sermon today. Perhaps you could speak at our Family Witness Day. You know, give your personal testimony, sort of thing. Tell us all how you came to find the Lord Jesus?'

She knew that this was the moment of real testing. If the conviction slipped from her eyes even momentarily she would lose her chance to be one of them, lose her chance really to be saved. She looked steadily into him, eye to eye, unblinking, fixing her mind on what it was she really wanted, needed.

'I'd love to,' she said. 'Just let me make a note in my diary.'

Dr Ropartz wrote in a small, neat, slanting hand that still somehow managed to fill every corner of the single sheet of notepaper. The envelope, however, was typed, official. She turned the two over and over in her grubby hands, looking through the back window, the newly piled-up garden debris ready for burning beyond the chickenwire.

All afternoon she had sweated out there in the unblinking sun, tearing her hands as she leaned her whole weight on the long, hard roots of ground ivy; raising a furious mass of red swellings on her ankles where she had blundered bare-legged, heedless, into nettle beds to drag out the brushwood of a year's plant deaths. When the dark began to move across the garden, she had leaned back on her heels with a feeling that was very near satisfaction. And now this cool, blue square of an envelope lay awaiting her on the scrubby doormat.

Dear Anne. How it turned her stomach, just to think of the responsibilities.

> Then again, *Dear Anne,*
>
> *A few quick lines to remind you that I am expecting the first instalment of your self-analysis project at some point during this next week. It goes without saying that we all hope you're settling in well and have gone some way to meeting your first attainment target: meeting others on their own ground and putting yourself forward as a member of the community in your own right. I'm sure you're coping better than you seemed to think you would.*
>
> *Please, don't, of course, forget that Dr Stone is on hand in Oxford should you need her. All the best, as ever.*

Patronising bastard! she thought, and immediately doubted the truth of the emotion. What, after all, could she take offence at? He was only trying to help, in his superior omniscience. How could he help his training, or the upbringing in a different tongue that had drawn an icy curtain across years of similar exchanges?

Where a dozen broken paperbacks spilled out of a case in the corner, she had thrown a brand-new spiral-bound notebook, bought that morning in the post office. Now she took it up and carried it to the typewriter, ready to transcribe her morning's work for Dr Ropartz's edification. The sun had made her head ache dreadfully, but she held in the jumping pulse with two fingers and with the other hand scrolled in a sheet of new paper. Consciously relaxing, she dropped her shoulders and lifted her hands to the keyboard. 'DREAMING – Night One,' she typed, and flipped over the first page of the notebook.

In fact it had been a straight replay, as it often was, centring on the garden. She'd always known it would from the first time she had nerved herself to investigate the shed.

The three of them in washed-out cotton frocks, cross-legged on the dirt floor, safely private in the cool of the toolshed beneath the ranks of dark bottles and half-empty tins. The tops of their dresses neatly pulled back to reveal a single childish nipple. To each was held the plastic lips of a doll, cold against the soft, hairless flesh – 'breast-feeding'.

'But *why* do we have to do it like this, Anne?'

That was Janey, her unbroken gaze not one of challenge, but trust – trust that Anne had the right answer, whatever it might be.

'Sarah-Jane Sinclair's mummy had a new baby and it drank out of a bottle.'

Anne pushed her hair behind her ears carefully and squinted up into the darkness of the cool, cobwebby ceiling. She wanted to explain it right.

'Sarah-Jane is not poor, Janey, but we are poor. Poor mothers have to feed their children from their breasts because that's the only milk they have. If Daddy was rich, we would have feeding bottles. We might even have three, then our poor babies wouldn't have to take turns.'

Robin's voice was like gravel. 'Not even now they don't have to take turns, because we can all feed them ourselves, like you said, Anne.'

Anne leaned across to squeeze her approval. 'That's right.'

'Anne, why are we poor?'

She thought, then, 'We are poor,' she said, 'because Mummy had three children, which is three children too many, and Daddy hasn't got a paying job. And because he's lazy,' she said after a pause.

'Daddy's not lazy,' said Robin mildly. 'He works hard in his study – all day – doing German into his tapes.'

'He's lazy,' Anne repeated patiently. 'And he's not nice to

Mummy, because he doesn't get a paying job like other people. And you know how I know?'

They looked at her, waiting, quietly, their shining eyes crossed with slanting light and shadow.

'Because Grandad told me.'

They were all quiet at that, because that, above everything, proved that Anne was right.

'And we're not to be a burden. Do you understand?'

They nodded solemnly, in unison, the dolls forgotten, each decided in her own mind what that meant: not to be a burden. Neither had to ask.

It meant sitting quietly in the toolshed when Mummy was crying and Anne fetched her hankies. It meant running upstairs quickly when you were asked – 'Tell your mother . . .' And back down again – 'And you can just tell your father . . .' Not getting tired, not complaining or sulking, but helping, until everything was all right again.

It meant you tried on the clothes from Mrs Mather's box – two of everything in the same size, because the Mather girls were twins – the fake fur winter coats, the velour one-piece pyjamas that stuck in your crotch all night, the washed-out summer cottons and yellowing underwear – and you *looked forward* to the surprises that might come out of it, and didn't moan at the things that scratched and looked funny – things they laughed at when you wore them to school. Once there had been a single white dress like a ballerina's with layers of neat petticoat and red hearts embroidered around the skirt hem. They had all sighed in delight. It was the right size for Janey now, too tight in the bodice for Anne.

And, 'We are poor,' repeated Anne, but somehow it was comforting to have it said. Grandad wouldn't say it, but Grandad was rich and wanted to spare their feelings. In his bedroom he had a stool made of blue velvet that pulled up to the dressing table; and the dressing table had a hole in the middle so you could sit with your legs under it while you looked in the mirror. It was a copy of the stool used by the Queen when she was crowned in Westminster Abbey, Grandad had said, and Robin gently ran her fingers over the nap after washing her hands – 'so they won't be sticky and leave marks,' Grandad said.

'Grandad, you must be rich,' they said, in awe, then Mummy arrived, collecting them in the Morris Minor. She made them say sorry. 'You don't talk about how much money people have got,' she told them. 'It's not good manners.' So none of them talked about it any more except among themselves.

Grandad had two big gardens and a tea service made from solid silver that he said he'd never use unless the Queen herself came to tea. On the wall in the dining room hung two famous paintings that Anne had seen on biscuit tins, by Constable. Grandad had had them specially painted. They'd cost a lot of money.

When Mummy shouted at Daddy and Daddy didn't answer but just locked himself in the study and when Mummy went upstairs and threw all his shirts on the lawn through the bedroom window, Anne and Janey would sit on Grandad's lap and tell him, and he would swear never, ever to tell anyone else – their secret was safe with him. 'But you must help Mummy and not be burdens,' he would say, and they would understand again, just as they always did.

There were four of them in the front seats, but she could see by hanging her head forward, looking sideways along the row, that she was the only one with her hands squeezed into fists, thumbs inside, scraping along the greasy palms. The organ paused from its meditative, foot-shuffling music and the pastor stepped forward with an open smile as he rotated his face slowly around the gathered congregation, chin out.

'My brothers and sisters, I welcome you this evening to the last service of our Family Witness Day.'

A shuffle of assent ran round the hall, like the breeze they had expected all day through the wide-open windows but which had never come.

'You have just sung the words of that great hymn, *Oh God, Our Help in Ages Past*. And I know that there are many of you here who *know* it, *believe* it in your hearts.'

He paused to lean forward heavily, palms flat on the pulpit edge.

'But there are still others of you out there who come seeking their Saviour tonight. And how shall He ever deny a child of His who calls upon Him in time of need?'

The joints at the base of Anne's thumbs ached as she pulled them into her palms tighter, tighter. She felt the presence of Don and Mary Shand, their knees inches from the small of her back, Mary's feather practically tickling her neck.

The pastor's voice dropped, so that the back rows had to crane forward to hear across the low-ceilinged, stifling room.

'I'm going to call now upon these young people sitting here below me,' – here, he smiled at each of the four, individually, taking them into his gaze, into his heart, into his private prayers – 'and I'm going to ask them to yield up their own story for you tonight.'

Another pause, then quieter still, his voice sinking in a straight line to earth, like a feather in the still air.

'The story of how they found the Lord *Jesus* and let Him into their lives as King over their sorry, human hearts. Anne, would you care to join me in the pulpit?'

Anne sucked in her heartbeat and used its strength to lever her off the sticky seat, propelling her around the baptismal pool – uncovered for use – and up the shallow steps into the circle of the pastor's outstretched arm.

'You are how old, Anne?'

'Twenty-two,' she said, and summoned a smile to flash at the blurry rows of faces below her.

'And new to the area, I believe.'

'That's right.'

'Now Anne, I'm just going to ask you to tell it how it is and let these people in on how you began your life with Him – be a witness for Jesus. Perhaps you could start by telling us how long you've had Him in your heart.'

Now was the time for all those doubts to be pushed under in one violent sweep. If she could only summon all her strength into that directed force and tell them with truth in her eyes, in her voice, that she was saved, then her new life could begin – at last. She *wanted* to be saved. She wanted a blessed unconsciousness so that He could rush in and use her as a channel to pour out His Spirit on these people. As a channel for His voice she had a purpose at last and could put the past behind her.

'Since I was twelve,' she said.

'Something very dreadful . . . happened to me when I was twelve, or perhaps I should say that I made something very dreadful happen. But the Lord stepped in and gave me peace, though I had to leave my father and my mother and go into a place where I was alone and friendless. Now the Lord is giving me a second chance through bringing me here, letting me live among the new friends gathered here tonight. And I believe He will use me as a channel to show He loves me still and is working out His purpose in my life. That bad thing in the past will be forgotten in the light of the glorious deeds He will perform through me.'

That was the last she clearly remembered. When, an hour

later, she came up out of the deep darkness into the uncertain half-light and the smell of floor polish, she was surrounded by gentle hands, easing, wiping, soothing, leaning her back in her hard chair. And she hoped that though it had been her mouth that formed the words, it had truly been His tongue that had spoken.

'And we were all so impressed, dear, by what you had to say, that I've brought Gordon along to meet you. I think he has something he'd like to ask you.'

She still couldn't remember and didn't want to. As she knelt half-in, half-out of the flowerbed, peering up at Mary and her visitor under the brim of her sunhat, she continued to feel something from that dark pool of peace that had remained with her for the last week, as though the long-awaited healing had finally begun. Years of analysis had taught her well enough what it was best not to recover from the maze of myth and memory that was her mind.

What she said was, 'Perhaps you'd better come in. I'll put the kettle on.'

Gordon was a shambling, apologetic man with freckles and sandy hair who sat well forward on the hard-backed chair, long arms outstretched across the narrow table, brushing the radio, the edge of a picture, a vase as he spoke. Shyness made it hard for him to hold her eye.

'Well, in short, it is out of the ordinary, but we were wondering if you'd oblige. Odd for a woman, I know, but there's nothing in the Bible to say a woman can't teach. Depends on the woman, of course, but as long as it doesn't form the main message of the Sabbath I think we'd find whatever you have to say can only add to the workings of the Spirit in the Church.'

He glanced at Mary for confirmation, here, glad to be

relieved of the pressure of talking to Anne alone, if only for a moment.

'Wouldn't you say, Mary?'

'We were wondering if you'd address a couple of the fellowship groups, you know, informally, at the evening service next week,' she continued, neglecting to reassure him by meeting his gaze, so anxious was she to put across her point.

'People haven't stopped talking. We haven't been this stirred up by a testimony for as long as I've been in the village, and this place has been my home ever since Don and I were married thirty-eight years ago, now.'

She paused to take a sip of her tea and catch her breath, laid her hands on the table. Anne felt, rather than saw the violet-scented fingers approaching and at last raised her eyes – shining, now – shining with being wanted, needed, useful.

'So you see, my dear, it's been a long, long time. What do you say, Anne? Will you come and give us some teaching?'

This time the letter ran to two sheets and she thrilled to his congratulations, his exhortations to further efforts, perseverance.

> *Do you see now, Anne, how God has not cast you out?*
> *In fact, for those who adhere to the Judaeo-Christian*
> *tradition (as you know I do not, personally, but let*
> *God stand as a cypher for a force of good in which I*
> *do put my faith), its core certainty is that there is*
> *nothing for which God cannot forgive you.* [Heavy
> underlining, so deep the next page bears its marks.]
> *Only allow that there is a force deeper, greater,*
> *better, more forgiving than yourself, and you will find*
> *a path to your own healing, as we have said all along.*

*You must learn to trust your own goodness. If this
chapel, this church, will provide you with that
certainty, then you are moving in the right direction.*

*I would be interested to learn why it is that you feel
you still cannot tell your fellow churchgoers about
your past. Can you still not believe that if they are of
God then they can be trusted to forgive in a godly
manner? It all happened a long time ago, Anne, and
you were still a child – past the age of reason, it is
true, if you believe in such things – but a child
nonetheless, without the ability or knowledge to take
an adult's measured decisions. Have courage, Anne,
and put the first foot on that bridge of trust.*

*I am still disturbed, however, by the continuing
power your dreams seem to have over your waking
life. Your last letter revealed a startling absence of
any of the rehabilitative effects I believed we had
accomplished so successfully during last year.*

The last letter had been difficult to write.

Mary had been helping her at the bottom of the garden all day, clearing bindweed from around the bottoms of the fenceposts. She had equipped Anne and herself with heavy gardening gloves, which were a revelation to Anne and made the work far quicker.

'Blooming terrible stuff,' Mary had said, dragging out another clinging clump of the curly tendrils and shaking it into the green plastic bag she had brought with her. 'Ought to get some weedkiller on it, Anne. It's the only way to get rid of it once it's got a hold.'

Anne had pretended absorption in her corner of the fence, but suddenly the headache was back. She straightened up quickly and headed for the house.

'Anne, dear?' Mary called, but Anne continued walking.

'Just remembered something,' she muttered, and couldn't even steel herself to look back over her shoulder.

While she stood with her cheek against the hall mirror, fighting down the pain, the panic, she would, she realised, also have to invent a reason for her sudden departure.

That night they had been back in the toolshed, the three of them, without their dolls this time, but still in the washed-out cottons, Robin and Janey holding hands as the light began to bleed away, leaving the knotholes in darkness.

'I don't really like it here in the dark, Anne,' said one, but she couldn't tell if it was Janey or Robin. The voice came from one, yet she knew with utter certainty that the thought had been spoken by the other.

'Then you'll have to go back,' she had whispered, dropping her contribution into the space between them, knowing the reaction it would elicit.

There was no doubting this time – they both stared back at her, horrified, and 'We can't,' they half-whispered, half-hissed in ragged unison, lowering their heads towards her so that the words came from their eyes and not their mouths. And back at the house their father was still locked in his study, the tapes of his own voice going round and round on his reel-to-reel – 'Die Schlagsahne – whipped cream; die Schlagsahne – whipped cream. Der Ausgang – exit' – the useless lists going on endlessly, never learned, while he did what? The disembodied voice plugged on, and their mother had gone away. They heard her start the Morris and steer across the spitting gravel, pause at the road, then roar away.

When the door finally slammed on her shouting, Robin had come rushing into the room Janey shared with Anne, clutching her stomach, her eyes round. 'It hurts,' she said, and together they had trooped down to the toolshed. The back-door handle had to be held down hard and the catch released very gently so there was no sound to betray their movements.

'Is it time now, Anne?' they asked, and she had nodded, lifting the plastic tea service from the shoebox behind a cardboard carton of old hymnals. There were dolls' blankets – leftovers from their own babyhood – wadding it round, and these she laid squarely on the dirt floor. A bottle of clear lemonade stood beside the shoebox, and she strained with slippery hands and then, successfully, with teeth, to unscrew the tight cap. They were silent, watching her, and from the house the German lists dribbled on into the gathering darkness.

You might think it would be an easy letter to write, the number of times she'd written it before, but back with a garden again, in this haven, it seemed the hardest thing she'd ever had to do to put it all down on paper – to see their eyes, feel their breath, smell the sick fizz of warm lemonade for the hundredth hundredth time. She closed her eyes and felt within herself for the dark pool that held her strength and her salvation.

They told her she had preached on a text from Matthew that evening, and the huge pulpit Bible in front of her when she came up from the depths was indeed open at Matthew. A deep, damp indentation at the edge of either page was proof that she had pressed her thumbs hard into the book as she spoke.

Had she looked at them with sightless eyes, though, or had she hung her head across the reading-desk so her hair fell forward to hide her face? If she hadn't felt so weak she might have been paralysed with self-consciousness, but they were pleased with her again, she could tell, and that made everything all right.

She looked closer at the passage. Matthew 14: Jesus on the shore at Galilee, calling Peter towards him across the surface of the water; telling him not to drop his eyes, but just to trust, and he would walk on the waters like his Lord. She felt as though she would have had a lot to say on the text herself, but couldn't remember a thing. What had He said tonight?

'Was I . . . ?'

They were all tending to her with their customary gentleness and care, but strangely silent. She tried again, ungumming her dry tongue from the roof of her mouth.

'Was it helpful?'

She felt surer than ever that she must not, must *never* tell them that she couldn't remember.

At last one of them looked at her, put a long arm across her shoulder. It was Gordon.

'Don't say a word more, my dear. You must just rest now, but we must go away and discuss this amongst ourselves, you understand. There's a lot to prepare if we're to do it right.'

Then they had slowly drifted away, leaving her somehow washed up outside the porch door, her bag under her arm, her hat straight on her head, pointed in the direction of home.

'And then,' she had written, 'you know the rest.'

'But write it out as we agreed or you may never know peace,' came by return of post. So she had taken her pen and notebook, abandoned the stiff machinery of the typewriter and written and written, while outside the garden burned brown and the sun boiled through the uncurtained glass.

She wrote how her teeth ached from biting down on the stubborn bottle cap, and how she dropped in the yellow pieces from the forbidden canister with the label, 'DANGER – Paraquat'. One by one they vanished in a waiting foam of lemonade, then she sat quiet while the fizz that obscured them died back into the bottle and they were all dissolved. She wrote how she poured it carefully into the red-and-yellow plastic

116

tea service and gave a cup to each sister as they lay wrapped in the dolls' blankets on the dirt floor. And finally she wrote how she lay down beside them with a curious lightness born out of their trust and the relief that they would no longer be a burden, and drank from her cup as they drank from theirs. And, 'Don't worry,' she had told them. 'It won't take long.'

There was shouting and running feet, and she couldn't, for a minute, remember where she was. But the faces of her mother and father flashed before her, stony with the raw loneliness that welded them together: new shades of meaning grafted suddenly on to their togetherness. And the image – or was this just memory? – of some heavy machine plugged suddenly into her veins and which seemed to bounce up and down with the beating of her heart, landing with a sickening lightness, only to jump back towards the strip-lit ceiling. And the voices: 'You are saved. Anne, you are saved.'

But they were still calling her name, and the faces resolved into shapes that were familiar, yet not her parents. The flat hair, the bobbing feather . . . She felt she should know. They leaned down over her and suddenly the names came swimming up like gifts. Don. Mary. The room, grouping and regrouping around her was theirs. She was back at the church, back with her new family. She had the feeling she had come in too late, at the end of the speech.

' . . . so they're gathered now, my dear, and with their eyes on Him they'll prosper in this miracle of latter days. We just thought you'd like to know, and we'll be back soon, Anne dear, because you know, it won't take long.'

How could they still tell her that there was no good, no evil when once more she knew herself a channel for the voices of persuasion that whispered in the darkness?

By dawn she finally understood what she had been called for this time – what she had called for them to do.

Twenty-seven fully-clothed bodies were dragged out from the middle of the reservoir, strangely, where it was deepest. They laid them side by side on the concrete shore, man beside woman and woman with her child.

The police couldn't understand at first how they'd broken in, with no gaps in the wire, no ladders – and then the staff identified one of the bloated dead as Don Shand, the keys to the compound still in his pocket. His eyes were staring straight before him and his cold lips curved in a smile of happy triumph.

It had taken them a while, walking foot to foot across the even darkness of the quiet, night reservoir. He must have been pleased they'd got so far.

Two strands of wire

Roger Stone

This is one of the things I hoped would happen. Roger Stone found a copy of Darklands *in his local Cardiff branch of Forbidden Planet and, as he read it, he realised it contained the kind of fiction he liked to write. So he sent me four stories, one of which I thought was extremely good and ideal for the second volume. He writes with rare confidence for someone who's placed only a handful of stories – in a Newent Arts Society anthology,* Writers' Monthly Magazine, *small press magazines* Xenos *and* Cambrensis, *the* South Wales Argus *and a forthcoming anthology* Shorts From Mid-Glamorgan, *which sounds more like an illustrated history of the Welsh trouser to me but there you go. This is his first appearance in a horror anthology. He's written one novel and is working on a second.*

Born in Mid-Glamorgan in 1952 and now living in Gwent, he is a chartered engineer but gains more pleasure from writing. He was turned on to it in his early teens by reading Poe and Kafka. 'H.G. Wells added a sense of wonder,' he says, 'Hemingway showed me I didn't have to use adjectives and Chandler showed me how much fun they can be.' There's something clever going on in this story which will make it quite uncomfortable for some readers, but once you're in you're trapped.

Two strands of wire

'Excuse me.'

She wants something. She's speaking to me, so she wants something. Women usually just smile, if they don't know you, and you struggle to tell what they mean, from the smile. Are they grateful for an opened door, embarrassed by a dropped umbrella, interested, coldly polite, superior? The smile says it all, if you read it right. But this is different. She's speaking to me, so she wants something. Tonight of all nights! Shit!

'Yes, love? What's the problem?'

'You haven't got a set of jump leads, have you?'

She's taking a few steps across the concrete, from her car, tucked away in the far corner, to mine, nearer the stairwell. Tentative steps; not so much to cover distance as to establish a connection, get me to identify with her. She's standing there, hands in pockets, quilted jacket, denim jeans, looking hopeful. There's a faint smell of lavender in the air, and a set of leads in the boot of my car.

'Sorry, no, I haven't.' Why the hell did I say that? I know it'll make me feel guilty, and Sarah won't mind if I'm a few minutes later. But that's the problem – *later*. She'll be standing on that corner in half an hour, getting wet and cold, and it'll take me at least forty minutes to get there. Perhaps I should fetch the leads anyway. No. It's too late now. She'd think I was acting strangely. First I tell her there aren't any, then there are.

'I'll help you push it to the exit ramp if you like. Maybe it'll start on the way down.' Now that really *is* stupid. It would have taken less time and effort to use the leads. All this agony over two strands of wire.

'No thanks. It's a lousy starter. That's why I flattened the battery. I'd hate to get stuck at the bottom and block the exit.'

She's smiling.

'Thanks anyway.'

At least I offered. But that hasn't removed the guilt. Should I offer her a lift? No. Don't dig yourself in any deeper. So what do I do? She's backing away now. I shrug and call out 'Good luck' and she's getting a bag out of her car and locking the door. I get into my own car, start it up, noticing the girl heading for the lifts as I pull out of the parking bay.

The ramps are deceptive. I have four floors to descend but the concrete seems endless. My concentration is diluted by the image of a young woman in a quilted jacket and denim jeans lifting a pale hand, thumb extended, into a stream of driving rain. On the second floor I grazed my front bumper against the spiral wall of the ramp.

Tonight the queue is short; only three cars. Just as I'm pushing the gear lever into first the man in front fumbles with his change. It falls noisily between the kiosk and the car, rolling underneath. He leans out and reaches, blindly. I drum my fingers on the wheel and swear under my breath. The girl in denim is forgotten and I mentally count the miles I have to cross to meet Sarah, check my watch, swear again.

Out on the street, I join the early evening traffic. Past the bus station, through the lights, and I'm waiting to turn into St Mary Street. Suddenly there's a noise, a rush of cold air, and a hint of lavender, and she's settling into the passenger seat, closing the door, and smiling.

'Are you going east – to Newport?'

The lights are green and the traffic is moving. I raise a hand in apology to the sounded horns and move off, stammering an uncertain 'Yes. Well, near there anyway.'

There's no time to question or to doubt; not even to look at her properly; the traffic doesn't allow it. I can only weave through the buses and pedestrians and accept that she's here. Out past the infirmary, heading for Roath Court, the pace eases and I look across at her for a second or two. She smiles but says nothing. The quilted jacket is shrugged off as the heater warms us up, her shoulders moving fluidly, and the garment lands on the back seat with a rustle of nylon. A pale green shirt, rough cotton, gives out the sweet aroma of female sweat. This is not the sweat of exertion, lubricating pumping muscles and bus-chasing legs. I look at her eyes. There's a . . . I don't know . . . a colour behind the blue, a focus beyond the lens. It flashes the air between us and I look away, at the traffic and the rain. Who's going to talk first?

'I leave the M4 at High Cross,' I say. 'Will that do you?'

After a pause she says, 'They're in the trunk, aren't they?'

I notice her accent for the first time. It's been well submerged, but the word 'trunk' makes it seem more obvious. Not New York, or West Coast. Not New England or Deep South. Too gentle for those. Canadian or maybe a border state. Her question draws out some sweat of my own around my collar.

'Sorry?'

This time she pauses for so long I look at her again to see if she's heard me. Her mouth smiles – just the mouth. It opens.

'The jump leads. They're in the trunk.'

I think about denying it. She won't know. What will she

123

do? Stop the car and search among the jumble of coats and boots? Denial is simple.

'How did you know?' I ask.

'You carry your conscience in your eyes, David.'

My name attaches itself so casually to the end of her sentence that I feel no surprise. There are two flows carrying me along now; one outside the car, one inside.

We drive for a while in silence. Outside, the traffic is heavy past faceless retail units; store-front signs calling out to the weary. The slip road sucks us up to the interchange and we glide back down on to the motorway, shielded from the other traffic by a cocoon of spray. I wait for her to speak again. She will. There's no need for me to take the initiative. The motorway recedes behind the curtains of water and I wait.

'I need to get a bus to Heathrow. There's a flight I want to get tomorrow.'

'Yes,' I say. 'But what about your car?'

There's a laugh, almost a giggle, but too throaty.

'Did you think it was mine? You did, didn't you? Really, David; a gentle little hatchback like that? That's not me at all. If I'd wired it right I wouldn't be here now.' I could feel her smile. 'Just think what we'd be missing.'

I check in the mirror to pull out around a slow-moving lorry. The lane is clear but I stay where I am. I'm looking at her more often now. The drop-off point is coming too slow, but I take my time. I'm unsure whether the knot in my stomach is anticipation or dread. She slides around in her seat. It moulds to her and holds her while she turns to face me. Her tongue slicks along her upper lip and the eyes open wider, penetrating and full of knowledge. My foot presses the accelerator and I move into the middle lane.

Lights blaze at me. An air-horn blasts through the closed windows while a shadow rushes to tower behind the car. My foot is already floored and I grip the wheel and wait for a sickening impact, a scream of dying metal that tears flesh. The shadow hovers and shouts, but slowly, unwillingly recedes, flashing angrily. The smell of perspiration is stronger now. I steer into the slow lane while the car is buffeted by the passing shadow. The spray swallows the threat and we are alone again.

I'm still looking at the receding hulk. I feel heat on my face. Her breath is quiet but feels loud. Somehow she is leaning across the car but not resting on her hands. They are on the back of my head and under my chin. I feel her tongue wiping the sweat from my cheek. She whispers the word 'salt' and takes the sweet water from my face, my jaw, behind my ear. Her tongue, quick and firm, flickers for a second near my lips and then she drops back into her seat. I look at her. She wipes lines of moisture from her neck with a finger and draws it along her lips, watching me.

She moves in her seat again, reaching for her boots. Zippers open. Leather creaks. White-socked feet lift to the dashboard and cross themselves.

'I overeat,' she says. Her fingers prod at her stomach. 'Can you see? *Fucking* jeans are always too tight.' She looks at me as she spits out the word, watching for a reaction. 'I've got to ease the pressure. Do you mind?' I don't answer, because there was no question, and I'm still unsure what I really want her to do. Her hands move to her belt buckle and open it carefully, fingers levering at the metal button at her waist. It unhooks with an audible sigh. The zip ripples open. She pauses to make sure I'm watching before she unpeels her legs, slowly, skilfully, to her ankles. I can see white cotton and a thin line of dark hair. She leaves the denim hanging from her calves, swinging gently as the car bumps across joints in the road. Finished with the jeans, her hands come to rest on her lower belly, pressing and smoothing as though to ease or spread a dull ache. I shift uneasily in my seat and focus on a set of hazy tail-lights twenty yards away.

'What's the matter, David? Are you uncomfortable? I think it's your trousers, you know? They're not meant for driving in, trousers. I always drive like this.' Her hand follows the curves of her inner thighs. 'It lets the air circulate.' She laughs again, but the humour has lost its pretence of being mutual.

The journey is half-over; the speedometer shows I'm keeping up a steady pace; but I feel as though time is slowing down, holding me in this ... bubble ... closed in by curved walls of driving and bouncing rain and faint images of traffic. There is nothing to say, no conversation to tread through, no pleasantries to exchange. She was a stranger to smile at and be polite to, a pretty face, a nice body. Now she is too close, too tight; inside me in a way that twists and gnaws. There were a few minutes when she looked like a diversion, acted like a cheap and amusing fantasy. Now the control has moved to the place it always was, not where I'd fooled myself into thinking I held it.

'I've only been in one of these once before,' she says. Her fingers are tracing the outline of the maker's sign on the dashboard. 'I was a passenger, like now. A man was giving me a lift, like today. But he was ...' she hesitates, '... a nuisance.' Her hand shoots out and holds me, presses me, where I'm hard and vulnerable; squeezes. 'He grabbed me, here, David, this man. Makes you jump, doesn't it? Takes you by surprise.' I nod, mutely. 'I don't get taken by surprise now,' she says. 'I don't allow other people to have control. Look.'

She takes my left hand from the wheel and pulls it across to her lap, pressing my fingers against her warm flesh. I feel sick; swallow down a burning mixture of vomit and fear. She moves my fingers, sliding them under the top of her briefs to the harshness of curls and the dark wetness beneath. 'This is what I like, David; what *I* like.'

I snatch my hand away. For a moment I lose my fear of what she might do. Damaged pride and the humiliation of exposed fantasies erect a barrier behind which I can be in control. But she regains it. Her laughter curves its way around the edges of the shield to toss it aside.

'David?' There is mockery in the voice. 'David? Do you think this is your game, that you're in control, that I'm *your* fantasy?'

I look at her, sliding about in her seat. Her eyes carry no message – there is nothing to read in them. Their emptiness catches my throat and I search in them for some emotion – anger, hatred, lust. Nothing. But I'm encouraged by the silence. I can feel the journey passing, the road speeding away beneath my feet. There can't be more then ten minutes to go – seven, maybe eight miles. I watch the road and convince myself that's all there is, just the road.

The silence vanishes under the sound of tearing cloth. The remains of white briefs are thrown across the car, landing somewhere behind me, and there is more tearing. I glance quickly to the side to see her shirt being pulled, violently, by bared teeth and green-nailed hands. She is laughing again and the shirt falls from her mouth to hang, gaping, around her breasts. Kneeling on the seat, now, facing me, her breathing rapid and shallow, her eyes shining. Words come, measured and harsh from lips that barely move from their fixed half-smile.

'Well, David. Nearly there. What shall we do now? Shall we pull on to the hard shoulder? I can climb over you, straddle you, take you deep inside. No one would know. Or shall I put my head in your lap, David? I'm good with my mouth. Would you like that? Could you drive us through the rain while I do it? Carry on to the next exit? Can you last that long? Or shall I just lie here until we leave the motorway, until you slow down at the top of the ramp, and then open the door and fall out, graze my knees and arms, cry on to someone's shoulder and remember your face, your name, your car? What shall I do, David? What would your fantasy do? If you could control it?'

The screen wipers count through the silence, tick away the pendulum-seconds. She is motionless at my side, breathing barely controlled, hot breaths. I wait for something – a word, a movement. The silence boils in my gut, blocks my throat, stifling words and decisions, making me wait, passively. Through the spray I can see the count-down signs to the exit ramp. I breathe deeply, the first breath I can remember taking, but it's an uneasy breath, not sure of its rights. We climb the ramp to the roundabout. She doesn't move. As I check to the right for traffic and peer at the dipped headlamps there's a flurry of movement, material rustling, the sound of zips. The car stops. I look around and face a blast of cold, wet air.

'Thanks for the lift, David.'

A young girl is smiling at me; denim jeans, boots, quilted jacket, slightly torn blouse. She is leaning in through the door.

'I can walk to the bus depot from here, or thumb a lift.' She tilts her head to one side. 'Thanks again. You were very helpful. Bye.'

The door slams and I feel myself being pulled out of a trance. I open my door – jump out. Cars sound their horns and people shout. I start after her but am reluctant to leave my own car, suddenly a haven.

'Wait,' I shout. 'How do you know me? Do you know a friend of mine? Is that it? Who are you?'

She turns, stepping lightly backwards as she faces me, rain

cascading down her cheeks, her shirt already soaked. 'The world is full of Davids, David. Just like you. But there's only one of me. For you there's only one of me.'

The rain swallows her and I stand, surrounded by traffic and noise, alone. I return to the car, close the door, and wind down the windows. By the time I reach the corner where Sarah waits, the faint smell of lavender has disappeared.

Coffee

Jean-Daniel Brèque

Born May 1954 in Bordeaux, Jean-Daniel Brèque spent two years teaching in Morocco as an alternative to military service and on his return to France found himself unemployed. Eventually he took a job in the tax office at Dunkirk where he stayed until 1987. Already a regular contributor of articles and illustrations to UK fanzines Fantasy Unlimited *and* Comics Unlimited, *his first short story sale (a collaboration), in 1984, was to* Fiction, *the now defunct French edition of* The Magazine of Fantasy & Science Fiction. *He tried his hand at small press publishing, producing an anthology,* Arachne, *and a Michael Bishop chapbook. The appeal of the tax office proved less than everlasting and he left to become a full-time translator of such names as Barker, Simmons, Koontz. His own short stories have appeared in* Fantasy Tales, Best New Horror 2, Brèves, Bouches d'Ombre, Antarès *and* Territoires de l'Inquiétude.

Jean-Daniel is a regular visitor to the British Fantasy Society's Fantasycon. A genial fellow possessing a luxuriant beard and excellent English, he is easily located on these occasions by the pungent and not unattractive smell of his pipe tobacco. Of Coffee, *he says, 'The first draft of this story was written several years ago and most of it is a straight rendering of what happened to me one Sunday afternoon when I ran out of cigarettes.' I would hope* some *of it, rather than* most. *See what you think.*

Coffee

I had just finished swilling the kitchen floor when I noticed I was almost out of cigarettes. Like most Sundays everyone on my landing was away and I realised I'd have to go out.

Bright sunshine had followed the bad weather we'd been having recently and as I headed in the direction of the Avenue de la Mer I could smell the last surviving flowers of the summer. Passing in front of an apartment building I saw a group of half naked children absorbed in a game. Their laughter seemed to greet me as I walked by.

The bar where I usually got my cigarettes was shut so I decided to go down as far as the esplanade in the hope of finding a café that might have some.

The beach was deserted, the strong wind and the approach of the autumn term having dissuaded the last remaining bathers. On the beach their reminders – empty, twisted Coke cans, fast-food wrappers, magazines bleached by the sea – were of endless fascination to stray dogs. In the distance, rollers of foam broke the surface of the sea and smoke from the factories at Dunkirk drew a veil across the sun. A trawler had anchored some way out and was swaying gently.

As I passed several cafés I peered through the windows for cigarettes but couldn't see any and after braving the windblown sand for a few hundred metres I went into a café where I vaguely recalled having seen someone buying a packet.

'Only if you're drinking,' the barman said to me.

'All right, give me a beer.'

I took the book of matches he left lying on the counter, lit a cigarette and swallowed a mouthful of beer. Behind me two old women were drinking coffee with the proprietress.

'I've told him time and time again,' the proprietress was saying. 'All right, your daughter is dead but you've still got your two sons. You can't spend the rest of your life crying about it. Look,' – she turned to one of the old women – 'your husband died but you don't sit there thinking about him the whole day, do you?'

The old woman shook her head without saying anything.

'Look at me, where would I be if I spent my time dwelling on the past? I've done things, I've got my family, my business, but I know that in the end none of it means anything . . .' She sipped her coffee. 'What are children, after all?' she continued. 'They're affectionate – up to a certain age – but they give you so much worry. Sometimes you want to hit them they're so annoying. And they always end up leaving you.'

In conclusion she tipped her cup back and emptied it. 'Will you have another, with a dash of rum?' she asked the woman next to her.

'Yes, but it'll have to be the last one.'

'That's right, you're going to leave us. Off down to the south and the sun. Come on then, have a rum in the last one.'

The proprietress got up and went behind the counter. Under the indifferent gaze of the barman, she served three coffees laced with rum, and came and sat down again.

'Cheers!'

I emptied my glass, paid the barman and left.

A large patch of oil darkened the surface of the sea. I walked a few steps, extinguished my cigarette and decided to take the long way back.

The wind had picked up even more and was flinging sand at my legs. In a restaurant window a little boy stared sulkily at a plate of mussels. The streets were deserted. In the square behind the town hall groups of children were playing boules.

A dog came towards me as I turned into the Rue de l'Hôtel de Ville and I crossed the road to avoid its look of complicity. Once I had passed it, however, the dog started following me. I turned round to scare it off with an aggressive stare but the sun, reflected in a window, dazzled me.

I approached the building where I'd seen the children playing. A little girl in a red bathing costume started crying and ran away from her friends.

'Go on and cry, sore loser!'

'Crybaby.'

'I'm going to tell my mum!' the little girl in red shouted back at them.

She ran towards the wasteground and hid behind a mound of earth. The dog, which had overtaken me, looked as if it was about to head towards her then looked in my direction and changed its mind. The other children forgot her and returned to their game.

I approached the mound, guided by her barely stifled sobs. I lit another cigarette and was seized by giddiness. The sun was dazzling.

'Are you all right?' I asked.

She looked at me with red eyes. I looked up at the sky but a bank of clouds had hidden the sun.

'They said I lost but I won,' she wailed.

The dog had stopped not far away to urinate on an abandoned tyre. As I crouched down next to the little girl the dog gave me a knowing look. I ignored it and glanced in the

135

direction of the other children but they weren't visible from this position. 'What's your name?' I asked.

She didn't reply; her eyes were fixed on the dog which was standing stock still. 'It's bad,' she said.

'What is?'

'The dog. The other day it bit David and he had to go to Villette Hospital.'

'Do you play here a lot? Isn't it dangerous?'

'My mum says we should stay inside. But it's not much fun.'

I nodded. Drinking coffee without rum isn't much fun either.

After giving me another look, the dog wandered away from the mound and headed off towards the other children. I made as if to get up and chase it or warn the little girl's friends, but she put her hand on my arm to stop me.

'No,' she murmured. 'I want to watch.'

Absorbed in their pebbles, which they were moving around on the ground according to an unknown set of rules, the children didn't notice the dog until it started to growl. They dispersed quickly and the dog chased the boy who'd run towards the main door. It bit him before he reached the step.

The child cried out and a man appeared at a first-floor window. A few seconds later he was in front of the building, unleashing a series of violent kicks at the dog, which ran off. Dazzled once more, I watched even though I was becoming confused.

Seeing me rubbing my eyes the little girl asked, 'Are you crying? I'll take you home.'

She took my big hand in her tiny one and, following my directions, took me as far as my building. Even when I'd opened my eyelids all I could see was red.

'What floor do you live on?'

'The first,' I mumbled.

'It served him right,' she said when we were in the lift. 'He shouldn't have made fun of me.'

She led me to the door of my apartment. I handed her the key and she opened the door.

Once inside, the red veil disappeared from in front of my eyes. The little girl sat down in my armchair.

'I'd really like a coffee,' she said with a confident grin.

'At your age?'

'My mum sometimes lets me drink coffee.'

As I went into the kitchen she got up and took down a book from my bookcase. With the coffeepot whispering away I got several bin liners out of the cupboard and spread them out carefully on the floor.

The coffee was ready. I laced it generously with rum and went back into the living room. She raised her eyes from the book open on her knees and gave me an intense look. Her cheeks were as red as her bathing costume.

'Thank you,' she said, taking the cup. She sipped her coffee.

Gradually, sleep overcame her. I went back into the kitchen and opened the drawer.

Translation by Nicholas Royle

Organ donors

Kim Newman

Not only is there something strange about Crouch End, North London, which makes the area attractive to horror writers, but there's also a very localised blip in the space-time continuum – localised to Kim Newman's flat. How else could he be so prolific? Ten novels sold since 1989. And as if that's not enough, he's also published a stack of short stories and countless book and film reviews, as well as his other non-fiction work. His short stories have appeared in every Interzone *anthology,* Fantasy Tales, Fear, Arrows of Eros, New Worlds *and many other books and magazines. His story* The Original Dr Shade *won the British Science Fiction Award for Best Short Fiction 1990. One way in which he cheats the clock, of course, is by splitting the workload between himself and Jack Yeovil. Kim does all the serious stuff while letting Jack loose on the outrageous fantasy novels and stories published by GW Books (and Pan in the case of* Temps*) – not that there isn't often a serious point lurking behind Yeovil's pyrotechnics.*

Born in 1959 in London, Kim Newman was brought up in the West Country, hence the pseudonym. In Bridgwater in the early 80s he wrote plays for the Sheep Worrying Theatre Group and played the kazoo in a cabaret band, Club Whoopee. He's an experienced broadcaster, most notably on Channel 4's Box Office *as regular film reviewer (1989–92). His published novels include* The Night Mayor, Bad Dreams *and* Jago.

Readers with back issues of Fantasy Tales *and* Interzone *may like to know that* Organ Donors *is 'the wind-up story of the series that began with* Mother Hen *and includes* The Man Who Collected Barker, Gargantuabots vs the Nice Mice *and (sort of)* Twitch Technicolor'. *Because of the way its ideas linger and grow in the mind, it may be Kim Newman's subtlest story.*

Organ donors

She came out of the lift into reception and heard there'd been another accident outside. Beyond sepia-tinted doors, a crowd gathered. People kneeled, as if pressing someone to the pavement. Heidi was phoning an ambulance. A man crouched over the fallen person, white shirt stained red, head shaking angrily. The picture was silent, a gentle whirr of air conditioning like the flicker of a projector. Sally walked to the doors, calmly hugging file folders to her chest. She looked through heavy brown glass.

Without shock, she knew it was Connor. She could only see feet, still kicking in the gutter. White trainers with shrieking purple-and-yellow laces. His furry legs were bare. Tight black cycle shorts ripped up a seam, showing a thin triangle of untanned skin.

A gulp of thought came: at least their where-are-we-going? lunch was off. She choked back relief, tried to unthink it to limbo. Then craziness kicked in. She dropped her folders and waded through paper, pushing apart the doors. Outside in Soho Square, noise fell on her like a flock of pigeons. Everyone shouted, called, talked. A siren whined rhythmically.

A dozen yards away, a van was on its side, a dazed and bloody man being pulled free. The bicycle was a tangle of metal and rubber. In the broken frame, she saw, squashed, the yellow plastic drinks container she'd bought him. A satchel of video tapes lay in the gutter.

'Connor,' she said. '*Connor!*'

'Don't look, love,' someone said, extending an arm across her chest.

People shifted out of her way, parting like stage curtains. Heat burst in her head, violet flashes dotted her vision. Her ankles and knees ceased to work. The ground shifted like a funhouse ride. Connor's head was a lumpy smear on the pavement, tyre track of patterned blood streaking away. She was limp, held up by others. Her head lolled and she saw angry blue sky. Buildings all around were skyscrapers. She was at the bottom of a concrete canyon. Darkness poured in.

At her first interview, Tiny Chiselhurst had been chuffed by her *curriculum vitae*. Like everyone else for the last twelve years, he didn't expect a private investigator to look like her. She told him yes, she still had her licence, and no, she didn't own a gun.

Her independence was a recession casualty. She wound up the Sally Rhodes Agency and escaped with no major debts, but there was still the mortgage. None of the big security investigation firms were hiring, so she was forced to find another job her experience qualified her for. Being a researcher was essentially what she was used to: phoning strangers, asking questions, rushing about in heavy traffic, rummaging through microfiche. There were even seductive improvements: working in television, she could rush about in minicabs and retire her much-worn bus-train-tube pass.

On her first day, she was ushered into the open-plan *Survival Kit* office and given a desk behind one of the strange fluted columns that wound their way up through the Mythwrhn

Building. Her work station was next to April Treece, an untidy but well-spoken redhead.

'Don't be surprised if you find miniature bottles in the drawers,' April told her. 'The previous tenant went alky.'

Sally had little to move in. No photographs, no toys, no gun. Just a large desk diary and a contacts book. Her mother had given her a Filofax once, but it was somewhere at home unused.

'Welcome to the TV trenches,' April said, lighting the next cigarette from the dog-end of the last, 'the business that chews you up and spits you out.'

'Why work here, then?'

'Glamour, dahling,' she said, scattering ash over the nest of Post-it notes around her terminal. The other woman was a year or so younger than Sally, in her early thirties. She wore a crushed black velvet hat with a silver arrow pin.

'They put all the new bugs next to me. Like an initiation.'

Their desks were in a kind of recess off the main office, with no window. Sally hadn't yet worked out the building. It seemed a fusion of post-modern neo-brutalism and art deco chintz. In reception there was a plaque honouring an award won by Constant Drache for the design. She suspected that, after a while, the place would make her head ache.

'Need protection?' April said, opening the cavernous bottom drawer of her desk. 'We did an item last series and were deluged with samples. Have some Chums.'

She dumped a large carton of condoms on Sally's desk. Under cellophane, Derek Leech, multi-media magnate, was on the pack, safe sex instructions in a speech balloon issuing from his grin.

'Careful,' she warned. 'They rip if you get too excited. We had the brand thoroughly road-tested. The office toy-boy was sore for months.'

143

Sally looked at the carton, unsure how to react. Naturally that was when Tiny Chiselhurst dropped by to welcome her to the team.

She woke up on a couch in reception. She saw the painted ceiling, a graffiti nightmare of surreal squiggles and souls in torment. Then she saw April.

'Bender tried loosening your clothes,' she said, referring to the notorious office lech, 'but I stopped him before he got too far.'

April's eye-liner had run but she'd stopped crying. Sally sat up, swallowing a spasm. Her stomach heaved but settled. April hugged her, quickly, then let her go.

'Do you want a cab? To go home?'

She shook her head. She buttoned up her cardigan and waited for a tidal wave of grief-pain-horror. Nothing hit. She stood, April with her. She looked around reception. Plants spilled out of the lead rhomboid arrangement that passed as a pot. Framed photographs of Tiny and the other presenters, marked with the logos of their programmes, were arranged behind Heidi's desk.

'Sal?'

She felt fine. The buzz of worry-irritation which usually cluttered her head was washed away. All morning, she'd been picking through viewing statistics. Her impending Connor discussion prevented concentration; she'd had to go through the stats too many times, filling her mind with useless figures.

She remembered everything but didn't feel it. She might have had total amnesia and instantly relearned every detail about her life. Her memory was all there but didn't necessarily have anything to do with her.

'Connor is dead?' She had to ask.

With a nod April confirmed it. 'Tiny says so long as you're

back to work tomorrow afternoon for the off-line, you're free.'

'I don't need time away,' she said.

April was startled. 'Are you sure? You've had a shock, lovie, you're entitled to be a zombie.'

Sally shook her head, certain. 'Maybe later.'

Although April introduced Connor as the 'office toy-boy', it was a joke. He was tall, twenty-one, and trying to earn enough as a bike messenger to go back to college. Like everyone (except Sally), he wanted a career in television. Zipping in and out of Soho gridlock biking memos, sandwiches, video tape and mysterious parcels between production companies was his way of starting at the bottom. He was one of the lean young people in bright Lycra who congregated in Soho Square, ever alert for a walkie-talkie call. He was freelance but Mythwrhn was his major employer. There were a lot like him.

Sally first slept with him on a Friday night, after a party to mark the first transmission of the series. It had been a long time for her and she was flattered by his enthusiasm. Besides he was kind of fun.

As he poked about her flat early next morning like a dog marking territory, she wondered if she'd made a mistake. She hid under the duvet as he wandered, unselfconsciously and interestingly naked, in and out of the room, chattering at her. He said he was 'looking for clues'. April had told everyone Sally used to be a private eye, and the Philippa Marlowe jokes were wearing thin.

She checked the bedside clock and saw it was before seven. Also on the table was the carton of Chums, one corner wrenched open. They'd come in handy after all. It'd have been hard to get aroused if she'd thought of Derek Leech leering off the pack at her. She turned the pack, putting Leech's face to the wall.

145

Connor jumped on her bed, eager to get to it again but she had to get up to pee. As she left the bedroom, she realised he must be looking at her as she had looked at him. Last night, it had been dark. Putting on a dressing gown would kill the moment, so she went nude into the bathroom. After relieving herself she looked in the long mirror and wasn't too disappointed. When she was Connor's age she'd been almost chubby; with the years, she'd exercised and worried away the roundness. April said she envied Sally her cheekbones.

When she got back to the bedroom Connor had already fitted another condom over his swelling penis.

'I started without you,' he said.

Tiny told her she didn't have to come to that week's production meeting, but didn't mean it. Sally was still waiting to wake up an emotional basket case but it hadn't happened yet. She slept through the alarm more often and had stomach troubles, as if suffering from persistent jet-lag, but her thoughts were clear. She even dealt with mental time-bombs like the travelling toothbrush left in her bathroom. Perhaps after all these years, she was used to weirdness. Maybe she couldn't survive without a stream of the unexpected, the tragic, the grotesque.

Networked on ITV at eight on Friday evenings, *Survival Kit* was an aggressive consumer show, proposing that life in the late 20th century was frighteningly random and unspeakably dangerous. Tiny Chiselhurst was at once editor and presenter, and the show, in its fifth season, was the cash-cow that kept Mythwrhn Productions, a reasonably successful independent, listed as rising. This series, Sally had helped Tiny, whose sarky humour was what kept viewers watching, expose a crooked modelling agency run on white slavery lines. Now she was switched to something that had little to do with the show itself and so was primarily an ornament at these meetings, called upon to report privately afterwards.

Tiny sat in the best chair at the round table as researchers, assistants, producers, directors and minions found places. He seemed to be made entirely of old orange corduroy, with a shaggy 70s mop and moustache. The meeting room was a windowless inner sanctum, eternally lit by grey lights, a crossbreed of padded cell and A-bomb shelter. After reviewing last week's programme, doling out a few compliments and making Lydia Marks cry again, Tiny asked for updates on items-in-progress. Useless Bruce, fill-in presenter and on-screen reporter, coughed up botulism stats. Tiny told him to keep on the trail. The item hadn't yet taken shape but was promising. What that meant, Sally knew, was that no sexy case – a ten-year-old permanently disabled by fish fingers, say – had come to light. When there was a pathetic human face to go with the story, the item would go ahead.

Finally there was the slot when people were supposed to come up with ideas. This was where performance could best be monitored, since ideas were the currency of television. She'd begun to realise actual execution of an item could be completely botched; what Tiny remembered was who had the idea in the first place. Useless Bruce was well known for ideas that never quite worked.

'I was talking to a bloke at a launch the other night,' said April. Someone said something funny, and she stared them silent. 'He turned out to be a corporate psychiatrist at one of the investment banks, talks people out of jumping off the top floor when they lose a couple of million quid. Anyway, he mentioned this thing, "Sick Building Syndrome", which sounded worth a think.'

Tiny gave her the nod and April gathered notes from a folder.

'There are companies which suffer from problems no one

can explain. Lots of days lost due to illness, way above the norm. Also, a high turnover of staff, nervous breakdown, personal problems, *sturfe* like that. Even suicides, murders. Other companies in exactly the same business with exactly the same pressures breeze through with *pas de* hassles. It might be down to the buildings they work in, a quirk of architecture that traps ill feelings. You know, bad vibrations.'

Sally noticed Tiny was counterfeiting interest. For some reason, he was against April's idea. But he let her speak.

'If we found one of these places, it might make an item.'

'It's very visual, Ape,' said Bender, an associate producer, enthusiasm blooming. 'We could dress it up with *Poltergeist* effects. Merchant bank built over a plague pit, maybe.'

Tiny shook his head. This was the man who'd stayed up all night with a camera crew waiting for the UFOs to make corn circles.

'No,' he said. 'I don't think that suits us.'

'Completely over-the-top,' Bender said, enthusiasm vanishing. 'We're a serious programme.'

'Thank you, April,' Tiny said. 'But Bender has a point. Maybe last series, we could have done this paranormal hoo-hah...'

'This isn't a spook story,' she protested. 'It's psychology.'

Tiny waved his hand, brushing the idea away. 'Remember the big picture. With the franchise bid, we mustn't do anything to make the ITA look askance. It's up to us to demonstrate that we pass the quality threshold.'

April sat back, bundling now useless notes. Sally was used to this: it was all down to Tiny and he could be as capricious as any Roman emperor at the games.

Roger the Replacement, one of the directors, had noticed a dry piece in the *Financial Times* about a travel firm considered a bad investment, which suggested further digging might turn up something filmable. British holidaymakers sent to unbuilt hotels in war zones. Tiny gave him a thumbs up, and, since April wasn't doing anything, assigned her to work the idea. The meeting was wound up.

In the ladies, Sally found April gripping a sink with both hands, staring down at the plug, muttering, 'I hate him I hate him I hate him hate hate hate hate.'

After her exercise class, they had al fresco lunch in Soho Square. In summer, it was a huge picnic area; now, in early autumn, office workers – publishing, film, television, advertising – melted away, leaving the square to tramps and runners. He had sandwiches while she dipped Kettle Chips into cottage cheese and pineapple. Connor always pushed his idea that *Survival Kit* do a week-in-the-life-of-a-wino item, unsubtly pressuring Sally to take it into a production meeting. She'd tried to tell him it'd been done before but his excitement always prevailed. Today he pointed out the 'characters' who pan-handled in Soho, explaining their fierce territoriality.

'You don't notice till you're on the streets, Sal. It's a parallel world.'

On a bench nearby sat two men of roughly the same age, a ponytail in a Gaultier suit and a crusty with filth-locks and Biro tattoos. Each pretended the other didn't exist.

'It's a pyramid. At the bottom, people get crushed.'

He was right, but it wasn't *Kit*. Besides, she was irritated: was he interested in her mainly as a conduit to the inner circle? With one of his lightning subject-shifts, Connor made a grab, sticking his Ribena-sweetened tongue down her throat. His walkie-talkie chirruped and he broke off the kiss. It was just past two and lunch hour was officially over. He frowned as a voice coughed in his ear.

'It's for you,' he said.

Knowing there'd be trouble, she took the receiver. Tiny had been after her to use a portable phone. She was summoned to the penthouse. Mairi, Tiny's PA, conveyed the message. Tiny wanted to chat. Sally assumed she was going to be fired and dutifully trudged across the square to Mythwrhn.

She stabbed the top button and the lift jerked up through the building. Tiny had a suite of offices on the top floor which she hadn't visited since her interview. Mairi met her at the lift and offered her decaf, which she refused. She wondered if the girl disapproved of her and Connor. She had the idea it wasn't done to dally outside of your age range or income bracket. At least, not if you were a woman. All the young middle-aged production staff had permanent lusts for the fresh-from-school female secretaries, runners and receptionists.

Tiny's all-glass office was a frozen womb. He sat behind his desk, leaning back. She noticed again the figurine on its stand: a bird-headed, winged woman, throat open in a silent screech. It was an old piece, but not as old as some.

'Know what that is?' Tiny asked rhetorically, prepared to explain and demonstrate his erudition.

'It's the Mythwrhn,' she pre-empted. 'An ancient bird goddess-demon, probably Ugric. Something between a harpy and an angel.'

Tiny was astonished. 'You're the first person who came in here knowing that . . .'

'I had an interesting career.'

'You must tell me about it sometime.'

'I must.'

The last time she'd seen a statuette of the Mythwrhn, she'd been on a nasty case involving black magic and death. It had been one of her few exciting involvements, although the excitement was not something she wished to repeat.

Without being asked, she took a seat. Apart from Tiny's

puffily upholstered black leather egg-shape, all the chairs in the office were peculiar assemblages of chrome tubing and squeaky rubber. As Tiny made cat's cradles with his fingers, she was certain he'd fire her.

'I've been thinking about you, Sally,' he said. 'You're an asset but I'm not sure how well placed you are.'

Her three-month trial wasn't even up, so she wasn't on a contract yet. No redundancy payment. At least the dole office was within walking distance of the flat. The poll tax would be a problem, but she should qualify for housing benefit.

'Your experience is unique.'

Tiny's confrontational, foot-in-the-door interviews with dodgy characters put him in more danger in any one series of *Survival Kit* than she had been in in all her years of tracing the heirs of intestate decedents, finding lost cats and body-guarding custody case kids. But he was still impressed by a real life private dick. April said the term was sexist and called her a private clit.

'You know about the franchise auction?'

The independent television franchises, which granted a right to broadcast to the companies that made up the ITV network, were being renegotiated. There was currently much scurrying and scheming in the industry as everyone had to justify their existence or give way to someone else. There was controversy over the system, with criticism of the government decision that franchises be awarded to the highest bidder. The Independent Television Authority, the body with power of life and death over the network, had belatedly instituted a policy of partially assessing bids for quality of service rather than just totting up figures. In the run-up to the auction, battles raged up and down the country, with regional companies assailed by challengers. More money than anyone could believe was being poured into the franchise wars. A worry had been raised that the winners were likely to have spent so much on their bids they'd have nothing left over to spend on the actual programmes.

'Mythwrhn is throwing in its hat,' Tiny said.

For an independent production company, no matter how financially solid, to launch a franchise bid on its own would be like Liechtenstein declaring war on Switzerland.

'We'll be the most visible element of a consortium. Polymer Records have kicked in, and Mausoleum Films.'

Both were like Mythwrhn, small but successful. Polymer used to be an indie label and now had the corner on the heavier metallurgists, notably the 'underground' cult band Loud Shit. Mausoleum distributed French art and American splatter; they were known for the *Where the Bodies Are Buried* series, although Sally knew they'd funnelled some of their video profits into British film production, yielding several high profile movies she, along with vast numbers of other people, hadn't wanted to see.

'Deep pockets,' she commented, 'but not deep enough.'

Tiny snapped all his fingers. 'Very sharp, Sally. We have major financial backing, from a multi-media conglomerate who, for reasons of its own, can't be that open about their support. I'm talking newspapers, films and satellite.'

That narrowed it down considerably. To a face the size of a condom packet, in fact.

'We're contesting London, which puts us up against GLT. So it's not going to be a walk-over.'

Greater London Television was one of the keystones of the ITV net, long-established monolith with three shows in the ratings top ten, two quizzes and a soap. In television terms, it was, like its audience, middle-aged verging on early retirement. Mythwrhn had a younger demographic.

'I'd like you to be part of the bid,' Tiny said.

152

She was surprised. 'I'm not a programmer or an accountant.'

'Your special talents can be useful. We'll need a deal of specialised research. In wrapping our package, it'd be handy to have access to certain information. We need to know GLT's weaknesses to help us place our shots.'

This sounded very like industrial espionage. As a field, IE never appealed to Sally. Too much involved affording the client 'plausible deniability' and being paid off to sit out jail sentences.

'You'll keep your desk and your official credit on *Kit* but we'll gradually divert you to the real work. Interested?'

Thinking of the Muswell Hill DSS, she nodded. Tiny grinned wide and extended a hand, but was distracted by a ringing telephone. It was a red contraption aside from his three normal phones, suggesting a hot-line to the Kremlin or the Batcave.

Tiny scooped up the receiver and said, 'Derek, good to hear from you . . .'

'Since the franchise schmeer,' April said, a drip of mayonnaise on her chin, 'the whole building has gone batty.'

Sally ate her half-bap in silence. She wasn't the only one diverted from usual duties and hustled off to secret meetings.

'They should put valium dispensers in the loos.'

When the consortium announced their intention to contest London, GLT replied by issuing a complacent press release. Ronnie Shand, host of GLT's 'wacky' girls' bowling quiz *Up Your Alley,* made a joke about Tiny's ego in his weekly monologue. High-level execs were heaping public praise on programmes made by their direst enemies. The dirty tricks had started when GLT, alone of the ITV net, pre-empted *Survival Kit* for a Royal Family special. As payback, Tiny had ordered Weepy Lydia to inflate a tedious offshore trust story involving several GLT board members into a majorly juicy scandal item. In the meantime, the best he could do was give five pounds to any office minion who called up the ITV duty officer and logged a complaint about a GLT show. It had the feel of a phoney war.

'Bender's wife chucked him out again last night,' April said. 'Found him writing silly letters to Pomme.'

Pomme was an eighteen-year-old PA who looked like a cross between Princess Diana and Julia Roberts. If it weren't for her Liza Doolittle accent, she'd have been easy to hate.

'He kipped in the basement of the building, blind drunk. Must have walked into a wall by the look of his face. I hope he keeps the scars.'

Six months before Sally joined the company, when April was young and naive, she had slept with Bender. It hadn't done either of them any good.

'Are you all right?'

People kept asking her that. Sally nodded vigorously. April touched her cheek, as if it'd enable her to take Sally's emotional temperature.

The funeral had been yesterday. Sally had sent a floral tribute but thought it best not to go. Connor's friends would think she was his aunt or someone. She had never met his parents and didn't especially want to.

From the sandwich shop, Sally saw the square. A knot of messengers hung about the gazebo, all in Lycra shorts and squiggly T-shirts. Sprawled on benches, they let long legs dangle as they worked pain out of their knees. Some, unlike Connor, had helmets like plastic colanders. Staff at Charing Cross Hospital had a nickname for Central London cycle messengers: organ donors. Scrapes and spills were an inevitable part of accelerated lives. And so was human wastage.

Ironically Connor had carried a donor card: he was buried without corneas and one kidney.

'Come on,' said April, looking at her pink plastic watch, 'back to the front...'

If she had doubts about the identity of the consortium's financial backer, they were dispelled by the front page of the *Comet,* tabloid flagship of Derek Leech's media empire. Ronnie Shand was caught in the glare of flashbulbs, guiltily emerging from a hotel with a girl in dark glasses. The story, two hundred words of patented *Comet* prose, alleged *Up Your Alley* was fixed. Contestants who put out for Shand (51, married with three children) were far more likely to score a strike and take home a fridge-freezer or a holiday in Barbados. An inset showed Ronnie happy with his family in an obviously posed publicity shot. Inside the paper, the girl, an aspiring model, could be seen without clothes, a sidebar giving details about 'my sizzling nights with TV's family man'. Shand was unavailable for comment but GLT made a statement that *Up Your Alley* would be replaced by repeats of *Benny Hill* while an internal investigation was conducted. Sally wondered whether they'd investigate the allegations or witch-hunt their staff for the traitor who'd tipped off the *Comet*.

Tiny was a bundle of suppressed mirth at their meeting and chuckled to himself as she reported. She'd carried out a thorough, boring check of the finances of GLT's component parts, and discovered profits from hit shows had been severely drained by a couple of disastrous international co-productions, *The Euro-Doctors* and *The Return of Jason King*. The interruption of *Up Your Alley* was a severe embarrassment. GLT must be hurting far more than their bland press releases suggested.

'If it comes to it, we can outspend the bastards,' Tiny said.

'We'll have to make sacrifices. Congratulations, Sally. I judge you well.'

There was something seductive about covert work. Setting aside moral qualms about the franchise system and relegating to a deep basement any idea of serving the viewing public, she could look at the situation and see any number of moves which could be to Mythwrhn's advantage. Taken as a game, it was compulsive. It being television, it was easy to believe no real people at all were affected by any action she might suggest or take.

'I've been looking at *Cowley Mansions,*' she said, referring to GLT's long-running thrice-weekly soap set in a Brixton block of flats. It was said GLT wouldn't lose their franchise because John Major didn't want to go down in history as the Prime Minister who took away the *Mansions*.

Tiny showed interest.

'I've not got paper back-up but I heard a whisper that GLT took a second mortgage to finance *The Euro-Doctors* and put the *Mansions* on the block.'

'Explain.'

'To sucker in the Italians and the French, GLT threw in foreign rights to the *Mansions* with the deal. Also a significant slice of the domestic ad revenues for a fixed period.'

Tiny whistled.

'As you know, TéVéZé, the French co-producer, went bust at the beginning of the year and was picked up for a song by a British-based concern which turns out to be a subsidiary of Derek Leech Enterprises.'

Tiny sat up.

'If I were, say, Derek Leech, and I wanted to gain control of the *Mansions*, I think I could do it by upping my holdings in an Italian cable channel by only two per cent, and by buying, through a third party, the studio and editing facilities GLT have currently put on the market to get fast cash. Years ago, in one of those grand tax write-off gestures, slices of the *Mansions* pie were given in name to those GLT sub-divisions and when they separate from the parent company, the slices go too. Then, all I'd have to do to get a majority ownership would be to approach the production team and the cast and offer to triple salaries in exchange for their continued attachment. I might have to change the name of the programme slightly, say by officially calling it *The Mansions*, to get round GLT's underlying rights.'

Tiny pulled open a drawer and took out a neat bundle of fifty-pound notes. He tossed it across his broad desk and it slid into Sally's lap.

'Buy yourself a frock,' he said.

In the lift, there was something wrong with a connection. The light-strip buzzed and flickered. Sally had a satisfaction high but also an undertone of nervous guilt. It was as if she had just taken part in a blood initiation and was now expected to serve forever the purpose of Kali the Destroyer.

As usual, there was nothing on television. She flicked through the four terrestrial channels: Noel Edmonds, tadpole documentary, Benny Hill (ha ha), putting-up-a-shelf. Like all Mythwrhn employees, she'd been fixed up with a dish *gratis* as a frill of the alliance with Derek Leech, so she zapped through an additional seven Cloud 9 satellite channels: bad new film, bad old film, Russian soccer, softcore in German, car ad, Chums commercial disguised as an AIDS documentary, shopping. After heating risotto, she might watch a *Rockford Files* from the stash she'd taped five years ago. James Garner was the only TV private eye she had time for: the fed-up expression he had whenever anyone got him in trouble was the keynote of her entire life.

The telephone rang. She scooped up the remote, pressing it between shoulder and ear as she manoeuvred around her tiny kitchen.

'Sally Rhodes,' she said. 'No divorce work.'

'Ah, um,' said a tiny voice, 'Miss, um, Ms Rhodes. This is Eric Glover . . . Connor's dad.'

She paused in mid-pour and set down the packet of spicy rice.

'Mr Glover, hello,' she said. 'I'm sorry I couldn't make . . .'

There was an embarrassed (embarrassing) pause.

'No, that's all right. Thank you for the flowers. They were lovely. I knew you were Connor's friend. He said things about you.'

She had no response.

'It's about the accident,' Eric Glover said. 'You were a witness?'

'No, I was there after.' When he was dead.

'There's a fuss about the insurance.'

'Oh.'

'They can't seem to find the van driver. Or the van.'

'It was overturned, a write-off. The police must have details.'

'Seems there was a mix-up.'

'It was just a delivery van. Sliding doors. I don't know the make.'

She tried to rerun the picture in her mind. She could see the dazed driver crawling out of the door, helped by a young man with a shaved head.

'I didn't suppose you'd know, but I had to ask.'

'Of course. If I remember . . .'

'No worry.'

There had been a logo on the side of the van. On the door.

'Good-bye now, and thanks again.'

Eric Glover hung up.

It had been a Mythwrhn logo, a prettified bird-woman. Or something similar. She was sure. The driver had been a stranger, but the van was one of the company's small fleet.

Weird. Nobody had mentioned it.

Water boiled over in the rice pan. Sally struggled with the knob of the gas cooker, turning the flame down.

A couple of calls confirmed what Eric Glover had told her. It was most likely the van driver would be taken to Charing Cross, where Connor was declared dead, but the hospital had no record of his admission. It was difficult to find one nameless patient in any day's intake, but the nurse she spoke to remembered Connor without recalling anyone brought in at the same time. Sally had only seen the man for a moment: white male, thirties-forties, stocky-tubby, blood on his face. The production manager said none of the vans had been out that day and, yes, they were all garaged where they were supposed to be, and why are you interested? As she made more calls, checking possible hospitals and trying to find a policeman who'd filed an accident report, she fiddled with a loose strand of cardigan wool, resisting the temptation to tug hard and unravel the whole sleeve.

April had dumped her bag and coat on her chair but was not at her desk. That left Sally alone in her alcove, picking at threads when she should be following through the leads Tiny had given her. She had a stack of individual folders containing neatly typed allegations and bundles of photocopied 'evidence', all suggesting chinks in the Great Wall of GLT. The presenter of a holiday morning kids' show might have a conviction under another name for 'fondling' little girls. A hairy-chested supporting actor on *The Euro-Doctors,* considered to have 'spin-off potential' even after the failure of the parent series, was allegedly a major player in the Madrid gay bondage scene. And, sacrilegiously, it was suggested the producer of a largely unwatched motoring programme had orchestrated a write-in campaign to save it from cancellation. In case Sally wondered where these tid-bits came from, she'd already found an overlooked sticker with the DLE logo and a 'please return to the files of the *Comet*' message; checking other files, she found dust-and-fluff-covered gluey circles that showed where similar stickers had been peeled off. So, apart from everything else, she was in charge of Tiny's Dirty Tricks Department. She wondered if G. Gordon Liddy had got sick to his stomach. This morning, she had thrown up last night's risotto. She should have learned to cook.

Bender popped his head into the alcove. When he saw only her, his face fell.

'Have you seen Ape?'

'She was here,' Sally told him. 'She must be in the building.'

Bender looked as if he'd pulled a couple of consecutive 24-hour shifts.

'No matter,' he said, obviously lying. 'This is for her.'

He gave her a file, which she found room for on her desk.

'She's not really supposed to have this, so don't leave it lying around. Give it to her personally.'

Bender, a tall man, never looked a woman in the face. His eyeline was always directed at her chest. In an awkward pause, Sally arranged her cardigan around her neck to cover any exposed skin. The associate producer was a balding schoolboy.

'We were all sorry about, um, you know . . .'

Sally thanked him, throat suddenly warm. She didn't know why Bender was loitering. Had April taken up with him again? Considering the vehemence of her comments, it was not likely. Or maybe it was.

'If you see . . . when you see Ape, tell her . . .'

160

There was definitely something weird going down. Bender really looked bad. His usual toadying smoothness was worn away. He had an angry red mark on his ring finger. It had probably had to be sawn free, and serve him right.

'Tell her to return the files asap. It's important.'

When he left, she decided to try work therapy. A minion named Roebuck was reputedly interested in being bribed to let Mythwrhn peek at GLT's post-franchise proposals. He'd contacted Tiny and it was down to her to check his standing. Being suspicious, she guessed Roebuck was her opposite number in GLT's Spook Department trying to slip the consortium dud information. She only had a name and she wanted an employment history. There were several people she could phone and – since everyone in television had at some point worked for, or at least applied to work for, everyone else – her first obvious choice was Mythwrhn's own personnel manager. If he had Roebuck's CV on file, it might have clues as to his contacts or loyalties.

As she bent over in her chair to reach her internal directory from her bottom drawer, her stomach heaved. Gulping back sick, she hurried to the ladies'.

One loo was occupied but the other was free. Apart from a mid-morning cup of tea, there was nothing to come up but clear fluid. It wasn't much of a spasm and settled down almost immediately. She washed her face clean and started to rebuild her make-up. The lighting in the ladies' was subdued and the decor was off, walls covered in waxy lumps like an ice cave. She supposed it had been designed to prevent loitering.

Pomme came in for a pee. She greeted Sally cheerfully, and, after a quick and painless tinkle, chatted as she made a kiss-mouth and retouched her lips.

'That bleedin' door is stuck again,' Pomme said, nodding

at the occupied stall. 'Or someone has been in there for a two hour crap.'

Sally looked at the shut door. There was no gap at the bottom to show feet.

'Have you noticed how that happens in this building?' Pomme said. 'Doors lock when you ain't lookin', or come unlocked. The lifts have layovers in the Twilight Zone. Even them security keys don't work most of the time. Must be bleedin' haunted.'

The PA left, her face requiring considerably less help than Sally's. Finally, Sally was satisfied. She put her make-up things back in her bag. Turning to leave, she heard a muttering.

'Hello,' she asked the closed door.

There was a fumbling and the 'occupied' flag changed. The door pulled inwards.

'April,' she said, looking.

The woman lolled on the closed toilet, eyes fluttering. She'd had a bad nosebleed and her man's dress shirt was bloodied. The bottom half of her face was caked with dried blood and flecked with white powder. Sally hadn't known she did coke. Or that things could get so bad with a supposedly 'fun' drug. April tried to speak but could only gargle. She pinched her nose and winced, snorting blood.

Sally wondered if she should get two tampons from the dispenser and shove them up April's nose. Instead, she wet a paper towel and tried to clean April's face. Her friend was as compliant as an exhausted three-year-old. Most of the blood was sticky on the floor of the stall.

'Pressure,' April said, over and over, repeating the word like a mantra. 'Pressure, pressure, pressure . . .'

Sally wondered how she was going to get April out of the building and home without anyone noticing. She told April to stay while she went and got her coat and bag. When she came back, April was standing and almost coherent.

'Sal,' she said, smiling as if she hadn't seen her for days, 'things are just fine up here. Except for . . .'

Sally tried to put April's hat on her, but she wasn't comfortable and kept tilting it different ways, examining herself in the mirror. Her shoulders heaved as if she alone could hear music and wanted to dance. Sally settled the coat around April's shoulders and steered her out of the loo.

The lift was on the floor, so she was able to get April straight in. If she could get her down to reception and out into the square and find a cab, she could say April was taken ill. A nasty gynaecological problem would go unquestioned. Those were mysteries men didn't want to penetrate.

She stabbed the ground floor button and the doors closed. If they got quickly past Heidi, she could limit the damage. But the lift was going up, she realised. To the penthouse. April was almost writhing now, and chanting 'pressure, pressure, pressure' until the word lost all meaning.

She slipped an arm around April's waist and tried to hold her still. April laughed as if tickled and a half-moustache of blood dribbled from one nostril. The doors parted and Tiny got in. He was hunched over in an unfamiliar position of subservience, grinning with desperate sincerity as he looked up to his companion. The other man, a human reptile of indeterminate age and indistinct features, was someone Sally recognised from the front of a condom packet.

'Sally, April,' Tiny said, so overwhelmed by his master's presence that he didn't notice their state, 'have you met Derek?'

Sally prayed to be teleported to Japan. The magnate, who kept going in and out of focus as if it were unwise to look at him with the naked eye, smiled a barracuda smile that seemed to fill the lift. She'd always thought of Derek Leech as a James Bond villain, with a high-tech hide-out in an extinct volcano and a missile silo concealed beneath his glass pyramid HQ in London's Docklands. A human spider at the heart of a multi-media web, he sucked unimaginable monies from the millions who bought his papers, watched his television, made love with his protection, voted for his bought-and-paid-for politicians. But in person, he was just another well-groomed suit.

Leech nodded at them. Sally tried a weak smile, and April, snorting back blood and residual traces of nose powder, radiated warmth and love before fainting. She slithered through Sally's grasp and collapsed on the floor, knees bunched up against her breasts.

'That's happened before,' Leech said. 'Embarrassing, really.'

Three days into April's 'leave', Bender went up to the penthouse while Tiny was out recording an interview about the franchise bid. After voiding his bowels on Tiny's granite-slab desk-top and hurling the Mythwrhn statuette through the picture window, he crawled out through shattered glass and stood on the narrow sill while a crowd gathered below. Then, flapping his arms like the failed Wright Brother, he tried to fly over Soho Square. Ten yards from the persistent smear that marked the site of Connor's death, Bender fell to asphalt, neck broken.

It had not been unexpected, somehow. Sally noticed people were marginally less shocked and surprised by Bender than they'd been by Connor. The office had a wartime feel; the troops kept their heads down and tried not to know too much about their comrades. Everyone secretly looked for jobs somewhere else.

Roger the Replacement went into hospital after a severe angina attack. He was thirty-eight. While he was away, his wife came to clear out his things and told Sally that he now planned to take a year off to consider his career options.

'What's the point?' the woman said. 'If he's dead, he can't spend it.'

'True,' she conceded.

Tiny took to wandering around chewing his moustache, checking and double-checking everyone's work. Still wrapped up 101 per cent in the franchise bid, he suddenly became acutely aware that Mythwrhn's current product would influence the ITA decision. The consequences of being blamed for failure would be unthinkable. Off to one side on 'other projects', she was spared the worst but the *Survival Kit* team suffered badly from the sudden attack of caution. Items toiled on for months were suddenly dropped, wasting hundreds of hours; others, rejected out of hand, were re-activated, forcing researchers to redo work that had been binned. In one case, the company was brought very close to Lawsuit County as a hastily slapped-together exposé of dangerous toys named a blatantly innocent designer rather than the shoddy manufacturer.

'I blame Derek Leech,' Useless Bruce said out loud in the meeting room as they waited for an unconscionably late Tiny.

'Shush,' Lydia Marks said, 'this place is probably bugged.'

'Tiny's completely hung up on the bid and *Kit* is suffering. Plus Leech has this Mephistopheles effect, you know. I swear reality bends wherever he stands.'

There were mumbles of agreement, including Sally's. There was something else she blamed Derek Leech for, considering the reputation of his products. She thought she was pregnant.

First, her doctor congratulated her in the spirit of female solidarity; then, interpreting her blank expression, she dug out a leaflet and said that at Sally's advanced age, she could probably justify an abortion on health grounds. So it was official:

thirty-five was 'advanced'. Also, Sally was unmistakably 'with child'. She wondered if her mother would be pleased. And whether she could stand another upheaval.

There wasn't time to talk with Dr Frazier, since she had to rush from the Women's Clinic to meet with the GLT Deep Throat. Miraculously, Nick Roebuck seemed to be a genuine defector. He wanted old-fashioned money and a shot at a position with the consortium if and when they took over the franchise. Someone reputedly sharp who knew GLT from the inside was convinced enough the consortium were going to win to gamble his career on it. That should be good news for Mythwrhn.

In the cab, Sally held her belly as if she had a stomach ache, trying to feel the alien lodged in her. A tiny Connor, perhaps, dribbled through a ruptured Chum? Or a little Sally, worm-shaped but an incipient woman? Half the time she thought her body had betrayed her; then she was almost won round by the possibilities. All her contemporaries who were going to have babies had already done so. She'd be the last of her generation to give in.

Roebuck had arranged to meet her at a sawdust-on-the-floor pub in Islington, well off the media beat. The cab cruised Upper Street, looking for the sign.

Sally had seen hard-edged women turn mushy-gooey upon producing a baby. She wondered if she'd ever even met a child she liked, let alone whether she was a fit mother. She corrected herself: fit *single* mother. Christ, should she even tell Connor's parents? There was some of their son left after all. Did she want to invite those strangers into her life, give them a part of *her* baby?

The cab drew up outside the pub and she paid the driver. Inside, a few glum men were absorbed in their pints. It was mid-afternoon and beer was half-priced to the unwaged. She supposed they called it 'the miserable hour'. A country and western song on the juke-box proclaimed 'If They Didn't Have Pussies, There'd Be a Bounty on Their Pelts'.

She spotted Roebuck at once, at a corner table. Shiny of suit and face, scalp red and glistening under thin strands of cross-combed blond hair. Apart from the barmaid, Sally was the only woman in the pub. She let Roebuck buy her a Perrier (until she decided what to do about the baby, she was off the gin) and listened to him gibber inconsequentially as he fiddled with the satchel he'd brought the papers in. He was nervous to the point of terror, as if he expected GLT shock troops in black balaclavas to burst in and execute him.

'May I?' she said, reaching for the goods. 'Just a taste.'

Roebuck looked appalled.

'It could be old copies of *The Independent*,' she explained.

Reluctantly, he handed over. The satchel was almost a schoolkid's accessory, not at all like the slimly imposing briefcases common in the business.

'I trust this will go in my favour,' Roebuck said.

'I'm sure the consortium will do well by you.'

She looked at a few sheets. There were authentic audience figures, with alarmed notes scrawled in the margins. A couple of thick documents marked 'HIGHLY CONFIDENTIAL' outlined proposed changes in GLT production and transmission schedules. Without a close examination, she guessed the purpose was to cut short term production costs to cover the losses GLT would sustain ponying up for a winning bid. She was almost satisfied to find a confidential memo from the board, insisting the company try to buy back its squandered percentages of *Cowley Mansions* before a raider took over completely.

'This seems to be in order,' she said.

Roebuck nodded, face burning. Palpable desperation

sweated off the man. He gripped the table to prevent his hands shaking. Sally wondered how low the consortium's unseen campaign would get. Roebuck had looked around throughout the meeting, as if searching for a familiar face.

'It'll stop now,' he said. 'Won't it?'

'I don't know what you mean.'

Disgust bulged through fear for a moment and he got up, barging out of the pub, leaving her with the satchel. A couple of others left almost immediately.

She gathered the papers. She'd win untold brownie points for this coup, but didn't know how much of it was her doing. As she left, she noticed an almost-full pint abandoned on a table by the door. The man who'd sat there had struck her as familiar. Broad, undistinguished, in overalls. With a spinescrape of fear, she wondered if he might be the van driver.

Out in the street, she couldn't see Roebuck or the nondescript drinker who could have been following him. So much to think about. She looked for another cab.

A man in a suit was dismantling April's desk, sorting through every scrap of paper and odd object in its tardis drawers. April had a system whereby every unwanted freebie and done-with document was shoved into a drawer until it disappeared. Tiny was either overseeing the job or ordered to be present at the dissection. The suit worked like a callous surgeon, calmly incising closed envelopes and packets. Sally wondered if he were from the drug squad.

'This is Mr Quilbert,' Tiny said, 'our new security manager.'

Quilbert smiled and shook her hand limply. She instantly pegged him as a cuckoo slipped into the Mythwrhn nest by Derek Leech. He had one of those close-to-the-skull haircuts that disguise premature baldness with designer style.

'We've lost an important file,' Tiny said. 'Bender might have given it to April.'

'I didn't think they were talking,' she said. 'Well, not recently.'

'Nothing scary,' Quilbert said, 'just stats about the building. There was a security survey in there.'

'We can get a copy from the consultants,' Tiny said, 'but it'd be embarrassing.'

Quilbert slit open a packet and slid out a pornographic magazine in Hungarian.

'That's from one of last year's items,' Tiny said. Quilbert smiled tightly and dumped it on the pile.

'Have you tried asking April?' she suggested.

'A bit tricky,' Tiny said. 'She's had a relapse. They've had to put her under restraint.'

She took the file, which she'd sincerely forgotten about, home, hoping it might help her understand the tangle of mysteries. Besides, an evening poring through arcane security lore seemed more comfortable than an evening phoning her mother and announcing a compromised 'blessed event'.

There was a new security guard, in a black one-piece bodysuit, installed in reception, presumably on Quilbert's orders. She was sure his X-ray vision would perceive the documents she was smuggling out but he was too busy trying to cosy up to Heidi. That hardly suggested fearsome efficiency.

She made herself tea and sat on her sofa, television on but with the sound down. The file Bender had given her for April was tied with red ribbon. She let it lie a moment and drank her tea. On the screen, an inter-racial couple argued their way to a cliff-hanging climax on *Cowley Mansions*. The soap's storylines had become increasingly bizarre: Peter, the gay yuppie, was discovered to be 'pregnant', a long-unborn twin developing inside his abdomen; Joko, the cool black wastrel, was revealed to be a white boy with permanently dyed skin, hiding out; and Ell Crenshaw, the cockney matriarch who ruled the top floor, spontaneously combusted the week the actress demanded a vast salary hike. Either the writers saw a Leech takeover as inevitable and were devaluing the property before the new landlord arrived, or GLT had ordered audience-grabbing sensationalism in the run-up to the auction.

After the soap came a commercial for the serialisation of Josef Mengele's Auschwitz diaries in the *Argus*, Leech's heavy paper. Then a caring, sensitive ad for Chums.

Sally undid the ribbon and didn't find a security survey. The first item was familiar: a glossy Mythwrhn press release, dated three years ago, about the redesign of their Soho Square premises. She paged through and found quotes from critics praising the features of the building that now drove people mad. The brochure also profiled Constant Drache, the award-winning architect entrusted with the commission. He'd been an unknown until Derek Leech chose him to construct the DLE pyramid, the black glass creation that now dominated Docklands. In a broody shot, Drache posed in black like the lead singer of a Goth group. A wedge of gibberish about his intentions with the building was printed white on black. It was silly, considering that a lot of Drache's 'severe edges' were now best known for ripping the clothes of passing people, but hardly worth Quilbert's search-and-destroy mission. Drache referred to buildings as 'devices', insisting each have its own purpose and be designed to concentrate 'human energies' towards the fulfilment of that purpose. Cathedrals, for instance, were designed to concentrate prayer upwards. Sally wondered what low ceilings and floor-level lighting were supposed to concentrate you towards, and, before she could stop herself, guessed Bender had probably worked it out.

She zapped to the Leech channel and found a scary scene from one of the *Where the Bodies Are Buried* sequels. A teenager screamed silently as Hackwill, the monster, slashed him with a cake-slice.

Under the brochure was a clipped-together batch of articles from a psychology journal. April hadn't abandoned her 'sick building syndrome' idea, or at least had got Bender to retrieve materials from the files before Tiny pulled the plug. Sally skimmed until her head hurt with jargon. Respectable psychology segued into the *Fortean Times* and even weirder quarters. She found pieces, with significant passages underlined in violet, on 'curses' and 'hauntings'.

The television monster laughed loud enough to be heard even with the sound down. The camera pulled back from a graveyard through which a girl was running to reveal that the tilted tombstones constituted a giant face.

The last items were thin strips of word-processed copy. A fine print tag at the bottom of each page identified the copy as having been generated for the *Comet*. Sally guessed that for a tabloid these pieces would constitute a heavyweight Sunday section article. She read them through, recognising the style and concerns of the Leech press. Dated a year ago, the article celebrated a major police infiltration into a nest of Satanic child abusers. Naming a few names, the piece was about decadent high society types turning to black magic to advance themselves. A 23-year-old stockbroker was purported to have made a million on Market Tips From Hell. A top model, who'd doubtless have posed nude for the illo, claimed drinking goat's blood landed her international assignments.

It was typical *Comet* drivel but had never appeared in the paper. Each strip of prose was individually stamped in red with a large NO design that contained, in tiny letters, the initials DL. She supposed this was Leech's personal veto. Why hadn't the piece appeared? It seemed a natural for the *Comet*. So, most likely, Leech had an interest in its suppression. She read everything through again and found it. There was a reference in the copy to the '£3.5 million modern home' which was the gathering point for the cult. In the margin, in faded pencil that looked as if it had been almost rubbed out, were the words 'Drache Retreat'.

'Where's the goon?' Sally asked Heidi. The security man wasn't at his post.

'Caught his hand in the lift,' the receptionist said. 'Dozens of little bones broken.'

Sally raised an eyebrow. A workman was examining the lift door, screwdrivers laid out on a dustcloth like surgical instruments.

'There was blood all over the floor. Disgusting.'

Carefully, she climbed the stairs, trying to keep her elbows away from Drache's 'severe edges'. If the architect had chosen to inset razorblades into all the walls, the effect might have been more obvious.

The *Survival Kit* offices were depopulated. Pomme told her everyone was off with a bout of the flu. Pomme's perfect complexion was marred by eruptions.

'Bleedin' worry, I reckon,' she said, scratching her blood-dotted chin.

April's desk had been put together again but was stripped clean. There was a padded envelope on Sally's desk, with her name printed on it. She opened it and found a bundle of twenty-pound notes. There was no compliments slip.

She took a giant-size bag of Kettle Chips out of her case and, after a furtive glance around, ate them rapidly, one by one. She was eating for two. The cash was for Roebuck's papers, she understood. A bonus, blood money.

She had just scrunched up the crisp packet and buried it in her wastebin when Pomme slid her head into the alcove.

'Remember Vindaloo?' she said, referring to the office cat who'd disappeared three months ago.

Sally nodded.

'The lift-repair man just found the bones at the bottom of the shaft. Ugh.'

All the black magicians she knew were dead, which was not something she usually found upsetting. She couldn't ask anyone to explain things to her. Nevertheless, she thought she'd work it out.

It was possible to climb past the penthouse and get on to the roof. The original idea had been to make it a party area but Drache insisted on a rubbery-leathery species of covering that made the light slope dangerously slippery.

Sally sat carefully and looked out at Soho Square, thinking. Her hair was riffled by the slight breeze. She wished she had more crisps. Down in the world, the organ donors were waiting to be sent out. Today, things had ground to a halt in the business. It was an armistice, a pause before the *putsch* of the franchise auction. Thousands would go under the mud in that armageddon, leaving the map of media London dotted with crushed corpses.

It was almost peaceful. Above the building, she felt a calm which was elusive inside it. The knot of worry which she'd got used to eased away.

'Chim-chim-a-nee,' she hummed. 'Chim-chin-a-nee, chim-chim-charoo . . .'

She decided she'd have her baby. And she'd leave Mythwrhn. There, two decisions and her life was solved.

Hours might have passed. The sun came out from behind a cloud and the roof heated. Should she give her blood bonus away? She'd been taking tainted money so long, she might as well keep this too. Soon she'd have to buy cribs and baby-clothes and nappies. Leech's money was no worse than anyone else's.

A few of the rubberised tiles nearby had been dislodged, and a dull metal was exposed. Beneath was a thick layer of lead, its surface covered in apparently functionless runes. She assumed they were symbolic. She picked free a further few tiles, disclosing more and more lead plates, all etched with hieroglyphs, incantations, invocations.

It confirmed what she had guessed. A cathedral was designed to direct upwards; the Mythwrhn building was designed to capture and contain. In psychic terms, it was earthed. She hoped she wasn't succumbing to the New Age now life was developing inside her. But for the past few months she had worked among enough negative energy to blacken anybody's crystal.

No wonder everyone in Mythwrhn was miserable. They were supposed to be. Misery was the cake, she supposed; all the blood was icing. Drache's Design must extend under the pavement into the street, to catch the drippings from Connor. If Bender had jumped from the roof rather than the penthouse, would he have escaped?

The Device worked like a scale. All the misery weighed one pan down, thrusting the other upwards. She could guess who would be sitting on the other pan. And what the uplift was for.

Under her crossed legs, the building thrummed with pent-up unhappiness. She was above it all. At once, she was centred. In her condition, she had power.

Over the years, she'd collected a library, mainly by ordering from the Amok Bookstore in Los Angeles, which was dedicated to 'extremes of information in print'. She skipped past William B Moran's *Covert Surveillance and Electronic Penetration,* G.B. Clark's *How to Get Lost and Start All Over Again* and Colonel Rex Applegate's *Kill or Get Killed: For Police and the Military, Last Word on Mob Control,* paused for an amused flick through one of John Miner's seven-volume *How to Kill* series, then selected Kurt Saxon's *The Poor Man's James Bond.*

Saxon, an extreme right-winger and authority on explosives, had authored a guide for the defence of the USA in the event of a Russian invasion, compiling information on sabotage, home-made weaponry and sundry guerrilla tactics. Although Saxon declared himself 'very pro-establishment and pro-law enforcement' and that he would 'not knowingly sell his more sensitive books to any left-wing group or individual', given the ever-decreasing likelihood of a Soviet invasion, the only conceivable purpose of his work was as a manual for the criminal.

Along with more conservative texts – Seymour Lecker's *Deadly Brew: Advanced Improvised Explosives,* the CIA's *Field Expedient Methods for Explosives Preparations* – Saxon's book gave Sally a wide variety of recipes to consider. She made a shopping list and went out to the chemist's, a DIY shop, a tobacconist's, Sainsbury's and Rumbelow's to buy the easily available ingredients she now knew how to convert into a functioning infernal device. The most hard-to-obtain items were the steel buckets in which she wanted to place her home-made bombs, to direct the blasts upwards. Everyone had plastic these days.

She was in her kitchen, attempting to distil a quantity of picric acid from ten bottles of aspirin, when her mother telephoned to see how she was getting on.

'I'm cooking, Mum.'

'That's nice, dear. Having a guest for dinner?'
'No. Just practising.'

'What's in the buckets?' Heidi asked.

'Live crabs,' she claimed. 'We're doing an item on the crooked pet racket.'

'Ugh.'

'You're telling me.'

The security guard was back at his post, hand mittened with plaster. Sally held up a bucket and he avoided looking into it.

'Careful,' she warned, 'the little bastards don't half nip.'

She was nodded through. On her lunch-hour she went back to Muswell Hill to fetch the other two buckets from her flat and went through the whole thing again.

That afternoon, there was enough blast-power under her desk to raise the roof. She hoped.

There was a confab going on up in the penthouse, a long-term post-franchise planning session. Sally would have to wait until everyone left. The idea of detonating some of the consortium along with the building was tempting, but she was more likely to get away with what she intended if no one was hurt. If the roof was blown off the Device, the energy should dissipate. She couldn't bring Connor or Bender back or restore April's mind or Pomme's complexion but she could spoil the nasty little scheme.

As the afternoon dragged on, she pretended to work. She ate three packets of Kettle Chips, shuffled papers around on the desk, phoned people back. She guessed this would be her last day. It'd be a shame to do without the leaving party and the whip-round present. She'd probably have qualified for paid maternity leave, too. Actually she'd be lucky to stay out of jail.

She had the idea, however, that Leech would not want her talking too much about the motive for her terrorist atrocity. A *Comet* think piece about how pregnancy drives women up the walls wouldn't serve to explain away her loud resignation notice.

The few *Kit* staff around drifted off about tea-time. Pomme invited her out for a drink but Sally said she wanted to get something finished before leaving

'You look a bit peaky, Sal,' Pomme said. 'You should get a good night's kip.'

Sally agreed.

'You've been driven to smoking?'

There was a packet of cigarettes on her desk. Sally coughed and smiled.

'Your face looks better, Pomme.'

'Fuckin' tell me about it, Sal.'

The girl shrugged and left. Sally realised she'd miss some of the others. Even Useless Bruce. She'd never worked much with people before, and there were nice things about it. From now on, she'd be alone again. Perhaps she would re-start the Agency.

Alone in the office as it got dark outside, she ate more crisps, made herself tea and sat at her desk with a new-bought occult paperback. She gathered the building was a magical pressure cooker and the accumulation of 'melancholy humours' was a species of sacrifice, a way of getting someone else to pay your infernal dues. It was capitalist black magic, getting minions to pay for the spell in suffering while the conjurors got ahead on other people's sweat. Obviously, some people would do *anything* to get a television franchise. Since catching on, she had been noticing more and more things about the Mythwrhn building: symbols worked into the design like the hidden cows and lions in a 'How Many Animals Can You See in This

Picture?' puzzle; spikes and hooks deliberately placed to be hostile to living inhabitants; numerical patterns in steps, windows and corners.

Sally divided the cigarettes into five sets of three. Pinching off the filters, she connected each of the sets into six-inch-long tubes, securing the joins with extra layers of roll-up paper. One test fuse she stood up in a lump of Blu-tak and lit. It took over five minutes to burn down completely. Long enough.

At eight o'clock, she put an internal call up to the penthouse and let it ring. After an age, Tiny's answering machine cut in asking her to leave a message. She double-checked by opening a window in the office and leaning out as far as possible into the well, looking up. No light spilled out of the penthouse.

The lift was still out of order, so she had to take the works up the stairs. First she went up and circumvented the suite's personal alarm. With some deft fiddling and her electronic key she got the doors open. The penthouse was dark and empty. It took three quick trips to get everything into Tiny's office and she arranged it all on his desk, working by the streetlight.

She felt ill. Since realising what was going on, she'd been more sensitive to the gloom trapped within the walls of the Mythwrhn building. It was a miasma. The water in the pipes smelled like blood.

Had Bender been trying to break the Device when he smashed the windows? If so, he'd made a mistake.

There was a hatch directly above the desk, just where it was indicated on the plans she'd borrowed. Above would be a crawlspace under the lead shield. She put a chair and the now-untenanted statuette stand on the desk, making a rough arrangement of steps, and climbed up to the ceiling. A good thump dislodged the hatch and she stuck her head into the smelly dark.

She'd assumed this was where all the energies would gather.

The cavity didn't feel any worse than the rest of the building and she had a moment of doubt. Was this really crazy?

After ferrying up the four buckets and the other stuff, she jammed through into the crawlspace. Here she could turn on the bicycle lamp Connor had left in her flat. She shone the beam around. She almost expected to find screaming skeletons and the remains of blood sacrifices, but the cavity was surprisingly clean. Meccano struts shored up the lead shield and crisscrossed the plastered ceiling. There was a slope to the roof, so the crawlspace grew from a two-foot height at the street edge of the building to four feet at the rear. If she placed her buckets near the rear end, the blast should neatly slide off the lead shield and dump it into the square. With luck, not on the heads of innocent passers-by.

She crawled carefully but still opened her palm on a protruding nail. The floor was studded with spikes, either one of Drache's devilish frills or a defensive feature. Crouching at the rear of the building, she pushed up, testing the shield. It was unresisting. Prominent bolts were spaced around the walls. With a monkey-wrench she loosened as many as she could reach. She banged her elbows constantly and skinned her right knuckles. Her hair was stuck to her face by sweat. This was not usually prescribed for expectant mothers.

With enough bolts loosened, she tried to push the shield again. It creaked alarmingly and shifted. Sally found she was shaking. She thought she could almost dislodge the lead without the bombs. But it was best to be safe.

She'd hoped the joists would be wooden, so she could screw in hooks to hang the buckets from. However, the metal struts came equipped with handy holes, so she was able to rig up the hanging bombs with stout wire. In each bucket of packed-down goo, she'd used Saxon's recommended dosage for disabling a Russian tank. She stuck the long cigarettes in each bucket and flicked a flame from her disposable lighter.

Once the fuses were burning, she intended to get down to her desk and alert the skeleton overnight staff. She'd say she'd seen smoke pouring down the stairs. With five minutes, she should be able to evacuate the building.

She lit the four cigarettes and wriggled back towards the hatch. Down in the penthouse, lights came on and voices exclaimed surprise. Knowing she was dead, she dangled her legs through the hatch and dropped into the office.

'What, no Leech?' she said.

Tiny was between the others, shaking and pale. The Device had been eating at him as much as his employees. Sally guessed he was only in the consortium as a Judas goat.

Quilbert was in charge, Drache was along for the ride, and the nondescript man holding Tiny up was the muscle. He was also the van-driver who'd knocked down Connor and the balls-squeezer who'd pressurized Roebuck. He looked more like a plumber than Satan's Hit Man.

'Ms Rhodes, what are you doing?' Quilbert asked.

'Raising the roof.'

Tiny shook his head and sagged into his chair. Drache strode around the office, examining his handiwork. He had a black leather trenchcoat and showy wings of hair like horns.

'The stand should be here,' he said, pointing to the dust-free spot where it had stood. 'For the proper balance. Everything is supposed to be exact. How often have I told you, the patterns are all-important?'

Quilbert nodded to the muscle, who clambered on to the desk and stuck his head into the crawlspace.

'Smells like she's been smoking,' he said.

'It's a secret,' she said. 'I quit but backslid. I have to take extreme measures to cover up.'

'I think I can see . . . *buckets*?'

Quilbert looked at Sally as if trying to read her mind. 'What have you done?'

'I've forestalled the Device,' she said. 'It was all wasted.'

Quilbert's clear blue eyes were unreadable.

'Only an innocent can intervene,' Drache said pompously. 'You've taken blooded coin.'

'He's right,' Quilbert said. 'You don't understand at all. Everything has been pre-arranged.'

'Not everything,' she said. 'I'm going to have a baby.'

Drache looked stricken but Quilbert and Tiny didn't get it. She supposed they found it as hard to believe as she did.

'There's something burning,' a voice mumbled from above. 'In the buckets . . .'

Drache flew around in a cold rage.

'If she's carrying a child, she's washed clean,' he said, urgently. 'It'll upset the balances.'

'What have you done?' Quilbert asked.

Sally smiled. 'Wouldn't you like to know?'

'Put out the fires,' Quilbert shouted up, 'at once!'

She should tell them not to tamper with the buckets in case the burning fuses fell. For the sake of her child, she couldn't die.

'Careful,' she said . . .

The ceiling burst and a billow of flame shot into the office, flattening everyone. A dead human shape thumped on to the desk, covered in burning jelly. Sally's ears were hammered by the blast. The stench of evaporating goo was incredible. Metal wrenched and complained. Hot rivets rained on to the fitted carpet. She heard screaming. A raft of steel and plaster bore down on Quilbert and Tiny. The windows had blown out, and the air was full of flying shards, glinting and scratching. She felt a growing power deep inside her and knew she would survive.

The cloud of flame burned away almost instantly, leaving little fires all around. Drache stumbled, a bloody hand stuck to half his face, and sank to his knees, shrieking. Sally was flat on her back, looking up at the ceiling. She saw night sky and felt the updraught as the accumulated misery of months escaped to the Heavens like prayers.

They kept her in hospital for weeks. Not the same one as Drache and Quilbert, who were private, and certainly not in the department that had received the still officially unidentified van-driver. She only had superficial injuries, but in her condition the doctors wanted to be careful with her.

She read the media pages every day, following the ripples. In the week before the auction, the consortium fell apart. Mausoleum Films, wildly over-extended, went bust, bringing down yet another fifth of the British Film Industry. Tiny promised *Survival Kit* would be back as soon as he was walking, but he'd have to recruit a substantially new staff since almost everyone who had worked in the now roofless Mythwrhn building was seeking employment elsewhere. Most wanted to escape from television altogether and find honest work.

The police had interviewed her extensively but she pleaded amnesia, pretending to be confused about what had happened just before the 'accident'. No charges against her were even suggested. Mythwrhn continued to pay her salary even though she'd given notice. After the baby, she would not be returning.

Derek Leech, never officially involved in the consortium, said nothing and his media juggernaut rolled on unhindered by its lack of a controlling interest in a franchise. GLT, somewhat surprised, scaled down their bid and fought off a feeble challenge at auction time, promising to deliver to the British public the same tried-and-tested programme formulae in ever-increasing doses. On *Cowley Mansions*, Peter the gay yuppie had a son-brother and, salary dispute over, the ghost of Ell Crenshaw possessed her long-lost sister.

Apart from the van-driver and Drache, who lost an eye, nobody had really been punished. But none of them benefited from the Device either. All the gathered misery was loose in the world.

The day before she was due out, April and Pomme visited. April was taking it 'one day at a time' and Pomme had discovered a miracle cure. They brought a card signed by everyone on *Survival Kit* except Tiny.

The women cooed over Sally's swollen stomach and she managed not to be sickened. She felt like a balloon with a head and legs and nothing she owned, except her nightie, fitted any more.

She told them she'd have to sell the flat and get a bigger one or a small house. She'd need more living space. That, she had learned, was important.

Lethality

Elizabeth Young

I'm not saying this story was a late submission, but I was halfway up the M1 to the printers in Newcastle when it came in and I had to go back. Small exaggeration. It was faxed to me in the middle of the night four days before press day and I knew after a couple of pages that it had to go in.

Elizabeth Young, born in Lagos, Nigeria, grew up under the dual influences of West African animist religions and the Free Presbyterianism of her Scottish parents. She attended the Mount, a Quaker boarding school in York, and, after a year at the Sorbonne, went to York University to study contemporary American literature. On leaving university she went to London at the beginning of the punk era and worked as a fiction buyer in Compendium bookshop. Married now and living in North Kensington, she contributes reviews to a number of books and magazines. Horror fiction, she believes, 'arises out of pity as much as fear, and writing it is a way to render bearable that which is psychically unendurable.'

Lethality is only her third adult horror story and the second to be sold (the first is in The Weerde II *published by Roc). She's at a loss to explain why so many of her fictional characters tend to be extremely unpleasant but stresses that it has nothing to do with their sexual orientation.*

Nightmare warning: avoid reading this one just before going to sleep.

Lethality

'There's prob'ly cancer snakes down there . . .'

'No such thing, snot-balls!'

'There is too – some come in Mum's garden – you know, the long thin red ones. Then she . . .'

They were standing beneath the pier. Its black wooden supports were shredded like lace. Round the groynes were feculent living growths of sewage and detritus patrolled by scavengers; dogs or monkeys with broken paws, their hair shaven off so that one could see the pastel internal organs moving feebly under the thinnest of skins. They coughed and whined and trailed excremental ropes like umbilical cords. Blowflies puffed languidly around each pitiful anus. The beasts had been 'liberated' from research stations or else had escaped when the funding stopped.

'Fuckin' scummy . . . toe-rags,' wheezed Bloat and chucked his can. 'They get in the houses and all. Your mum . . .' he turned to Jacko. 'Your mum – them cancer snakes . . . went into—' he started choking, 'up her . . .' He couldn't get the word out. 'Pss. Puss . . . Pss.' He gobbed. 'Dint they, dint they!!?' Bruce elbowed him sharply. Jacko turned away.

Look as far as you might, there was no sea.

No one had seen it for years.

The nineteenth century sewage pipes had collapsed away

but one could see how far and how deep they had travelled before disgorging their load. Now it lay over the entire beach. Miles of tissue paper waved in every sluggish breeze. Huge blood clots, siphoned from the clinic trucks, covered the old stone steps. If Bloat saw an embryo he ran to pop it like a jellyfish but that made Jacko sick.

Bloat whirled round and held his nose. 'Phew! What a Scorcher!' he said. 'Geddit? Phew? Pee-oo.'

The sun poured down relentlessly. Free now of all restraint it coated the land like glue, seeking out each last drop of moisture. Storms were frequent but the rain, swollen with radiation from abandoned power stations, was often black as liquorice. It could leave sticky insect tracks on skin and was worse than useless.

Underneath their bandannas and shades the boys' skin was red and cracked. Everyone was the same.

It was the last year of the century. Thousands of voyagers had been sent on reconnaissance missions in space. Voluntary and involuntary: some were paid and some paid handsomely for the privilege. Now no one could get them down and on cloudless nights one could see flocks of the little space ships, like pods or bonnets, circling hopelessly against the indigo backdrop. Each tiny coloured light winked pathetically until finally, helplessly, it would go out. The night sky was like Christmas all the time.

There were rumours. A giant white bull had appeared in central Europe, its horns draped with ribbons and garlands, and it repelled all comers. Refrigerator refugees, desperate for the touch of ice on their lips, were marching north. Big cats from Surrey with candles on their heads had colonised the malls. Like a dick in a tight twat the stories would grow and just as suddenly collapse. It was always someplace else. Things changed so slowly. What was strange one day was habit by the next. On the television news – when the electricity was working – all was serene: there were cures and companies and mergers and rock music. Just like it ever was. The stores were full or empty but when the goods were there they came from all places and seasons. And if academics sobbed at dinner parties and panic whispered softly through an office as the wind flattens dried grass before a fire, or if the rainy nights were full of echoes from the past, who was to care?

Some things never changed: London boys, sturdy invaders, down by the sea for the weekend.

Jacko stood by the railings sucking a Mini-Milk lolly.

'Lookit him suck that mini dick!' Bloat strode over in his big leather motorcycle boots. 'What you need, my son, is a good shaggin'. Give him one, Bruce!' Bloat took out his asthma inhaler. No one said anything.

Bruce and Jacko were named after long-forgotten entertainers who surfaced now only on cable reruns. Old heroes floating through blue rooms on moonless nights. Families sprawled like paraplegics, gasping in the heat, listening to the slow thump of a cranky generator. Old heroes lookin' good. All that effort, Jacko used to think, it had been for money, hadn't it? Money couldn't buy what you wanted now.

'S'fuckin' boring here.' Bloat swaggered towards the promenade. 'IF YOU'RE LOOKIN' FOR TROUBLE, YOU'VE COME TO THE RIGHT PLACE! As my old dad used to say!'

'Your dad Elvis,' said Bruce, robotically. 'Your dad Elvis the, uh—'

'HANWELL HOMBRE!'

Jacko trailed after them. They always picked on him, grabbing his bum, calling him a biscuit-bandit and a turd-packer. That was their big joke. Their only joke. Jacko sighed. You had to hang with the neighbourhood, specially nowadays.

With your family and the street. Bunsen Road was all he knew. Once before he'd been away for the day but he was just a kid. He'd seen lions though. None of the other boys had done that.

He watched Bruce and Bloat charging up the esplanade, headed for a synagogue outing for the physically challenged.

'Oy, oy, oy!' yelled Bloat, scattering the wheelchairs. 'See the front-wheelers go, go, go!'

Bruce tried a half-remembered football chant, gave up and whirled amongst the old folks, offensively rubbing his thumb and first fingers together in their faces. Yarmulkes and hairpins spun down the street. Frail women were tipped sideways into the litter and offal that crammed the gutters. The crowd surged forwards. A flatus of hasty prayers rose towards the heavens.

You got a whole lot of God-botherers at the seaside now. They lived there and they liked to die in public. Most of them were cults and sects waiting through the hungry spangled nights for what they called the Rapture when they would be swept into the bosom of God. The Evangelists were the noisiest. They could really pump up the volume on that gospel glad-handing. It seemed, mused Jacko, that the darker your skin, the less troubled you were by lassitude and lesions. He couldn't care less – everyone was muddled up together now – but Bruce and Bloat had been raised very differently and it made them seethe with jealousy and hate. You still got the first edition God-squad though. Today it looked like the whole lot were out in force. The Papists were bowling through the holiday throng in their black skirts or soliciting outside the pubs. There was even a C of E wedding by the bandstand. The bride handled her illusion veil as if it were a pair of headphones. White paper rosebuds ripped off and circled lazily in the reeking breeze.

''kin hell!' gasped Bloat, stumbling breathlessly out of the crowd. 'That was a fuckin' rapt'cha an' all!'

'Raptcha'd their knickers off,' grinned Bruce, handing Jacko a six-pack.

For the rest of the afternoon the boys staggered up and down the promenade. They elbowed each other, groped for butt and balls and lurched with laughter. They played the slot-machines and pin-balls or, alternatively, kicked them to shit.

By the time the evening lights came on they were well pissed. Fairground music gusted across the quietening town.

'What now?'

'Club?'

They strolled on.

'Wassis? Lookit this! Them gippoes – them travellers – come right into town now. Shouldn't be allowed!'

They stood before a small market-trader's stall. Beside it a pink silk curtain was hung across a shopfront. A hand-chalked cardboard sign read, 'MARIE LAVEAU. FORTUNES! PALM READING! LUCK, HEALTH, HEALING. GeT GOOd LUCK TodAY!'

'Getta good fuck today!'

'Whey-hey!'

'Let's gyp the gippoes!'

Bruce and Bloat blundered into the curtain, shrouding their heads.

'Woo-agh! Woooeee . . . It's the ghostbusters!'

'The ghosts, gnat-prick!'

The curtain billowed and they vanished, as if sucked into the stall. Jacko hesitated. Looked at the meagre wares on display. Coloured candles in glass vases with crude paintings of skulls and dice and cats and horseshoes on them. A jumble of gnarly roots in little packets with labels. High John the Conqueror Root, Twitchgrass Root, Tonka Beans, Sampson Snakeroot. Bottles of oil: Compelling Oil, Fiery Wall of Protection Oil. What was this stuff? Suddenly there was an uproar from within. Jacko heard furniture crashing and Bloat's hoarse shout, 'It's a nig-nog!'

Jacko ran through into the shop. A pink shaded lamp was swinging wildly overhead and a card-table lay upended on the floor. Tiny candles rolled and winked over the carpet on which were chalked two drawings of enormous snakes. Beside them someone had sketched simple stars and crosses, as children do.

Bruce and Bloat, huge black leather mountains, were facing two women. One, who was white and middle-aged, had an anorak hood pulled up over untidy grey hair. She was kneeling on the floor, trying to gather up cards and candles. A young West Indian woman wearing a blazingly white turban and a blue polka-dot dress was standing beside her.

'Well, well, well,' said Bruce, slowly. 'Nice little party.'

'Please go away.'

'C'mon,' said Jacko. 'There's nothing here.'

'I think there's a *lot* here.' Bloat sniffed the air elaborately. 'A lot of . . . cunt. A lot of cuntish tricks.'

'Cheatin' inn'cent people,' added Bruce. 'Load of rubbish.'

Pathetically, the lady on the floor was holding out a bundle of notes.

'You can't bribe me to grab yer gippo gash grandma! 'sides, we're not greedy, *are* we, boys?' Bloat looked around, smiling widely. 'Not like some.'

Bruce held a candle to the silk curtain. It caught with a roar. The girl screamed, quickly.

'What'cha gonna *do* 'bout it? Put a spell on us? Nah!'

Bloat, hands on belt, was steering himself towards the girl. Jacko put his arm out – 'No!' – and Bloat knocked him over. The curtain was drifting away in soft spirals of black ash. The veil of the temple was torn and the whole world could see the rose light of the open shop.

'Brothel,' growled Bloat. Bruce reached down the side of his boot. The girl seemed to make a decision: she stepped forward and raised her arms.

'Damballah-W'édo,' she said clearly.

The woman crouched on the floor had been muttering for a while. Jacko, struggling to rise, could hear her repeating, over and over, 'Damballah-W'édo, gadé pitites ou yo hé! Aïda-W'édo, min pitites ou yo hé! Damballah, min z'enfants ou là . . .'

Several things happened at once. There was a very loud knocking on the ceiling, from above. The girl looked up and smiled. 'No!' shouted Jacko, involuntarily. Bloat looked up as well, startled. The noise was like thunder and then it *was* thunder as a sudden storm swept across the bay. There was a squall of hail which hit them with the force of marbles, followed instantly by the dank blast of the rainstorm. All the lights in town went out. The back door opened and a group of children ran in, singing, giggling. They wore white dresses. The pastel lights of the sky pods washed over them so that they looked like sugared almonds. Jacko could hear a furious hissing noise, very loud, very close at hand.

Bloat and Bruce tore off their shades, trying to see properly. The girl shimmered like a silken rope unfolding through the multiverse. There was a slithering noise – *where?* – as if corpses were tumbling down the back stairs. Bruce and Bloat plunged towards the slippery esplanade.

Jacko helped the older woman get up. He said 'It wasn't me' and felt the girl's soft breath on his cheek. 'Shit goes to shit. When shit is at the centre. All are the same.'

The town generators kicked in and fairground music rose like a dirge.

Jacko reached out and was driven backwards by a sudden dazzle of white light. He found himself on the pavement.

The rain plastered his bandanna to his skull. He could hear his friends kicking cans across the empty parking lots. 'Slit-slavering bitch!' 'Up her fuckin' cunt with a pineapple!' 'Ream her out!'

A crazy lady staggered past, flowered skirts hitched around her waist. 'Salmon and springbok!' she called. 'Come out of the rain, come out of the rain!' An army of hooded monks rounded the corner. Their leader held a crucifix aloft as they intoned the terrible chant. *'Quomodo sedet sola civitas.'*

Jacko ran.

By the time they were sprawled on the sticky, plastic banquettes of the town's one nightclub, Bruce and Bloat were fully restored. 'We showed that bitch, dint we?' Only Jacko still felt disturbed about the incident but even he could barely think what with the harsh electro-pulse of the music and the liquid warmth of the pills they had taken spreading through his brain. Bloat had bought the Dippy Dazzlers off a dwarf with hair like straw at the entrance. The tribes and travellers – those with no money at all – along with those deemed too anti-social to have a city pass, were supposed to stay in the reservations outside the boundaries but the Bill were too uncoordinated now to do much serious policing. At night the dealers and black marketeers would leave their deadbeat patchwork tents and customised bulldozers and creep into town. They had to. Without proper shelter or clothing everyone, especially the children, burnt up fast. No doctor was going to pick their way through the open sewers and ash-pit conflagrations of shantytown where disease hung thick in the air and a knife in the guts was as likely as not.

A tall girl with a silver wig and white velvet hotpants tottered past the boys, radiating diamond-blue light in the fluorescence. 'Hey girl, not so fast,' blustered Bloat. 'What'choo havin'? What's yer name?' To Jacko's surprise, she sat down, said her name was Emily-Charlotte Jenkins and she'd like a large snowball please. Bruce gazed at her hungrily till Bloat returned. Jacko knocked back his sixth – or was it seventh – Super Strength 52. S'funny, he thought, as everything else weakened, the drink and drugs seemed to get stronger, almost as though they were feeding off the rest.

Then, for the second time that day, Jacko heard a gentle voice at his ear.

'You're really cute,' it said. The man at the next table had edged his chair over. It was hard to see him through the random scintillation of the spotlights. Jacko could only make out a large hat and a face as blank and flat as a knife, partially obscured by the sort of round, mirrored sunglasses that people wore in old films. The stranger took these off and placed them on Jacko's nose.

'Ooooh! At first sight they have changed eyes!' The large woman sitting on the other side of the table stood up, wriggled provocatively and pitched herself neatly into Bruce's lap. 'And which of these chewy chickens is mine then?' Jacko wrestled the glasses off – 'Bloody things' – looked over and froze. That *lady* with her burnished mane of hair and exaggerated pout was obviously a man. Even in here Jacko could see the biceps straining the ruched silk of her evening dress and thick black hair struggling through the gold mesh of her stockings. Did Bruce not realise? There was no blood on the floor yet. In fact, Bruce was gazing at his prize with a pleased, soupy expression as though someone had given him a very large and useless gift; a velvet Easter egg perhaps. God, these places got worse all the time. Fuckups and freaks and deviators, wall-to-wall. After dark they all came creeping and crawling into the cellars of the cities, like the vermin they were. Still, once the boys got down the clubs they liked to leave their prejudices behind and get as fucked up as the next guy. Why ruin a night out? Besides, some of these deadly nightshades could be harder than they looked and do you a dreadful injury.

'Leona's just an old-fashioned girl,' said the man next to Jacko. His unshaded eyes were two purple bruises. Funny accent.

'You American?' asked Jacko grudgingly.

'We certainly are. Been visiting with friends in London.'

'Why come *here*?'

'Duty calls.'

Emily-Charlotte leaned forward tipsily and took the stranger's hand. 'You done these really nice,' she said, tapping his fingernails which were lacquered maroon. 'I can tell. I'm in *maquillage* and they say' – she wiggled her own set of silver scalpels – 'that my manicures'll take me far.'

'All the way to my room, babe!' growled Bloat. He was in a jumbo-sized good mood. 'What's your name?' asked Emily-Charlotte prettily of the stranger, as Bruce's paw drew her back into the booth.

'Vector.'

'Oh, Victor.'

'Vector.'

'*Harr-ee*, you're hurting me,' Emily-Charlotte squealed as Bloat engulfed her.

The rest of the evening passed in an alcoholic haze. Leona pouted and teased. *Leona, you're making an exhibition of yourself. Oh it's all water off a quack's back to me, Miss Morbid*. Bruce sat as if stuffed, his expression at once pleased and puzzled.

The Dippy Dazzlers and knock-out lager had shot through Jacko's synapses like a runaway train. When it crashed he found himself on his knees in the deserted car park, vomiting a lurid rainbow of junk food, like any idiot under-age drinker.

The rains had passed and the air was a heavy soup of sewage. He could hear the others over by the sea-wall.

'It's so pretty here at the seaside. Look – all those lights in the sky. You don't see those in town. It's just great! Makes you feel free.'

'C'mon girl, snap your garters! We've a way to go.'

'I'll bet you're a Taurus, Harry.'

'Is Brucie going to walk a lady home then? Is that a ciggie-poo for Cinders?'

Jacko struggled to his feet, dizzy as a battered moth. The strange man in the big hat was staring at him.

'God, I'm dead,' said Jacko.

'Life-challenged,' corrected the man.

There was a pause.

'Hey, you're really sick, aren't you? Poor kid. I know what to do. Come with me. Do you always drink so much?'

'We had like, a rough day.'

The others had vanished. Jacko allowed himself to be led along the shore-front, deserted now. Tin cans rolled along the empty street.

Jacko, now that was a cute name. Where did he live? Were those his friends?

Jacko, dazed and humiliated, began to respond to the gentle questioning. The man's face was white as bone under the streetlights.

'I don't even know your name, Mr—?'

'Doctor. Dr V. Latter. From the French – la terre. My friends call me V.'

'What's your job then?'

The man threw his keys in the air and caught them. 'I'm a gambler, I guess.'

'You play cards?'

'Mmm. Sometimes, you know, I think I was always a

gambler. In the past, on the Mississippi riverboats. Or a plantation owner. My mother came from the South. She was a Creole. She's gone now.'

'My mum's gone too.'

V drifted closer and tried to take Jacko's hand.

Jacko shook it free. 'Someone tried to touch my brother like that once. He threw kettle de-scaler in his face.'

'Kettle de-scaler, huh?' V glided back closer, silent as a ghost. Jacko felt himself weakening. The guy was totally weird but . . . His mates called him those names. He'd always wondered about it.

'*You* don't really mind, do you?'

Jacko found he didn't, not really. No one had paid that much attention to him since his mum died. 'It means you're a . . . queer, dunnit? I never met one before. Not close to.'

V laughed. 'Sure, I like boys.' An icy hand stroked Jacko's neck and this time he didn't pull away. 'What's bothering you, kid? Is it me?'

'No. It was this thing this afternoon.' And Jacko told him about the fortune-telling booth and the storm and the snakes on the floor.

'That's just those ladies' religion, sweetheart. They believe that the great serpent is the father of all living things – like your God. His other half is the lady serpent, Aïda-W'édo. Sometimes she's a rainbow. When they're together, when they make love all is in harmony. They create the world and coil around it, to protect it, as if it were an egg. They are powerful gods.'

'Is it black magic?'

'Some say so. We call it *vodun*.'

'Do you know that lady?'

'Not exactly.'

'She hated us. That religion though, that magic stuff – it's all rubbish, yeah?'

'It has proved effective in the past.'

'Everything's gone so weird. It's like the *Twilight Zone*.'

'I know . . . I know.'

V's hotel was grander than anything Jacko had ever seen. V closed the shutters in his room and wrapped a rose silk scarf round the bedside lamp. Jacko dropped his T-shirt on the floor and flopped face-down on the white lace coverlet. V sat beside him, stroking him and talking softly. It was soothing. The blazing horrors of the day seemed to recede and just as the last sea tide had drawn away from the world with a muted sigh, so the sorrows were drawn from his mind and he was able to fall asleep. He awoke briefly to find himself naked in the bed with V's arms around him. 'I won't hurt you,' whispered V, and he didn't, not at first. Jacko felt a long, cold body pressed close to his own and a long, cold organ parted him and dipped towards his innermost core. Then he felt nails break his skin. A voice snarled, '*This* is what you wanted, isn't it?' and Jacko saw white, white, white, a choir of children like blanched almonds rotten in the rain and their bones sang death. He ejaculated on the sheet and sleep swept him up again.

He woke up to the head-battering yolk of the sun. V, with his back to the bed, was shaving in a mirror. He had a shock of white hair that fell to his shoulders. Flakes of skin were drifting from his skeletal back. Jacko managed to focus on the television set at the end of the bed.

The newsreader smiled a tight red smile. 'We are pleased to report that several of the space capsules have been brought safely to earth. Unfortunately, prolonged weightlessness has caused deterioration of the long bones and musculature.' The camera cut to a space pod. The door opened and what looked like a plastic bag full of melted jelly babies flubbed down the steps. A woman was weeping for joy into her handkerchief. 'Our Henry was held hostage by the skies. Now he'll be at home with us in Hinckley Point. We've had cards from well-wishers all over the world.' The newsreader smiled again. 'Late last night a gang of thieves broke into a sub-post office in Luton. They took several thousand pounds in cash after skinning the postmaster and bagging the valuable yellow fat. His wife was expertly de-veined and her vulva minced up in a rotating egg-slicer. Both are said to be doing well. Shares have fallen by . . .'

Jacko sat up, his head pounding. 'That's not the news! It's all wrong.'

'Sounds the same as usual to me, babe.' V pressed the remote and the picture vanished. 'Happy now?'

'Something's still wrong!' Jacko writhed in the sticky sheets. His arse itched intolerably and he began scratching it. After a while he tried to stop and pull his hand away. He couldn't. His fingers were stuck. He pulled harder and kicked at the sheets. Somehow he just couldn't get his hand free. He wriggled his fingers furiously, tearing his own blood-vessels, but they were caught fast.

'Oh my God! You've given me a disease! In my bum. You fucked me and—'

'No I didn't.' V turned round. His robe hung open. Beneath the tuft of silver pubic hair hung nothing. Just a few shreds of bloodied flesh.

'You left something up me!'

'Not me, sweetheart. It was just an old dildo.' V chucked it on the bed and walked to the window. Opening it, he sat on the ledge and began to eat what looked like buttered cigarettes. His face was thickly powdered, white as a moonstone. He had painted in the purple shadows around his eyes.

At that moment Jacko's arse took the first serious bite out of his fingers. He screamed.

'Hush now. We don't want that everyone comes running.'

Jacko's struggles grew more tortured and terrified as he sought to wrench his hand free from an anus now running with blood.

V gazed out over the dying world. 'The serpent eats his tail,' he observed placidly.

'It's you! You did this! Oh God I can't – it's your fault!'

'Live in shit, die in shit.'

'You know! You must! And Bruce – he went with that Leona lady.'

'Makes no odds probably. You're all the same.'

'Help me! Please. I beg you. Stop it! Stop it if you can!' V sighed and shook his head. Jacko felt something sharp close around his wrist and draw his arm deep into his bowels.

Then he heard Bloat's voice outside the window, sounding for once uncertain. 'I'm looking for my mates. Jacko Linden and er—'

'Bloat,' he screamed. 'Don't touch your—'

But V had whipped across the room and slammed his hand over Jacko's mouth. 'Let this be our little secret for a while, shall we?' He groped for the T-shirt and, lifting his hand, shoved the cloth deep into the back of Jacko's throat.

Jacko's elbow vanished and his face crashed against his knees. V walked to the window and, leaning out, called, 'Hey Bloat! Harry! Nice morning! I'll be right down.'

The skin of Jacko's abdomen had ballooned out. It was rippling and churning from the turmoil within. His arm had been absorbed up to the shoulder. His head was now banging repeatedly against his knees as he was jerked further into himself. Great gouts of blood were being discharged and pooling on the sheet. His back was arched tight as a bow. V swept up his hat and shades. The boy on the bed was a contortion of hair and legs. His head was moving frantically now, trying to resist the devouring fury of his lower bowel, but already the first soft black curls were being ingested. His back cracked with a sound like a pistol shot.

'So long.'

The door slammed and V ran quickly down the stairs singing, 'Thumbelina, Thumbelina, tiny little thing, Thumbelina dance, Thumbelina sing . . .'

The sun rose higher on another pitiless day.

The elevator

Garry Kilworth

Garry Kilworth was born in 1941 in York. He has spent much of his life abroad, his formative years in South Arabia, and later working in Singapore, the Maldives, Africa, Aden, Cyprus, Malta and Germany. He has worked in the RAF as a cryptographer and for Cable and Wireless. Since 1982 he has been a full-time writer, living in Hong Kong for a time but he is now back in Essex.

He won the Gollancz/Sunday Times Short Story Award in 1974 and went on to publish more than 75 short stories and ten novels. Writing across the spectrum – sf, horror, fantasy, young adults' and general fiction – his favourite medium is the short story. Hunter's Moon (A Story of Foxes), *a fantasy novel, reached the best-seller lists, while* In the Hollow of the Deep-Sea Wave, *a general fiction book, sold fewer copies but is being made into a film for Channel 4. His most recent books are* Dark Hills, Hollow Clocks, *a collection of dark faerie stories for young adults and* Frost Dancers (A Story of Hares).

In the introduction to his excellent collection The Songbirds of Pain *(1984), he writes: 'A short story should be as precise and accurate as an acupuncture needle in hitting the right nerve. There the analogy stops, for the nerve should jangle, not deaden.' In* The Elevator *he pinpoints the right nerve with his unfailing accuracy, and then when you reread, he gently slides the needle in several inches deep. You will enjoy it, almost as much as he obviously did.*

The elevator

The small silk-lined elevator had a magnetic effect for her. It seemed purpose-built for her slim form. All she had to do was step inside, press the button and descend to the cellar. It was a simple act, yet she hesitated. Trust and a little courage. That's all it took. She had the latter but could she trust the stranger who had been her husband?

Autumn, thought Julia, was neither one thing nor the other. If you had the car window closed, it became stuffy inside. If you had it open it was chilly. Autumn took so long to burn itself out in England. When she had visited Canada, there had only been a three-week gap between summer and winter, during which the fall swept past in a blaze of fiery colours. That brief conflagration of the trees was more dramatic and far less tedious than this lingering death of a season. She shivered and wound the window up again.

It had been in Canada where she had met Sabash, her Indian prince. It hadn't mattered that he had been a prince, of course, though her mother was delighted at being related to royalty. It might have been romantic, except that Sabash had been an old man when she met him. Now he was dead, only three months after their wedding. He must have known he was dying and she wondered why, after a lifetime of bachelorhood, he had made the decision to marry. Such a strange old man anyway. Reserved and enigmatic, she had not got close to him in those three months. Her own reasons for marrying were obvious: she was forty-five, uneducated and, frankly, poor. It had not been a love match on either side – more of an arrangement that suited both of them for their own particular reasons. When she thought about it, it sounded cold and callous but as long as nothing is hidden, that each partner knows the situation for what it is, there is no reason why a mutual arrangement such as theirs should be considered unethical.

The low sun burned itself into her eyes and she flicked down the shade as the car sped along. Her brother had not approved of the wedding. Or rather, he had not approved of Sabash as a husband.

'I'm sorry, Julia. There's something shifty about the bloke. I can't explain it – something about the way he looks at you. Hell, you know I'm not prejudiced, or anything like that. And I couldn't give a damn about his age. It's something about his face – or rather his eyes. They have a kind of carnivorous look in them when they're resting on you. Like a python or something. It sounds silly but all I'm saying is look after yourself. Don't trust him . . .'

The elevator waited, like a sentient thing, both attractive and repulsive in its aspect.

Well, she hadn't needed to trust him. Sabash had died shortly after that remark, over which she had become extremely angry with Alex. Now she was on her way to fulfil her obligations regarding the will. Sabash had requested, out of respect for him, that she spend one month at the mansion which was to serve as his surrogate mausoleum. Though she had never seen it, Sabash had once lived there and all his favourite possessions had been arranged, room by room, for viewing by visitors. She remembered his words: 'Also, at the mansion, there is a jewel. A ruby. In order that you should have something to do during your time at the house, I have hidden the stone and you are to look for it. A kind of game, you see . . .' His eyes had been feverish at the time and glowed with an intense light. It had frightened her but she supposed it came from his illness and mentally reprimanded herself for being foolish. 'It is a very large ruby. Very beautiful. It will suit your complexion.'

Sabash had been wrong there. It would not suit her at all. She had red hair and had the stone been an emerald it might have been worn by her, but not a ruby.

'Such a stone,' he had sighed. 'It burns with an inner fire. You will see . . .'

Suddenly the car entered the village of Ashdown and she had to apply sharp pressure to the brakes to avoid speeding in a thirty-mile-an-hour zone. The tyres screeched and the smell of burning rubber assailed her nostrils. There was no one about, though, to witness her bad driving. Only one or two small boys building a bonfire in preparation for Guy Fawkes night. The house was supposed to be just beyond Ashdown, in a low valley. She stopped the car on a rise just outside the village to look down the slope that curved beneath.

There. There was the house. The dying sun was caught in the mansion's windows and seemed trapped there, like the cold fire of rubies. It made the house look strangely uninviting: a live thing that was waiting to consume her. She realised such thoughts were the product of an overactive imagination, and were not to be heeded, but a strong sense of self-preservation took hold of her. The prospect of spending a month alone in such a place was not pleasant. It was not her house – it had belonged to a stranger. Yes, she had to admit that Sabash had still been a stranger to her when he died. She could be honest with herself at times like this. What was she to do? She had given him her promise. To turn around and run home to mother because of . . . well, let's face it, she thought, superstition was ridiculous. Surely her unease was the result of unusual circumstances and not premonition. What was she afraid of? The house? That was laughable. It was brick and mortar, nothing else.

The elevator's somnolent interior invited entrance. A step, no further.

She parked the car in the driveway and made her way to the front door of the house. Now that she was close to it, the feeling increased in strength. There was a panic in her breast that she found difficult to fight down. Perhaps there would be someone there? One of those servants that used to follow Sabash around like silent phantoms.

She fumbled for the key in her bag, found it and unlocked the big double doors. Leaving them open she entered the main hall. His presence was definitely there, in the musty odour that emanated from the tapestries and carpets, from the furniture and fittings. It was the smell of age and decay. She took one or two steps inside and shivered. So cold too. Old houses trapped the winter inside their stones. They leaked the coldness through their cracks and gripped the atmosphere with invisible fingers.

As she stood there, just inside the doors, the darkness began to descend and shadows moved out of the corners, expanding their dominions to include the whole inner world of the house. Suddenly her eyes caught sight of the light switch and she crossed to it immediately, turning it on. Instantly, the shadows were gone. The house flooded with light and she realised it was a master switch. Her panic began to subside.

Looking around her she was aware of cabinets lining the hallway, full of ivory carvings. Near the door to one of the rooms was a gun rack holding a row of gleaming rifles. Everything was quite ordinary in its way and remarkable only in its exotic origins.

'Hello!' she called. 'Is anyone here?'

The sound echoed up the stairway which lay ahead. On impulse she decided to explore a little before she left. She owed Sabash that much and perhaps the ruby would reveal itself without too much trouble.

She began wandering from room to room. There was a library full of leather-bound books, which probably had not been read since they had been purchased. The next room was full of paraphernalia concerning horses: photographs adorned the walls and there were crossed polo sticks over the fireplace. Overall the place smelt faintly of saddle polish. Then there was a large dining room with the traditional long wooden table, highly waxed. It was all very ordinary.

It was like a nest. A soft warm nest. How stupid she was to hold back.

Upstairs she found bedrooms, bathrooms and even a nursery, all lavishly furnished. The nursery, she realised, was not for any newcomer to the household. It contained photographs of a little Indian boy and what were obviously his childhood toys. Sabash had set up a shrine to his infant years, presumably for the benefit of visitors. Nevertheless, it was the weirdest room in the house. It was the kind of self-indulgence one associated with monomaniacs whose obsession is with their own egos. She picked up one of the photographs in order to study it closer and a piece of paper fluttered down from behind it. It was a note.

'Warm. You're getting warmer, my dear.'

Warm? What on earth did that mean? Then she remembered. The ruby. He was giving her clues. She began going through the drawers of the chest on which the photo stood, without success. Then she found another note, which said much the same thing, behind a second photo of Sabash. That was it then. It had something to do with images of himself.

For the next hour she went round the whole house looking behind paintings and photographs, collecting messages which told her she was getting warmer, until she came to a lifesize portrait in one of the living rooms. This has to be it, she thought. Feeling round the edge of the painting she eventually found a button which, when depressed, made the portrait slide aside to reveal an elevator the size of an upright coffin.

The cellar! The jewel was in the cellar. She lit a cigarette with trembling fingers and burnt herself in the process.

'Hell! That hurt.'

She rubbed the place and studied the portrait at the same time. The artist had managed to capture that strange light in Sabash's eyes. *'Don't trust him!'* The words of her brother sidled into her brain. Well, after seeing the house, she had to agree with Alex. There was something very peculiar about the man she had married.

She looked at the elevator again. Now. It had to be now. No more shillyshallying or weak excuses. It was not the stone itself now, nor the value it represented, it was the challenge.

She stepped into the elevator, turned to face the room, and pressed the button. The portrait slid back in front of her smoothly, leaving her in total darkness. Panic welled up in her throat as she heard the whirr of machinery below her. The elevator began a smooth descent. There! she thought, fighting down her fear. Nothing to it. I'm excited, that's all. Nothing more than that.

From somewhere in the subterranean depths came a rushing sound, followed by a muted roar.

What was that? The panic returned, like a cornered beast wheeling and baring its teeth savagely. Down, down, slowly, slowly, at funerary pace. Click, click, click, click. She was suddenly aware of soft sitar music coming from a speaker above her head. It had a sinister sound to it. She sensed undertones of nefarious rites in the mournful dirge that accompanied her descent.

The air inside the elevator was getting warmer. She stabbed at the button. Tried to halt her progress downwards. Each second was full of disbelief, desperate hope and unspeakable horror. Click, click, click, click.

'*You're getting warmer, my dear!*'

God! Please God, no. The lift descended. Hints, clues. Her throat constricted. Warmer and warmer. Then hotter. She was waiting in terror now. The heat became insufferable. Too late she remembered. He had been a prince. An Indian prince. The machinery edged her down, towards the furnace that had been triggered to life simultaneously with the activation of the elevator. She tried to claw her way up the silk-lined walls, her mouth contorted in a scream far too high for the pitch of the human ear. *Agni*. Fire. An ancient custom. The burning of the dead prince's wife, alive, on a pyre. The smell of hot varnish was in her nostrils. Melting silk filled her fingernails and the pain was excruciating.

'Sabash!' she shrieked. 'You . . .'

But the voice of the furnace, hot enough to melt rubies, smothered her final words.

The alternative

Ramsey Campbell

Ramsey Campbell was born in Liverpool in 1946. He sold his first short story, The Church in High Street, *to August Derleth's* Dark Mind, Dark Heart *in 1962, the same year as he left school. Two years later his first book,* The Inhabitant of the Lake and Other Less Welcome Tenants, *appeared from Arkham House. He worked in the Inland Revenue and Liverpool Public Libraries, gathering source material for a wealth of stories. His first sale to an original British anthology came in 1968, with two stories in* Tandem Horror 2, *one of them the restrained but terrifying* Reply Guaranteed. *His latest books are the novel,* The Long Lost, *and a new collection,* Alone With The Horrors.

*Ramsey Campbell is like a dentist whose probe finds traces of caries in teeth you thought were perfectly healthy. He pulls down the overhead lamps to get a better look and then starts to drill. It turns out the whole tooth has rotted from the inside. The rot is everywhere: in the brightly lit office (*Boiled Alive*), the orange city streets of dusk (*The Sneering*), the noonday lush green of the countryside (*The Pattern*). Anywhere we allow our perceptions to reinterpret our surroundings in terms of nightmares.*

As background on The Alternative, *Ramsey Campbell sent me the following: 'The idea of worldly success which is somehow dependent on nightmares had been lying dormant in one of my notebooks for years. Your request for a story probably roused it, as did a review of* Dark Feasts *which suggested that underlying some of the stories was my hidden scepticism about my own success.'*

During the period of writing The Alternative *he experienced his worst ever nightmares, panic dreams about things going wrong with his family and his home. They stopped when he finished the story.*

The alternative

Highton was driving past the disused hospital when the car gave up. On the last fifty miles of motorway he had taken it slow, earning himself glances of pity mingled with hostility from the drivers of the Jaguars and Porsches. As he came abreast of the fallen gates the engine began to grate as though a rusty chunk of it were working itself loose, and the smell of fumes grew urgently acrid. The engine died as soon as he touched the brake.

A wind which felt like shards of the icy sun chafed the grass in the overgrown grounds of the hospital as he climbed out of the Vauxhall, rubbing his limbs. He was tempted to leave the car where it was, but the children who smashed windows were likely to set fire to it if he abandoned it overnight. Grasping the wheel with one hand and the crumbling edge of the door with the other, he walked the car home through the housing estate.

All the windows closest to the hospital were boarded up. Soon he encountered signs of life, random windows displaying curtains or, where the glass was broken, cardboard. A pack of bedraggled dogs roamed the estate, fighting over scraps of rotten meat, fleeing yelping out of the communal entrances of the two-storey concrete blocks.

His skin felt grubby with exertion when at last he reached

his block. A drunk with an eyeshade pulled down to his brows was lolling at the foot of the concrete stairs. As Highton approached, he staggered away into the communal yard strewn with used condoms and syringes. Someone had recently urinated at the bend of the staircase, and the first flat on the balcony had been broken into; a figure was skulking in the dark at the far side of the littered front room. Highton was opening his mouth to shout when he saw that the man at the wall wasn't alone: bare legs emerging from a skirt as purple as a flower were clasped around his waist above his fallen trousers. The couple must have frozen in the act, hoping Highton wouldn't notice them. 'Have fun,' he muttered, and hurried past six doors to his.

The 9 on the door, where the red paint had been sunbleached almost pink, had lost one of its screws and hung head downwards from the other, like a noose. When he pushed it upright, it leaned drunkenly against the 6 as he let himself into the flat. The dim narrow corridor which led past three doors to the kitchen and the bathroom smelled of stale carpet and overcooked vegetables. He closed the front door quietly and eased open the first inner door.

Valerie was lying on the bed which they had moved into the living-room once the children needed separate bedrooms. Apart from the bed and the unmatched chairs the room contained little but shadowy patches lingering on the carpet to show where furniture had stood. At first he thought his wife was asleep, and then, as he tiptoed through the pinkish light to part the curtains, he saw that she was gazing at the corner which had housed the television until the set was repossessed. She gave a start which raised the ghost of a ring from the disconnected telephone, and tossing back her lank hair, smiled shakily at him. 'Just remembering,' she said.

'We've plenty to remember.' When her smile drooped he added hastily 'And we'll have more.'

'You got the job?'

'Almost.'

She sighed as if letting go of the strength which had helped her to wait for him. As her shoulders sagged, she appeared to dwindle. 'We'll have to manage.'

He lowered himself into a chair, which emitted a weary creak. He ought to go to her, but he knew that if he held her while they were both depressed she would feel like a burden, not like a person at all. 'Sometimes I think the bosses choose whoever travelled furthest because that shows how much they want the job,' he said. 'I was thinking on the way back, I should have another try at getting jobs round here.'

Valerie was flicking a lock of hair away from her cheek. 'If I can rewire a few properties,' he went on, 'so people know they shouldn't associate me with those cowboys just because I was fool enough to work for them, the work's bound to build up and we'll move somewhere better. Then we can tell Mr O'Mara that he's welcome to his ratholes.'

She was still brushing at her greying hair. 'Where are Daniel and Lucy?' he said.

'They said they wouldn't be long,' she responded as if his query were an accusation, and he saw her withdraw into herself. He was trying to phrase a question which he wouldn't be afraid to ask when he heard the door creep open behind him. He turned and saw Lucy watching him.

He might have assumed Valerie was mistaken – that their fourteen-year-old had been in her room and was on her way out, since the front door was open – if it weren't for her stance and her expression. She was ready to take to her heels, and her look betrayed that she was wondering how much he knew – whether he recognised her cheap new dress as purple as a

217

flower. She saw that he did, and her face crumpled. The next moment she was out of the flat, slamming the door.

As he shoved himself off the chair, his heart pulsating like a wound, Valerie made a grab at him. How could she think he would harm their daughter? 'I only want to bring her back so we can talk,' he protested.

She shrank against the headboard of the bed and tried to slap away the lock of hair, her nails scratching her cheek. 'Don't leave us again,' she said in a low dull voice.

'I'll be as quick as I can,' he promised, and had a fleeting impression, which felt like a stab of panic, that she meant something else entirely. The clatter of Lucy's high heels had already reached the staircase. He clawed the front door open and sprinted after her.

He reached ground level just in time to see her disappearing into the identical block on the far side of the littered yard. The drunk with the eyeshade flung an empty bottle at him, and Highton was afraid that the distraction had lost him his daughter. Then he glimpsed a flash of purple beyond a closing door on the balcony, and he ran across the yard and up the stairs, on tiptoe now. As he reached the balcony he heard Lucy's voice and a youth's, muffled by the boards nailed over the window. He was at the door in two strides, and flung it open. But his words choked unspoken in his throat. The youth on the floor was his son Daniel.

The fifteen-year-old blinked at him and appeared to recognise him, for a vague grin brought some animation to his face as he went back to unwinding the cord from his bruised bare scrawny arm. Highton stared appalled at the hypodermic lying beside him on the grimy floorboards, at the money which Lucy was clutching. He felt unable to move and yet in danger of doing so before he could control himself. He heard Valerie pleading 'Don't leave us again,' and the memory seemed to release him. 'No,' he tried to shout, and woke.

He was alone in bed, and surrounded at some indeterminate distance by a mass of noises: a hissing and bubbling which made his skin prickle, a sound like an endless expelled breath, a mechanical chirping. When he opened his eyes, the room looked insufficiently solid. 'Valerie,' he managed to shout.

'Coming.' The hissing and bubbling grew shriller and became a pouring sound. As he sat himself up she brought him a mug of coffee. 'Don't dawdle in the bathroom or your father will be late for work,' she called, and told him 'You seemed to want to sleep.'

'I'm just drying my hair,' Lucy responded above the exhalation.

'Finish on the computer now, Daniel. You know not to start playing before school.'

'It's not a game,' Daniel called indignantly, but after a few seconds the chirping ceased.

Valerie winked at Highton. 'At least all that should have woken you up.'

'Thank God for it.'

She stooped and holding back her long black hair with one hand, kissed each of his eyes. 'Have your shower while I do breakfast.'

He sipped the coffee quickly, feeling more present as the roof of his mouth began to peel. The dream had been worse this time, and longer; previously it had been confined to the flat. It must have developed as it had because he would be seeing O'Mara this morning.

As usual when Lucy had used it, the bath was full of foam. Highton cleared the mirror and tidied away Daniel's premature electric razor before sluicing the foam down the plughole with the shower. By the time he went downstairs, Valerie was waving the children off to school. When the microwave oven beeped he grabbed his breakfast and wolfed it, though Valerie wagged a finger at him. 'You'll be giving yourself indigestion and nightmares,' she said, and he thought of telling her about his recurrent dream. Doing so seemed like inviting bad luck, and he gave her a long kiss to compensate for his secrecy as he left the house.

All along the wide suburban streets the flowering cherry was in bloom. Highton inhaled the scent before he drove the Jaguar out of the double garage. He had an uninterrupted run along the dual carriageway into town until the traffic lights halted him at the junction with the road which led to the disused hospital past the flats which O'Mara had bought from the council. When the lights released him Highton felt as if he were emerging from a trance.

The only spaces in the car park were on the ninth floor. Beyond the architectural secrets which the top storeys of the business district shared with the air he saw the old council estate. He put the sight out of his mind as he headed for his office, mentally assembling issues for discussion with O'Mara.

O'Mara was late as usual, and bustled into Highton's office as if he had been kept waiting. He plumped himself on the chair in front of the desk, slung one leg over the other, rubbed his hands together loudly and folded them over his waistcoated stomach, flashing a fat gold ring. Throughout this performance he stared at Highton's chair as if both men were on the wrong sides of the desk. 'Tell me all the good news,' he demanded, beginning to tap the carpet with the toecaps of his brogues.

'We've identified a few points you overlooked in your accounts.'

A hint of wariness disturbed the heavy blandness of O'Mara's round face. 'So long as you'll be making me more than I'm paying you.'

'It depends whether you decide to follow our advice.'

Highton picked up the sheet on which he'd made notes for discussion, and blurted out a thought which seemed just to have occurred to him. 'You might consider a programme of repairs and improvements to your properties as a tax expense.'

O'Mara's face reddened and appeared to puff up. 'I can't afford to splash money around now I'm no longer on the council.'

'But surely—' Highton said, and heard his voice grow accusing. How could he forget himself like that? It wasn't his job to moralise, only to stay within the law. The dream must have disturbed him more than he knew for him to risk betraying to O'Mara his dislike of the man. 'Let me guide you through your accounts,' he said.

Half an hour later the landlord was better off by several thousand pounds, but Highton couldn't take much pleasure in it; he kept seeing how exorbitant the rents were. He showed O'Mara to the lift and made himself shake hands, and wiped off the man's sweat with his handkerchief as soon as the lift door closed. The sympathetic grins his partners and the secretaries gave him raised his spirits somewhat, and so did the rest of the day: he set up a company for a client, argued the case of another with the Inland Revenue, helped a third choose a pension plan. He had almost forgotten O'Mara until he returned to his car.

He leaned on the Jaguar and gazed towards O'Mara's streets. Could they really be as bad as he'd dreamed? He felt as if he wasn't entitled to go home until he had seen for himself. When he reached the junction at the edge of the estate he steered the car off the dual carriageway.

Concrete surrounded him, identical streets branching from both sides of the road like a growth which had consumed miles of terraced streets. The late afternoon sky was the same dull white. From the air the place must resemble a huge ugly crystal of some chemical. Perhaps half the windows he passed were boarded up, but he didn't know if he was more disturbed by the spectacle of so many disused homes or the thought of tenants having to live among the abandoned flats. The few people he passed – children who looked starved or unhealthily overweight, teenagers with skin the colour of concrete, older folk hugging bags tightly for fear of being mugged – either glared at him or dodged out of sight. They must take him for someone on O'Mara's payroll, since the landlord never visited his properties in person, and he was uncomfortably aware that his wallet contained a hundred pounds which he'd drawn from the bank at lunchtime. He'd seen enough to show him the district was all that he'd imagined it to be; but when he turned off the main road it was to drive deeper into the maze.

Why should he assume that he was following the street along which he'd turned in his dream? Apart from the numbers on the doors and over the communal entrances, there was little to distinguish one street from another. He was driving past the low nine hundreds; the block on the far side of a junction scattered with broken glass should contain the flat whose number he had dreamed of. He avoided the glass and cruised past the block, and then the car shuddered to a standstill beside a rusty Vauxhall as his foot faltered on the accelerator.

It was by no means the only faded red door he'd seen since leaving the dual carriageway, nor the only door on which a number was askew; but the sight of the 9 dangling upside-down as if the final 3 had been subtracted from it seemed disconcertingly familiar. He switched off the ignition and got clumsily out of the car. Glancing around to reassure himself that nobody was near, he ran across the road and up the stairs.

Of course the concrete staircase looked familiar, since he had already driven past a host of them. He peered around the corner at the top and hurried along the balcony as fast as he could creep. There were seven doors between the stairway and the door with the inverted 9. One glance through the gap between the curtains next to the door would quieten his imagination, he promised himself. He ducked his head towards the gap, trying to fabricate an explanation in case anyone saw him. Then he froze, his fingers digging into the rotten wood of the window-sill. On the carpet a few feet from the window was a telephone, and he'd recognised the number on the dial.

Even stronger than the shock which caused him to gasp aloud was the guilt which overwhelmed him at the sight of the room, the ragged pinkish curtains, the double bed against the wall beyond the unmatched chairs. He felt responsible for all this, and unable to retreat until he'd done his best to change it. He groped for his wallet and counted out fifty pounds, which he stuffed through the slot in the front door. Having kept half the cash made him feel unforgivably mean. He snatched the rest of the notes from his wallet and shoved them into the flat, where they flopped on the hall floor.

The sound, and the prospect of confronting anyone from the flat, sent Highton fleeing like a thief. How could he explain to Valerie what he'd just done when he could hardly believe that he'd done it? He swung the car screeching towards the dual carriageway and drove back to the business district, where he withdrew another hundred pounds from the dispenser in the wall outside the bank.

As he let himself into the house Valerie was coming downstairs laden with the manuals she employed to teach her students word processing. 'Hello, stranger,' she said.

Highton's stomach flinched. 'How do you mean?'

'Just that you're late. Though now you mention it, you do look a bit strange.'

'I'm home now,' Highton said, feeling even more accused. 'I had something to tidy up.'

223

'You can't fool me, you've been visiting your mistress,' Valerie said smiling. 'I've had to eat so I can run. Everything for you three is by the microwave.'

He was relieved not to have to face her while his thoughts were in turmoil, but his relief felt like disloyalty. He listened as the dreamy hum of her car receded, fading sooner than he was expecting. When the oven peeped he called the children downstairs. Lucy came at once, her extravagant earrings jangling; Daniel had to be shouted for three times, and would have worn his personal stereo at the dinner-table if Highton hadn't frowned at him. 'Let's hear about your day instead,' Highton appealed to both of them.

Daniel had scored a goal in a football match against a rival school and been praised for his science project, Lucy's work on local history had been singled out to be shown to the headmistress. 'Now you have to tell us about your day,' Lucy said.

'Just the usual, trying to balance the books.' Feeling trapped, Highton went on quickly: 'So are you both happy?'

Daniel looked puzzled, almost resentful. 'Expect so,' he said and shrugged.

'Of course we are. You and Mummy see that we are.'

Highton smiled at her and wondered if she was being sensitive to his emotional needs rather than wholly honest; perhaps it had been an unreasonably direct question to ask people of their ages. Once the dinner things were in the dishwasher Daniel lay on his bed with his headphones on while Lucy finished the homework her class had been set in advance to give them more time at the school disco, and Highton poured himself a large Scotch and put a compact disc of Mozart piano sonatas on the player.

The stream of music and the buzzing in his skull only unsettled him. Had he really donated a hundred pounds to someone he didn't know, with as little thought as he might have dropped a coin beside any of the beggars who were becoming an everyday sight in the downtown streets? In retrospect the gesture seemed so flamboyant as to be offensive. At least the money had been in old notes, and couldn't be traced to him; the idea that whoever lived in the flat might come to the house in search of an explanation terrified him. Worse still was the thought of their asking Valerie or the children. His growing confusion exhausted him, and he would have gone to bed if that hadn't seemed like trying to avoid Valerie when she came home. He refilled his glass and switched on the television, which was more likely than the music to keep him awake, but he found all the programmes discomforting: newscasts and documentaries about poverty and famine and a millionaire who had never paid tax, a film in which a policeman had to hunt down a jewel thief who had been his best friend when they were children in the slums. He turned off the set and waited for the financial report on the radio, in case the broadcast contained information he should know. The programme wasn't over when he fell asleep in the chair.

The next thing he knew, Valerie was shaking him. 'Wake up, I want to talk to you. Why won't you wake up?'

He found himself clinging to the arms of the chair as if by staying immobile he could hold on to his slumber. One of his fingers poked through a tear in the fabric, into the spongy stuffing of the chair. The sensation was so disagreeable that it jerked his eyes open. Valerie was stooping to him, looking in danger of losing her balance and falling back on the bed. 'Don't keep going away from me,' she begged.

Highton grabbed her wrists to steady her. 'What's wrong now? Is it the children?'

'Lucy's in her room. I've spoken to her. Leave her alone,

Alan, or she'll be running off again. She only wanted to give Daniel what she could because she can't bear to see him suffer.'

Highton blinked at Valerie as she tried to toss back her greying hair. The light from the overhead bulb glared from the walls of the room, except where the shadow of the lampshade lay on them like grime, yet he felt as if they or he weren't fully present. 'Where is he?'

'Gone.'

'Where?'

'Oh, where do you think?' Her resignation gave way momentarily to anger, and Highton felt deeply ashamed of having left her to fend for herself. 'There was some money in the hall,' she said as though she was trying to clarify her thoughts. 'A hundred pounds that must have been put through our door by mistake. Whoever did that can't be up to any good, and they'll turn nasty if they don't get it back, but Daniel wouldn't listen. He was away with it before we could stop him.'

Highton felt that he ought to know where the money had come from, as if he had foreseen it in a dream. The impression was too vague to grasp, and in any case he hadn't time to do so. 'How long ago?'

'Ten minutes, maybe quarter of an hour. We didn't see which way he went,' Valerie said like an accusation.

'You wouldn't be safe out there this late.' Highton squeezed her shoulders through the faded grey checked dress and stood up. 'You look after Lucy. I'll find him.'

He wouldn't return until he had, he vowed to himself. He closed the front door and picked his way along the unlit balcony to the head of the stairs. Through the windy aperture in the rear wall he could see across the yard. Some of the windows that were lit shouldn't be; he glimpsed the glow of an upturned flashlight beyond one set of makeshift shutters, the flicker of candlelight through another. Daniel and youngsters like him would be in one or more of the abandoned rooms while their suppliers hid at home behind reinforced doors and windows. The knowledge enraged Highton, who launched himself at the stairs, too hastily. His foot missed the step it was reaching for, and he fell headlong.

He was bracing himself to hit concrete, but his impact with the carpet was a greater shock. His fists and his knees wobbled, and the crouch he had instinctively adopted almost collapsed. He stared bewildered at the chair from which he'd toppled forwards, the radio whose voice had grown blurred and distant, the glass of Scotch which seemed exactly half empty, half full. The room and its contents made him feel dislocated, unable to think. He stumbled to the telephone and dialled the number which had lingered in his head.

The number was disconnected. Its monotonous wail reached deep into him. He was pressing the receiver against his ear, and feeling as if he couldn't let go until he had conceived a response to the wail for help, when Valerie came into the room. 'Who are you calling so late?'

He hadn't realised she was home. He clutched at the earpiece to muffle the wail and fumbled the receiver onto its rest. 'Nobody. Nobody's there,' he gabbled. 'I mean, just the speaking clock.'

'Don't look so disconcerted or you'll have me thinking you're being unfaithful.' She gazed at him for several protracted seconds, then she winked. 'Only teasing. I know you've just woken up,' she said, and went upstairs.

Her affectionateness made him feel guiltier. He switched off the mumbling radio and sat trying to think, until he realised how long he had been sitting and followed Valerie. He was hoping they could make love – at least then he might feel closer to her without having to talk – but she was asleep.

He lay beside her and stared up at the dark. His desire for sleep felt like a compulsion to dream. He didn't know which disturbed him more, his fear of finding out what happened next or his need to do so. Why couldn't he accept that he had simply acted on impulse this afternoon – that he'd donated his cash to some of O'Mara's tenants to compensate for his involvement with the man? Given how cramped the flats were, the presence of a bed as well as a few worn-out chairs in the front room didn't require much imagining, and was he really certain that he had dreamed anything more specific about the place before he had looked in the window today? Had he genuinely recognised the phone number? The memory of seeing it through the window was vivid as a photograph – so vivid that it blotted out any memory of his having seen it before. Trying to recall the dream felt like slipping back into it, and he kept recoiling from the promise of sleep.

When at last he dozed off, the alarm seemed to waken him so immediately that he could hardly believe he was awake. As long as sleep had caught up with him, why couldn't the dream have reached a conclusion? He dozed again, and when he was roused by Daniel and Lucy calling their goodbyes he thought he was dreaming. He sprawled on the floor in his haste to be out of bed and under a reviving shower.

Whatever temperature he set it to, the downpour felt more distant than he would have liked. The breakfast Valerie put in front of him was almost too hot to taste, but he mustn't linger or he would be late for work. He kissed her cheek and ran to the car, feeling obscurely treacherous. Because of his unsettled night he drove as slowly as the traffic would allow. At the junction from which the concrete flats were visible he felt in danger of forgetting which way to go, and had to restrain himself from driving townwards while the lights were against him.

Julie brought him a mug of coffee and the news that a client had cancelled that morning's appointment because one of her boutiques had been looted overnight. Highton set about examining a hairdresser's accounts, but he didn't feel safe with them: in his present state he might overlook something. He dictated letters instead, trusting the secretaries to spot mistakes. Since he had no appointments, should he take the afternoon off and catch up on his sleep? Once Rebecca had collected the tape of his dictation he cleared a space among the files on his desk and propped his hand against his mouth.

The phone jolted him awake. He wondered how they had been able to afford to have it reconnected until he saw that was in the office. 'It's Mrs Highton,' Julie's voice told him.

'Yes, I want to talk to her.'

A moment later Valerie's breathing seemed to nestle against his cheek. 'Next time it will be,' he said.

'What's that, Alan?'

'I was talking to someone here.' Despite his confusion he could lie about that, and say 'What can I do for you?'

'Do I have to make an appointment? I was going to ask if you wanted to meet for lunch.'

He couldn't say yes when he hadn't had time to think. 'I'm already booked,' he lied. 'I'm awfully sorry.'

'So you should be,' Valerie retorted, and laughed. 'I just thought when you went out you looked as if you could do with easing up on yourself.'

'I will when I can.'

'Do, for all our sakes. See you this evening. Don't be late.'

'Why should I be?' Highton demanded, hoping that didn't sound guilty. He dropped the receiver onto its cradle and pinched his forehead viciously to quicken his thoughts. He knew why he'd greeted Valerie as he had: because on wakening he'd found himself remembering the last words she

229

had addressed to him. 'Why did it have to be money? Why couldn't it have been something that might have meant something to him?'

She meant the cash Daniel had taken from the flat. Highton must have dreamed her words at the moment of wakening, but he couldn't recall doing so, which made them seem unassailably real. He wouldn't be able to function until he had proved to himself that they weren't. He told the secretaries that he wouldn't be more than an hour, and hurried to his car.

By the time he reached the junction he had a plan. He needed only to be shown that the tenants of the flat weren't the victims of his dream. If sounding his horn didn't bring someone to the window he would go up and knock. He could always say he had mistaken the address, and surely nobody would take him for a thief.

The pavements were scattered with chunks of rubble. Icy winds ambushed him at intersections and through gaps in the architecture, carrying tin cans and discarded polystyrene into the path of the Jaguar, dislodging an empty liquor bottle from a balcony. As he came in sight of the block where he'd posted the notes, a wind raised washing on the line outside the flat as if the clothes were welcoming him. Closest to the edge of the balcony was a dress as purple as a flower.

He clung to the wheel and sent the car racing onwards. Not only the purple dress was familiar; beside it was a grey checked dress, more faded by another wash. He trod on the brake at last, having realised that he was speeding through the duplicated streets with no idea of where he was. Before he found a route to the dual carriageway his head felt brimming with panic. He succeeded in returning to the car park without mishap, though he couldn't recall driving there. He strode almost blindly into his office, shouting 'Leave me alone for a while.' But when Julie tapped on the glass to inform him that the rest of the office was going home he was no closer to understanding what had happened or where it might lead.

He depressed the accelerator hard when the lights at the junction with the dual carriageway turned amber, and was dismayed to find that he wasn't so much anxious to be home as even more nervous of being sidetracked. He steered the car into the driveway and was unlocking the garage when Valerie opened the French windows and stepped onto the back patio. 'You may as well leave your car out, Alan.'

'Why, are we going somewhere?'

'You haven't forgotten. You're teasing.' Her amused expression disguised a plea. 'You're getting worse, Alan. I've been saying for months that you need to take it easier.'

When he didn't respond she marched into the house, and he could only follow her. The sight of Lucy still in her school uniform released his thoughts. 'I *was* joking, you know,' he called after Valerie. 'It's time to meet Lucy's teachers again.'

'Don't bother if it's that much trouble,' Lucy said.

'Of course it isn't,' Highton replied automatically, hearing Valerie tell Daniel 'Make sure you're home by nine.'

As the family sat down to dinner Highton said to Lucy 'You know I like seeing your schoolwork.' He saw that she guessed this was a preamble, and he hurried on: 'But your mother's right, I've been having to push myself lately. Better too much work than none, eh? Would you mind if I stayed home tonight and had a rest? I can catch up on your achievements next time.'

She suppressed her disappointment so swiftly he might almost have believed he hadn't glimpsed it. 'I don't mind,' she said, and Valerie refrained from saying whatever she had been about to say to him, rationing herself to a frown.

She and Lucy drove away before Daniel made for the youth club. Now that Highton had created a chance for himself – the only time he could foresee when he was certain to be alone in the house – he felt both anxious to begin and nervous of betraying his eagerness to Daniel. Hadn't he time to conduct an investigation which should already have occurred to him? He leafed through the phone directory to the listing for Highton, but none of the numbers alongside the column of names was the one he'd seen in the flat. Nor could Directory Enquiries help him; a woman with a persistent dry cough explained patiently that she couldn't trace the number, and seemed to suspect he'd made it up.

Whatever he'd been hoping the search would prove, it had left him even more confused. As soon as Daniel had left the house, Highton ran Valerie's Toyota out of the garage and unlocked the boot, then he carried Daniel's computer out to the car. The boy wouldn't be without it for long, he told himself, and the insurance money might pay for an upgraded model. He felt unexpectedly mean for removing only the computer, and so he rushed through the house, collecting items which he felt ashamed to be able to afford: the telephone extension in his and Valerie's bedroom, the portable television in the guest room. Dumping them in the boot, he ran back to the house, trying to decide which window to smash.

A burglar would enter through the French windows, but the prospect of so much breakage dismayed him. The thief or his accomplice could have been small enough to climb through the kitchen window. He was picking up a tenderiser mallet to break the glass, and a towel to help muffle the sound, before he realised the he couldn't use anything in the house. He dashed out, locking the front door behind him, and ran on tiptoe around the house.

He mustn't take long. He had to leave the items on the balcony outside the flat and drive to the school in time to appear to have decided to see Lucy's work after all. Once they were home he would discover that he'd been in such a hurry to get to the school that he had forgotten to switch on the burglar alarm. There were tools in the garden shed which an unprepared burglar might use, but how would the burglar open the padlock on the door? Highton had been straining for minutes to snap the hasp, using a branch which he'd managed to twist off the apple tree, when he wondered if he could say that he had left the shed unlocked, though wouldn't he be claiming to have been too careless for even pressure of work to explain? He ran to the garage for a heavy spanner, with which he began to lever at the hasp and then to hammer at it, afraid to make much noise in case it attracted attention. He was still attacking the padlock when the Jaguar swung into the drive and spotlighted him.

Lucy was first out of the car. 'They couldn't turn off the fire alarm, so everyone had to go home,' she called; then her cheerfulness wavered. 'What are you doing?'

He felt paralysed by the headlights. He couldn't hide the spanner. 'I lost the key,' he said, and remembered that Valerie knew it was on the ring with his keys to her car. 'I mean, I snapped it. Bent it. Had to throw it away,' he babbled. 'I was going to come to the school after all when I—' He had no idea how he would have continued if he hadn't been interrupted, but the interruption was anything but welcome. A police car had drawn up behind the Jaguar.

Valerie climbed out of his car as the two policeman approached. 'I wasn't speeding, was I?'

'We weren't following you, madam,' the broader of the pair assured her, staring at Highton. 'We received a report of someone behaving suspiciously around this house.'

'There must be some mistake. That's my husband.' But as she laughed, Valerie's gaze strayed to the open boot of her car. 'It's all right, Lucy,' she said – too late, for the girl was already blurting 'What are you doing with Daniel's computer?'

'I'm sure there's a perfectly reasonable explanation,' Valerie said in a tone so clear that she might have been addressing not only Lucy and the policemen but also the neighbours who had appeared at several windows. 'In any case, it's a domestic matter.'

The police stood their ground. 'Perhaps the gentleman would like to explain,' the thickset policeman said.

'I was just pottering. Can't I potter around my own property?' Highton felt as if the lights were exposing his attempt at humour for the defensiveness it was, and the police obviously thought so; they stepped forwards, the man who was built like a bouncer declaring 'We'll have a look around if you don't mind, to make sure everything's in order.'

They stared hard at the spanner and the padlock, they examined all the downstairs locks and bolts. They lingered over the contents of the boot of the Toyota. 'These are yours, are they, madam?' the wiry policeman enquired, and looked ready to ask Valerie to produce receipts. Eventually the police left, having expressed dissatisfaction by their ponderousness. 'There won't be any reason for us to come back, I hope,' the broad policeman commented, and Highton knew that they'd concluded they had cut short an insurance fraud.

Once they had driven away, Valerie glared at the neighbouring houses until the pairs of curtains fell into place. 'Don't say anything, Lucy. Help me carry these things into the house.' To Highton she said 'You look terrible. For God's sake try and get some sleep. Tomorrow we'll talk about what has to be done. We can't go on like this.'

He felt too exhausted to argue, too exhausted even to be afraid of sleep. He fumbled through washing his face and brushing his teeth, and crawled into bed. Sleep held itself aloof from him. In a while he heard Daniel and Lucy murmuring in the back garden, obviously about him. The unfamiliar smell of smoke made him flounder to the window, from which he saw them sharing a cigarette. 'Don't start smoking or you won't be able to give it up,' he cried, and they fled around the house.

Later, as he lay feeling that sleep was gathering just out of reach, Valerie came to bed. When he tried to put an arm round her she moved away, and he heard muffled sobs. He had the notion that somehow her grief wouldn't go to waste, but before he succeeded in grasping the idea, sleep blotted out his thoughts.

Then she was leaning over him and whispering in his ear. 'Come and see,' she repeated.

Her voice was too low for him to distinguish its tone, but when he opened his eyes he saw she had been crying. He swung his legs off the bed, on which he had been lying fully dressed. 'What is it?'

'Nothing bad,' she assured him, and he realised that her tears had been of relief. 'Come and see.'

He followed her into the hall of the flat and saw a portable television near the front door. 'Where did that come from?'

'That's part of it. Have you really been asleep in there all this time?' She was too full of her news to wait for an answer. 'He didn't spend that money on drugs. That's why you couldn't find him. He bought the television for us and something for himself to keep him straight.'

She put a finger to her lips and beckoned him to the door of Daniel's room. Daniel and Lucy were sitting together on the chair in front of the rickety dressing-table, which bore a computer with a small monochrome screen. Both of them were engrossed in the calculations which it was displaying. 'I'm teaching them how to use it,' Valerie said in his ear. 'Once they're old enough to get a job doing it, maybe I can go back to mine.'

Though Highton recognised that he shouldn't enquire too closely into how or where Daniel had been able to buy a computer and a television for a hundred pounds, it looked like a miracle. 'Thank God,' he said under his breath.

She squeezed his arm and led him back to the front room. 'It won't be easy,' she said with a strength which he'd feared had deserted her. 'The next few days are going to be awful for him. He swears he'll straighten himself out so long as we don't leave him alone for a moment. He means you particularly, Alan. He needs you to be here.'

She wasn't referring only to the present, Highton knew. 'I will be, I promise,' he said, trying to grasp why he felt less sure of himself than he sounded. 'Do you mind if I go out for a stroll and a think, seeing as I won't be going anywhere for a while? I won't be long.'

'Don't be,' she said, and hugged him fiercely.

He would go back to her, he vowed as he descended the dark concrete stairs, just as soon as he understood why he was harbouring any doubt that he would. Not far now, not much farther, he kept telling himself as he tramped through the dark between the broken streetlamps, trying to relax enough to think. When at last he turned and saw only darkness and looming blocks of flats he was seized by panic. Before he could run back to the flat, he awoke.

Valerie had wakened him by sitting up. When he reached for her, desperate to feel that she was there, she slid out of bed without looking at him. 'I'm sorry,' he mumbled, rubbing his eyes.

She gave him a wavering glance and sat on the far end of the bed. 'I don't even want to know what you thought you were doing, but I need to know what's wrong.'

'It's as you've been saying, pressure of work.'

'You're going to have to tell me more than that, Alan.'

He couldn't tell her the truth, but what else might convince her? 'I'm not happy about some of the clients I have to work for. One in particular, a landlord called O'Mara.'

'You used to talk to me about anything like that,' Valerie said as if he had confirmed his disloyalty. She nodded at the open door, past which Lucy was padding on her way to the bathroom. 'Wait until we're alone.'

Once the bathroom was free Highton made for the shower. If he closed his eyes he could imagine that the water was lukewarm rain, surging at him on a wind between the blocks of flats. He hurried downstairs as soon as he was dressed, not wanting the children to leave the house until he'd bidden them goodbye.

They were still at the table. They stared at their food and then smiled at him, so brightly yet so tentatively that he felt like an invalid whose condition was obvious to everyone except himself. As Valerie put his plate in front of him with a kind of resentful awkwardness, Lucy said 'Don't worry about Mr O'Mara.'

The side of Highton's hand brushed against the hot plate. The flare of pain was too distant to bother him. 'What do you know about O'Mara?'

'Only that he says you're the best accountant in town,' she said, flinching from his roughness. 'I didn't mean to listen to what you and Mummy were saying.'

'Never mind that. Where have you come across him?'

'I haven't yet. His son Lionel told me what he said. Lionel goes to our school.' She lifted a forkful of scrambled egg to her lips before adding defiantly, 'He's taking me to the disco.'

Highton could see that she was expecting an argument, but he didn't want to upset her now, particularly since there was no need. He finished his breakfast and waited near the front door to give her and Daniel a hug. 'Don't let life get you down,' he told them, and watched as they walked away beneath the sunlit cherry trees and turned the corner.

Valerie was switching on the dishwasher. 'So tell me about this O'Mara,' she said with more than a hint of accusation.

'You look after Lucy. I'll deal with him.'

'Not in your present state of mind you won't. You need to see someone, Alan. Maybe they'll prescribe some time off work, which we can afford.'

That was true, especially since she was a director of the firm. 'At the very least I have to tidy things up,' he said.

She seemed resigned, even relieved. 'Shall I drive you to the office?'

A surge of love almost overwhelmed him, and he would have pulled her to him if he hadn't been afraid that the violence of his emotion would rouse her suspicions. 'I don't know how long I'll be,' he said. 'I'll come back as soon as I can.'

Having to be so careful of his words to her distressed him. He yearned to linger until he had somehow communicated his love for her, except that if he stayed any longer he might be unable to leave. He grabbed his overcoat and made for the front door. 'We want you back,' she said, and for a moment he was certain that she had an inkling of his plan; then he realised that she was referring to the way he had become unfamiliar. He gave her a wordless smile which he just managed to hold steady, and hurried out to the car.

The lights at the junction on the road into town remained green as he approached them, and he drove straight through. For years he had driven through without considering where the side road led, but now there was barely room for anything else in his mind. It wasn't the money he'd left at the flat which had changed the situation, he thought; it was the balance of fortune. Life at the flat had started to grow hopeful because life at the house had taken a turn for the worse. He parked the car and marched himself to the office, thinking how to restore the balance.

'I'm going to have to take some time off. I wish I could be more definite.' His partners reassured him that they could handle the extra workload; they didn't seem surprised by his decision. He discussed with them the cases about which they needed information, and when they left him he grabbed the phone. 'No, I can't leave a message. I want to speak to Mr O'Mara in person.'

Eventually the landlord picked up the car phone. 'I hope I'm going to like what you have to tell me, Alan.'

'You won't,' Highton said, savouring the moment. 'I want you to tell your son to stop sniffing around my daughter. I won't have her feeling that she needs to prostitute herself for the family's sake.'

For some time O'Mara only spluttered, so extravagantly that Highton imagined being sprayed in the face with saliva. 'He won't be going near her again,' O'Mara shouted, 'but I'll be wanting a few words with her father in private.'

'Just so long as you don't send your thugs to do your talking. I'm not one of your tenants,' Highton said, and felt reality lurch. 'And if you come anywhere near my house the police will want to know why.'

When O'Mara began spluttering obscenities Highton cut him off and held onto the receiver as if he couldn't bear to let go until he'd placed one last call. He dialled and closed his eyes, waiting for Valerie's voice. 'Look after one another,' he said, and set the receiver on its cradle before she could respond. Snatching a fistful of old financial journals from the table in the reception area, he headed for his car.

The lights at the junction seemed almost meaningless. He had to remind himself not to turn left while they were against him. As soon as they changed he drove through the rubbly streets until he found a courtyard entirely surrounded by boarded-up flats. With the tyre-iron he wrenched the number-plates off the Jaguar, then he thrust the rolled-up magazines into the petrol tank. Once they were all soaked he piled them under the car and set fire to them with the dashboard lighter. As he ran out of the courtyard he shoved the plates between the planks over a window, and the numbers fell into the dark.

He was nearly at the flat when he heard the car explode. Surely that would be enough misfortune for his family to suffer. The sound of the explosion spurred him onwards, up the smelly concrete steps, along the balcony. The door of the flat swung inwards as he poked a key from his ring at the lock. 'I'm home,' he called.

Silence met him. The cramped kitchen and bathroom were deserted, and so were the untidy bedrooms and the front room. The small television in the latter, and the computer in the boy's room next to it, were switched off. He prayed that he wasn't too late – that Daniel had gone wherever Lucy and his mother were so that they could watch over him. Thank heaven the phone wasn't working, or he might have been tempted to make a call which could only confuse and distract him. He lay down on the bed and closed his eyes, wondering if he might dream of his life in the house while he waited for his family to come to him.